Breathe

The Cure

Lauren Spinks

1.

Una

Light was burning through my eyelids and I could hear the shrill cry of an eagle high above me. I opened my eyes to see clear blue sky and two eagles soaring above. I think they were they waiting for us. Waiting for their chance to scavenge the meat from our bones, like I had seen them do to other animals many times before. I slowly sat myself up, taking in the view around me.

We had fallen asleep between two large rocks, watching the Northern Lights dance across the sky. My older brother, Jordan, now sat on top one of the rocks, looking back toward the direction of home, his knees up in front of him, resting between his elbows. We had run for miles in the dark, our mother having pushed us out of the house through a back window, screaming at us to go.

I didn't want to leave her, but Jordan had grabbed hold of me, dragging me away from the house.

When Mama's screams had stopped, someone had given chase to us, but we were too quick, we knew the land much better than them. We had stopped running a few miles away from the house, once we were sure they had given up looking for us. The glow of their torches disappeared back the way we had come. Now the sun was shining on us as I climbed up the back of the rock, and took a seat next to Jordan.

'Can you see anything?' I asked him. 'Shall we go back?'

His brow furrowed.

'I don't know' he said. 'Mama said that if they came, we had to run away and not go back.'

'But where will we go?'

He shrugged his shoulders, slightly shaking his head, but saying nothing.

'What do they want with us?'

Jordan turned to face me. The wind blew one of his blonde curls across his face and he tucked it back behind his ear.

'They take whole families like ours. People who live outside of towns, by themselves, with no one around to help. Mama says they only want the children, but they take everyone so that there's no one left to get help, no one to come looking for them.'

'What do they want children for?'

He looked back out toward the horizon.

'They're trying to find a cure for something, I don't know what. Mama thought we would be safe here. They haven't taken anyone that lived this far north before.'

I didn't think it was true about Mama thinking that we were safe here. I think she was making plans to leave. We lived a few miles outside a small fishing town in Greenland. It was all I had ever known, but Mama and Jordan had lived somewhere else before. I had heard Mama talking to someone the last time we were in town, talking about selling the house. I think she wanted to move on again. Jordan and I continued to sit there, not saying anything until the sound of my stomach growling broke the silence.

'I'm hungry.'

Jordan nudged me with his elbow.

'You're always hungry Una.' He stood up on the top of the rock. 'Come on, we need to get going.'

Once we were within half a mile of the house, Jordan crouched down behind a rock, pulling me with him. I peered around one side, scanning the barren landscape, looking for any sign of the intruders from the night before.

'Jordan, Mama told us not to go back you said.'

'I know what I said Una, but we can't go anywhere in our pyjamas and we need food. And what if Mama is still in there? What if she's hurt?'

I turned away from the house and sat with my back to the rock. Jordan did the same.

'Look, we just need to get changed and pack some food and then we can get to the village and get on a boat. We can hide on board.'

'On a boat? And then what?'

He shrugged his shoulders again.

'I don't know, I haven't thought that far ahead yet. Once it's as far out as it's going to go we'll jump off and swim the rest of the way.'

'The rest of the way to where Jordan?'

'I don't know, to Canada, we can probably do it in a few days, a week maybe. We can find our way north from there.'

'Canada? But we've never been out that far without Mama. How will we even know which way to go?'

'Una for goodness sake, stop asking so many questions. We'll work it out. We can't stay here, we have to go. Mama said we had to leave.'

His harsh tone stung and so I nodded, trying not to let my lower lip wobble.

'Right come on Una, follow me and make sure you stay close.'

We walked the last half a mile to the house, stopping behind larger rocks here and there so that Jordan could look around. There were no boats in the water only large floating ice rocks. Had they really gone?

Once we finally reached the house, I could see that the back window we had jumped from still hung open. We made our way around to the front of the house and climbed the wooden steps to the front door, which swung back and forth in the wind.

'Stay here.'

Jordan left me at the bottom of the steps and slowly made his way to the door. After looking inside, he disappeared behind the door. I waited a few seconds, then made my own way up the steps, one by one. The door had swung back behind Jordan, but hadn't completely closed and from inside the house, I heard a sniff.

'Jordan?'

'Don't come in here Una, stay outside' he shouted back to me.

'Jordan what is it? Is Mama in there?'

'NO UNA, just stay where you are.'

I knew something was wrong, he sounded so scared, so frightened. I put my hand on the door handle, pulling it outward. The inside of the house was gloomy, with no lights on and the curtains still drawn, not letting in any light from outside. I took a step inside. Jordan turned toward me.

'Una, I told you to stay outside.'

In front of him, a blanket covered something on the floor and by his feet were the scissors Mama used for cutting fabrics. From underneath the blanket I could see a hand, white as snow. I walked slowly toward Jordan, then I knelt down beside him in front of the blanket. I realised Jordan had been the one who had put the blanket down.

'Is she…'

I looked up at Jordan. He nodded. I could see where her head would be and I gently leaned forward and pulled the blanket away from her face. Tears stung my eyes. Her long blonde hair was still neatly braided just like mine, her eyes were closed and her pale white skin was bruised on her left cheek. She had tried to fight. She had fought to save us, bought us the time to get away. I gently touched her face and could see on her neck the bruises that had been left behind, showing how they had killed her. I pulled the blanket back over her face and wiped my tears with my sleeve. Jordan went to a cupboard, pulling out a rucksack.

'Get dressed' he told me firmly.

He began taking cans from the kitchen and filled the bag. He took money from the drawer where Mama always kept it and wrapped it tightly in a plastic bag, stuffing that into the rucksack too. I went to my room and put on clean clothes, making sure I wore my swim suit instead of underwear. I put plimsoles on my feet, hoping I would be able to swim okay with them on. Did Jordan really think we could make it to Canada on our own? And what would we do when we got there?

Back in the kitchen, I ate bread and cheese whilst Jordan got dressed in his room. Jordan soon reappeared, clothed and ready to go. He pulled the rucksack onto his back and I handed him two chunks of bread with cheese and ham in between. I watched him eat in silence, trying not to look down at Mama's lifeless body, still covered by the blanket on the floor. He finished and stepped toward the door, he stopped with his hand on the handle, turning back into the room once more.

'Goodbye Mama' he said.

I reached out and took his other hand in mine, squeezing gently. He wiped his eyes, then pushed the door open. The bright sunlight hurt my eyes after being inside the dark house for a while. As I let my eyes adjust, Jordan stopped abruptly at the top of the stairs, almost making me bump into him.

'Jordan, what the…'

But then I saw them, just standing there, waiting at the bottom of the stairs. They hadn't left after all.

2.

Vivienne

'MORGAAAAAAAAAAAN.'

I shouted as loudly as I could, hoping he would hear me from wherever it was that he had disappeared to in the cottage. I waited, listening in the silence for the sound of movement. Where had he got to? I reached for my phone to text him when a knock on the kitchen window made my head jerk up.

'What?' his voice was muffled through the glass.

'What is this? Why do we have a dozen bottles of wine and no food?'

I motioned to the shopping bags he had abandoned in the kitchen.

'What do you mean what is it? I've got loads of food there. There's cheese, crackers, paté, what else do you need?'

'I told them I was cooking for them.' I shook my head in disbelief. 'What are they going to think of this? I wanted to do the special salmon thingy that Sereia loves.'

He disappeared from the window and after I heard the front door open and shut he reappeared behind me.

'They will think that they enjoy spending time socialising with you rather than just talking to me whilst you slave away in the kitchen. A cheese and wine night is far more enjoyable than fancy shmancy food in my opinion.' I stood up and he snaked his arms around my waist, pulling me into a tight embrace. 'You seem stressed Viv, have you not had a swim today?'

I pushed his arms away from me.

'Yes I have thank you very much, now go away again so I can start getting things ready.'

I turned away, reaching for a shopping bag and he grabbed my arm pulling me back.

'Well thanks to me, you don't really have to do anything before they get here, so… why don't we go and have a little lie down, get some rest before tonight? Or better yet, lets go for a swim.'

He slid his fingers underneath my t-shirt and into the small of my back, then pulled me back in toward him. He nuzzled his face between my head and shoulders, softly brushing his lips against my neck.

'I can't help but feel like you have an ulterior motive Mr Whidden.'

We had been married for six months and much to my enjoyment, we were still living up to the stereotypical newlywed image.

'What on earth would make you say that Mrs Whidden? You've had a long day at work, surely you could do with a rest before an evening of entertaining our friends? Plus, I can't imagine we will be able to get out for a swim tonight, you'll be far too intoxicated.'

He pulled his face away from my neck and raised an eyebrow with a smirk.

'I seem to remember you being the one who can't hold your drink.'

I finally gave in and wrapped my arms around his neck as he leaned down to kiss me. Before he could reach me, a harsh knock on the door made me jump. Morgan sighed heavily.

'I'll get it' he said as he rolled his eyes, then disappeared out of the kitchen.

I could hear muffled voices at the front door whilst I busied myself putting the cheese and meats and sparkling wine in the fridge, then filling the wine rack with the various bottles of red Morgan had also purchased. He was right as always though, it would be much nicer to simply spend the evening gathered in the living room together, instead of being stuck in the kitchen preparing food and cleaning up afterwards. Sereia and her boyfriend Adam were joining us to celebrate New Years Eve. Today marked one year since I'd met Sereia. She had mistaken me for my mother on an Asrai boat party in London, when the reason I was actually there was to find the person who had killed my mother and my father.

The months prior to that could only be described as a rollercoaster. I had moved here, to Zennor to be with my grandmother Emmy. After meeting Morgan, I had found out that I was an Asrai. I wasn't human, I could breathe underwater, I could heal quicker than humans and I would never get sick. I also found out that my parents' death wasn't an accident. So last New Year I had decided to find out why. So much had happened in the weeks that had followed that night. I had found out that I was half human or 'un-pure' as many Asrai referred to us as. My biological father had been a human, resulting in me being infertile.

I would never get a chance to meet him now, for he had been murdered before I was born, by the same man that killed my parents over two years ago. That man would go on to murder Emmy, my dear sweet grandmother, for which I still blamed myself every single day. If I had never gone looking for answers about my parents, Abraham would never have come here. He would never have taken Emmy and thrown her from the cliff top. I would never have ended up killing him. I pulled open the junk drawer and looked at the knife again. The knife that Emmy had given me to protect myself with. It really, truly had protected me that night. I never carried it with me anymore. It was just a reminder of what I had done and that I had lost Emmy too.

I had replayed that night in my head many, many times. I thought for hours about all the things that I could have done differently to save her. What I should have done to stop him. But it was getting easier now. I thought about it slightly less and just remembered Emmy as she was, as she had always been. I owed it to her to try and be the same way that she always was. Happy. She had always been happy and for the most part, I really, really was.

I spent my days working in the aquarium with Morgan, always making sure I got in an early morning swim by myself and then our evenings were spent lounging around the cottage, before taking a late night swim together. Sereia was living in the place Morgan owned a short distance away and we would see each other most weekends. That was unless her boyfriend Adam was visiting, in which case she would barely leave her room. I was surprised when she'd taken me up on the offer to spend New Years Eve with us and I couldn't wait. I hadn't seen Sereia since before Christmas as she'd spent it in London with Adam and I was really excited to hear all about it.

Once everything was put away, I headed into the living room. Noticing that Morgan had now disappeared outside, I busied myself fluffing cushions and clearing the coffee table. Wiping down the mantle above the fire place, I caught my reflection in the antique mirror that had always hung there. I stopped and stared for a moment. As impossible as it seemed, I looked younger now. My skin seemed to glow and my cheeks gave off a subtle pink sheen. The dark circles under my eyes had long gone and my dark, curly hair seemed longer and shinier than it had ever been. I traced my fingers down the frame of the mirror, following the intricate strands of hair sculpted into the metal, the way Emmy had always done.

I stared past my reflection in the mirror, wishing that I could see Emmy's reflection in it too. I touched my fingers to the glass and realised that it also had a fine layer of dust. After grabbing glass cleaner and paper towels from the kitchen, I gently sprayed the entire mirror. As I reached toward it with the paper towels to wipe it clean, I noticed that the mirror shimmered blue and glittery underneath the spray. The more I looked, the more colours I could see, not just blue, but green and gold too.

I checked the bottle, there was nothing to say that it was a shimmer or glittery window cleaner. I didn't want to make it worse by rubbing it in, so I went to the window of the living room and sprayed a little on there. Nothing shimmered or glittered there and when I wiped it off, no residue was left behind. I shrugged to myself, how very strange. It must just be the way it looks on a mirror. Crossing the room back to the mirror, I wiped it clean with the paper towel, revealing only the clear mirrored surface, shining underneath.

'It's only Sereia and Adam, they're not going to be inspecting the windows when they're here.' Morgan came up behind me. 'The mirror definitely did need a clean though. Sorry, I meant to do that the other day.'

'That's okay,' I said. 'But look at this.'

I sprayed the glass cleaner at the mirror again, using a bit more this time. Adam cocked his head to one side as the liquid ran down the face of the mirror, noticing the shimmer and glitter effect.

'That's weird, why would they put glitter in glass cleaner, kind of defeats the object really.'

'That's the thing, there isn't anything in it and it doesn't do the same thing on the windows.' Adam took the bottle out of my hand and inspected it, whilst I reached up with more paper towels and wiped the mirror clean again. 'Then it just disappears when you wipe it off, but there's nothing on the paper towel, look.' I held the damp paper towel out in front of him. 'It must just be the way it reacts on a mirror perhaps, pretty cool huh. Anyway, who was at the door?'

'Oh it was Bill Flett's son Martin. He's going around the village checking that everyone has enough grit to get their cars in and out. He's convinced the snow is going to settle tonight.'

'That's very considerate of him. How is Bill anyway? Is he managing to get out on the boat in this weather?'

'If his wheelchair doesn't stop him, some rough seas certainly won't. Do you remember that story he told at the wedding we went to?'

I smiled at the memory of it.

'Of course I do. But I didn't like it when that awful bloke that Emmy was speaking to was really rude to him about it. Did you believe him?'

'Without a doubt' he smiled broadly. 'He was definitely saved by an Asrai and I'd put money on it being Emmy.' He smiled to himself. 'I bet there are hundreds of stories like that all over the world. You've got one of your own.'

He pulled me toward him once more.

'Am I the only damsel in distress you've ever saved?' I said, raising my eyebrows at him questioningly.

He made a face and looked around as if trying to recall a memory, until finally nodding.

'So far yes, you've been the only one.'

I feigned pushing him away and he tightened his grip on me, slowly bending his head down and kissing me softly on the lips. 'Come on' he said. 'It's time for that swim.'

Sereia and Adam arrived on time at seven that evening. Morgan and I had set the food out on the coffee table in the living room, along with chopping boards, knives and plates. After choosing drinks and settling ourselves into comfy seats, we all helped ourselves. Adam and Sereia filled us in on their Christmas week in London, eating out and wandering the Winter Wonder Land with all its attractions, plus the Christmas markets.

They looked so adoringly at each other whilst recalling funny stories, it was obvious that Sereia was head over heels in love. Her Keeper, Olivia, had joked that every man she met was 'the one' within a few weeks, but she soon got bored and they were always gone after a few months. If only she could see her now. Thinking of Olivia made me wonder where she and Mathew were right at this moment.

Keepers were the only Asrai who lived on land amongst humans, who knew the location of ancient Asrai colonies. Olivia was the only one left now. Both Mathew and Sereia had been born at The Last Colony, but were raised on land to learn the ways of human life. Mathew's Keeper had been killed many years ago and he had had no way of returning to The Last Colony until we had met Sereia and her Keeper Olivia a year ago.

Mathew and Olivia had left for The Last Colony not long after, so we could only assume that they had made it safely. The only thing I knew about its location was that most Asrai believed it to be in the North. Olivia wasn't even permitted to tell anyone how long it would take to get there, or what the journey would entail. Whatever they had been through to get there, I suspected that she and Mathew were just as happy and wrapped up in each other as Sereia and Adam were.

'Your hair has grown out so much Morgan' said Sereia. 'It really suits you.'

Morgan ran his fingers through his mousy brown hair, which he now kept short on the sides and longer on top.

'It's a bit of a change from a skinhead isn't it?' he said with a smile. 'Emmy used to shave it for me so…'

An awkward silence settled across the room, everyone looked at me. Not wanting to bring the mood down, I broke the silence.

'Your hair has grown loads too Sereia' I said, with as much cheeriness as I could muster.

'Do you think so?' she said whilst grabbing the ends of her bright red hair with her fingers. 'It needs a cut really.'

Adam put his hand behind her head and gently stroked her hair.

'Really? I like it long' he said.

Sereia sat up straighter, smiling at the compliment.

'Maybe I won't get it cut just yet then.'

She leaned in and kissed Adam on the lips. Then, realising she had an audience, she sank back into her seat, covering her eyes. We all giggled with her and I was relieved that the mood had been so easily lightened again.

Once we'd eaten our fill of cheese, meats and crackers, Sereia and I cleared the coffee table and prepared desserts in the kitchen together.

'So' she said. 'Tell me how you've been, how's everything here? How are your turtles?'

'They're not really my turtles Sereia, they belong to the aquarium, but I do really love helping out there and looking after them. Definitely beats sitting at a computer all day. Although I do seem to have taken on the role of Morgan's administrative PA'. I jokingly rolled my eyes. 'So I'm not avoiding computers completely, but at least I get to spend lots of time with my husband.'

Sereia grabbed me out of nowhere and pulled me into a tight embrace, squeezing hard.

'I'm sorry' she said, pulling away from me and holding me at arms length. 'I'm just so, so, *so* happy for you. After everything you went through, it's just so wonderful that you and Morgan can be here, together. Together and happy.'

'And what about you?' I said as she finally let me go. 'You and Adam look seriously loved up, it's very cute.'

She busied herself taking plates out of cupboards whilst I began to slice the cheesecake.

'I know, I seriously am very loved up right now. He is just perfect in every way. The only thing that could make it even more perfect would be if he was

Asrai. It would be so much fun if we could all go out swimming together you know?'

'And you're definitely sure that he's not? I remember you thinking that he could be. How do you know?'

'I think it was just wishful thinking on my part. Plus he's really fit and have you ever met an Asrai that wasn't fit?' She smiled to herself, but then frowned a little. 'But he doesn't swim, like never ever and definitely not in the sea. How many Asrai do you know that don't swim.'

'I never used to swim in the sea until I came here.'

'Yes, but you didn't know you were an Asrai and you didn't live near the sea. You still swam though didn't you? You told me you would swim in a pool nearly every day.'

'Yeah I did, I just didn't realise why I liked it so much.'

'Well he won't even come to a pool with me if I suggest it, he won't even swim at the spa in the gym he trains at. It's actually making me wonder if he can swim at all you know? Was he one of those unlucky kids that never got a chance to learn?'

'It's a shame though isn't it. You meet your dream man and you can't tell him what you really are. Or do you think you'll tell him one day?'

'Maybe one day, if we ever got married or anything. Can you imagine though, he'll probably think I'm an absolute lunatic trying to explain all that to him.'

She passed me plates and I delicately placed slices of cheesecake on each one.

'Trying to explain what to me?'

Adam's head leaned in around the door frame of the kitchen. Sereia froze. Her eyes darted nervously to mine.

'Uh…' I stammered. 'That um, she… that she has a… um, an irrational fear of bears.'

I looked at Sereia, eyebrows raised, trying to hide my grimace.

'Bears? Why on earth would you be afraid of bears in England?' A look of utter confusion took over his face.

Sereia turned to face Adam, palms raised.

'That's why it's irrational' she said in a mock sarcastic tone, slowly shaking her head.

Adam stepped further into the kitchen, his face indicating that he was considering her statement.

'I guess that kind of does make you a lunatic I suppose.'

He grabbed her hand, pulling it toward his mouth and kissed her on the knuckles. Her body visibly relaxed. He believed her, he hadn't heard too much. Dropping her hand, he turned toward me.

'I've been sent for the fizzy stuff' he said. 'It's nearly midnight.'

We watched the second hand slowly tick around the clock on the wall in the living room. As it reached the ten, Sereia started the count down as we all stood around, holding champagne flutes of sparkling wine.

'four… three… two… one… Happy New Year' she raised her free hand in the air as we all clinked glasses.

Morgan put his glass on the coffee table and took my face in his hands. He pulled me toward him, our noses touching.

'Happy New Year Vivienne.'

'Happy New Year Morgan.'

Our lips touched and a surge of excitement shot through me. Would a kiss like this always feel as good as the first kiss we shared? The memory of it made me wish we were on the beach right now, our skin wet from the sea, the wind howling around us, the cold, wet sand underneath our feet. Our lips parted for a moment, but then I felt his kiss return, deeper this time. I felt my breath get heavier until a soft 'ahem' brought me back to reality. Morgan's face pulled away from mine and we both turned to find Sereia and Adam awkwardly averting their gaze. I couldn't help but laugh out loud.

3.

Slowly opening my eyes, I turned my head toward my bedside cabinet and squinted at the clock. It was only seven in the morning. We had spent the rest of the evening playing cards and board games, laughing at each others' bad luck and my terrible jokes and despite only going to sleep a few hours ago, I felt surprisingly fresh. I rolled over onto my side and found myself facing Morgan's naked back. I could see the lines of his muscles, the ridges of his spine and light freckles dotted here and there.

I cuddled up to him as close as I could, sliding my hand around his waist and onto his bare stomach. I let my hand smooth upward toward his chest and buried my face in his back, breathing in the smell of his skin. He was dead to the world and now the faint salty smell of his skin made me realise I was itching to swim. I slid out of bed and chucked on some clothes, then brushed my teeth and hair in the ensuite. Sereia and Adam had stayed in the guest room, so despite Morgan being out for the count, I tried to keep as quiet as possible. As I crept through the cottage toward the front door, I found Adam in the living room. He was standing in front of the mirror with a mug in his hand.

'Hey, good morning' I said. 'You're up early.'

He turned to face me.

'Oh, good morning.' He paused and shrugged his shoulders slightly. 'I can never sleep when I'm hungover really. What's your excuse?' he said, smiling at me.

'Same thing I guess. Can I get you anything before I head out? Breakfast? Pain killers?'

'No I'm fine honestly. Hope you don't mind,' he raised his mug toward the fireplace. 'I'm just admiring your mirror. I've never seen anything quite like it.'

I stepped into the room, smelling his strong coffee as I did so.

'I don't really know much about it. It's an antique. My Gran's mother gave it to her.'

'It really is beautiful. You should get it appraised, see if you can find out where it came from, who made it.'

I shook my head.

'Oh I would never want to sell it.'

His eyes widened as he realised what he'd said.

'I'm sorry, I didn't mean like that, I just meant it would be nice to know where it came from, how old it is you know? What's its history.'

I nodded.

'Yes, maybe… perhaps one day.'

He took a few steps toward me.

'I'm sorry, sometimes I put my foot in it like that.'

'It's okay, honestly. No harm done.'

I smiled at him, Looking at his handsome face, I suddenly became curious of the scar, running across his eyebrow and cheek. It wasn't hugely noticeable unless you were relatively close to him.

'How did you get that? Your scar on your face?'

His hand quickly rose to his face, gently touching his eyebrow and following the line of the scar down his cheek.

'This little thing? I was bitten by a shark.'

A wide grin spread across his face.

'Oh, so that's why you don't like the sea.' I smiled back at him.

'Who said I didn't like the sea? I just find it a bit too cold for my liking is all.'

He sipped his drink, still smiling at me.

'Was it a big shark then?'

I laughed as I said it, then Adam laughed too. But then his face went slightly more serious.

'Let's just say I upset someone that I shouldn't have.'

I raised my eyebrows. That certainly sounded ominous.

'Well on that note, I'm off out for a walk.'

'In this weather? Vivienne, you do know it's snowing outside don't you? You haven't even got a coat on.'

I left the living room and headed toward the front door. I always forgot how humans were surprised by a high tolerance to the cold. Asrai generally felt more comfortable in colder temperatures.

'Uh yeah…'

I looked around, surely there would be a coat I could pretend to need somewhere around here. I opened the hallway closet and found the big coat Morgan used when he occasionally had to pretend he felt the cold at work.

'Here it is.'

I shrugged it on, knowing full well it was absolutely huge on me. Adam leaned in the door frame of the living room.

'That's your coat?' His face was sceptical.

'I uh, I lost mine. Left it down the pub a few days ago. This is quite obviously Morgan's coat. But it keeps me nice and snuggley warm.'

I pulled it in tight around me, doing my best to look like one of those women who managed to look really small and feminine in their partner's clothes. I doubted very much that it was working as Adam seemingly looked me up and down before laughing to himself.

'Cute' was all he said, before heading back through the cottage toward the guest room.

Adam had been right, it was snowing this morning. The lightest flutter of snow fell around me, each flake melting as soon as it hit the ground. I made my way to the cliff path that would take me down to Pendour Cove. The wind today did not feel too strong and the water looked no more rough than usual for a cold winter morning. I had begun to feel quite warm in Morgan's huge coat and it flapped around me once I stopped hugging it in tight to my body.

Once on the sand, I found a crevice in the rocks to stuff my clothes into, hoping they wouldn't get discovered and cause alarm to anyone else that may wander down for an early New Years Day walk. With any luck, the threat of snow and ice was enough to keep all the other villagers tucked up nice and warm inside their homes. I looked up toward the top of the cliff and seeing no one around, I jogged to the water's edge. The icy water almost felt like a sting on my feet as I ran through the shallow waves and I couldn't wait to feel it over my entire body. As soon as the water was at my thighs, I dived underneath the surface, kicking my legs behind me and taking a huge gulp of water.

Not swimming properly late last night like we normally would have, had really made me long for the water today. The crisp coldness on my skin made me feel so alive and as always, every nerve in my body tingled with satisfaction. It almost felt like a drug to me and now I just wanted it more and more. I got as far as the buoy before breaking through the surface again. Taking in deep breaths of air, I realised I was out of breath, which was unusual for me.

But I was getting faster and faster every day, I had really been pushing myself on my morning swims. The exhilaration, the adrenalin. It all just made me feel so… so me. This had always been where I belonged. After catching my breath, I ducked back under the surface of the water. As I headed out in the direction of the horizon, I stayed close to the seabed and felt the seaweed tickle my legs. The sand gave way to large pebbles and rocks, the species of fish I encountered got bigger and bigger and the surface of the water got further and further away from me.

I found myself reaching a cluster of larger rocks, covered in underwater plants and seaweed. I came to a stop at the base of it and using my hands, I pulled myself around it slowly, looking at all the plants and starfish. My eyes settled on a starfish as big as a dinner plate and I reached my hand toward it. I stopped short of touching it at the sound of a faint whistling coming from somewhere. Looking around, I could see nothing that would explain the sound and so began to pull myself up the rocks to the top. Holding on at the top of the rocks, I searched the seabed below me. Nothing. But then the noise came again, louder this time and not so much of a whistle, but fast clicking. As it got faster and louder I looked up to find five silhouettes above me. Dolphins.

I pushed myself away from the rocks and up toward the surface. The closer I got to their dark silhouettes, the louder the clicking sounded. As I came close to breaking through the surface, I found myself being circled by the dolphins, clicking in what seemed like a playful way at me. I reached out my hands and gently stroked the side of one of them, its smooth, rubbery skin gliding across my fingers.

The dolphin dived down and swam away, before rushing back and nuzzling my arms. Stretching my arms out again, I stroked either side of its head until I felt a nuzzle in the back of my head. Turning around, I found another of the dolphins. So this one wanted a turn too huh? I spent the next few minutes stroking and smoothing which ever dolphin was nudging me the hardest. Each one would periodically swim off and break the surface, getting more air.

Eventually, I felt that it was time to head back and after waving goodbye to each dolphin, I broke the surface myself to get my bearings and headed back in the direction of land. Swimming just under the surface, I soon found myself surrounded by the dolphins. They would swim fast ahead of me and then slow down whilst I caught them up, were they trying to make me race them? There was no way I would ever be able to keep up, but it was fun nonetheless.

The dolphins soon got bored of racing ahead and eventually dropped their pace to match me. Were they hoping to follow me somewhere? The one to my right began to nuzzle under my arm, lifting my hand up with its nose, what was it trying to do? I tried to bat it away, but it just kept coming back, nuzzling my arm and hand. Not knowing what it could want, I held onto it by the dorsal fin and stroked the side of its face with the other hand. At once, I could sense the dolphin moving faster and I let it go, not wanting to upset it in any way. It shot off into the distance, then slowed and returned to me, nuzzling my arm once more. Did you want me to hold on? I thought. Is that what you want? Is that fun to you?

I reached out and held onto the dorsal fin with both hands. Again the dolphin started moving at speed as soon as I had a firm grip on the fin. As it gained momentum, my body was pulled in line with its own and I could feel the fast motions of its tail underneath my legs. The dolphin swam closer to the surface and then ducked down lower repeatedly, being mimicked by the other dolphins keeping pace around us. It was difficult not to scream out loud with excitement. Faster and faster we went until suddenly, the dolphin broke through the surface of the water. I held on as tightly as I could as we crashed back underneath the water.

My heart was beating faster than ever as the dolphin's tail whipped faster underneath me and we breached the surface once again. I let out a scream of delight as the other dolphins dived in time with us, crashing in and out of the water over and over again.

4.

'Wow, I have't seen dolphins in forever' Sereia said.

It was a week later and she and Adam had come to the aquarium.

'I don't remember ever seeing them in real life, but Olivia says we did, back when we made the journey from…' her voice trailed off and she looked at Adam, who was listening intently. 'Uh, made that boat trip down in Porthcurno.'

I knew what she had been about to say. She was referring to her journey from The Last Colony many years ago. She had been so young at the time that she didn't remember it herself.

'That long ago huh?' I gave her a knowing look.

She sipped her coffee and nodded.

'Yup, so long ago.' A smile crept across her face. 'You're so lucky Viv, how exciting.'

'So where did you see them exactly?' said Adam. His face, once again, looked quite skeptical.

'Down on the beach at The Cove. When I went for a walk on New Year's Day. You guys had gone by the time I got back, so I couldn't tell you about it then. The tide was in and they were really close to the beach. I bet I could have touched one if I'd actually gotten in the water.'

I gave Sereia a sideways glance as she covered her face with her coffee cup, concealing a smile.

'They came in that close huh? Not something you hear about every day. Especially not at this time of year' Adam said.

He set his coffee cup down, eyebrows raised. I shrugged.

'I guess not. I doubt I'll ever be lucky enough to see them again. I just wish I'd had my phone with me so I could have taken a picture or video, but never mind.'

The cafe was quiet today. The Christmas break was over and the children had returned to school. There was only a spattering of visitors in the cafe and the manager Deborah was scanning the room for empty cups and plates. She approached our table, apron tied tightly across her middle.

'Can I get you guys anything else?'

She smiled broadly, hands on hips. With her short grey hair, she reminded me of Mrs Claus. We all shook our heads in unison.

'No we're fine thank you Debs. I've got to get back to work now really anyway.'

She nodded her head.

'Well I hope that that husband of yours isn't working you too hard. You need to look after yourself if you're going to give us some little babies soon.'

I flinched as the words came out of her mouth. Sereia noticed and opened her mouth as if to say something.

'You know Morgan Debbie, he never works anyone too hard' I said with a smile. 'But like I said before, we've got a lot to concentrate on here for now and we may travel a bit first too so…'   I shrugged my shoulders and gave a little shake of my head. Her smile widened.

'Well don't wait too long my dear. I can't wait to have another little Whidden running around. It will be just like when Morgan was a young lad.'

She smiled to herself and headed back to the counter. Adam stood up.

'Excuse me for a moment ladies, I just need to visit the gents.'

As he headed off in the direction of the toilets, Sereia turned toward me, taking my hand and giving it a squeeze.

'Are you okay Vivienne?'

I smiled and nodded.

'Yes, I'm fine.' She raised an eyebrow. 'I am, really I am. I get it all the time, I'm used to it now.'

'Have you talked about what you might do? Have you thought about adopting?'

I shook my head.

'I don't know. It just seems so... there are so many children out there that need a family, how do you pick one? What gives me the right to pick?' I shrugged my shoulders again. 'I think I'd rather have to be chosen if I'm honest. I wouldn't feel so awful about all the children I'm not choosing if you know what I mean?'

She nodded now.

'I know, but you can't think of it that way.' She squeezed my hand again.

'Don't you think you'd feel the same way Sereia?'

I felt the sting of tears in my eyes and blinked it away as best I could. Sereia's head turned as Adam returned to the table. She let go of my hand.

'So' he said. 'Are you going to show me around your aquarium or what?'

Sereia and Adam wandered around the aquarium a few steps ahead of me. They walked hand in hand, like Morgan and myself often did. Sereia's red hair shone in the light every time her head looked left or right as she practically skipped along, keeping pace with Adam's long strides. Every now and again he would pull her in close and she'd look up at him, beaming from ear to ear. When he leant in to kiss her, I would look away, not wanting to intrude on their romantic moments.

Sereia practically squealed with delight as we went through the huge glass tunnel where the fish and sharks swam all around and overhead.

'Wow, this is amazing' she said. 'It almost feels like I'm really there, really out in the ocean again.'

'Again?' Adam turned to face Sereia, eyebrows raised, before continuing. 'You've been swimming with sharks before?'

Sereia turned her back toward him and touched her fingers to the glass.

'Yes, it was amazing. I did one of those shark cage things on holiday years ago.'

Sereia turned her head toward me as I joined her peering through the glass and we shared an awkward glance. Adam wandered off to the end of the tunnel, following a shark that swam along, close to the glass.

'You really need to be more careful' I whispered. 'That's twice recently that you've nearly dropped yourself in it.'

She waved me away with her hands.

'I may have to tell him soon you know.'

'Really why?'

I looked over her shoulder, making sure he was still at the other end of the tunnel, out of earshot.

'He's been talking a lot about our future. He's thinking of moving here. I don't know, I just feel like I can really trust him and if he does turn out to be the one' she raised her hands into quotation marks, rolling her eyes 'and we're together forever, I think he should know.'

I nodded toward Adam as he had turned around and was slowly making his way back to the where we were standing, following the same shark back again.

'Right' he said, 'when do I get to see those turtles I've heard so much about?'

That evening, as Morgan and I wandered slowly down to The Cove in the dark for our nightly swim, I recounted the day's events. Morgan grimaced as I told him of Sereia's slip ups and the possibility that she may choose to reveal her true self to Adam.

'She really does need to be more careful. We don't know if he really can be trusted. He could go running off telling anyone. I think it's better not to tell them at all really, human partners I mean.'

'My mother told David.'

I remembered that David, my biological father had known what she was.

'She was pregnant with you though. Maybe she thought she didn't have a choice. Sereia still does.'

She may have told him before. I saw a picture of them on a beach. It looked really cold, he was wrapped up warm, but mum and the others didn't have much on. I assumed they had been there for a swim. But you're right. I don't know that for sure, he may have had no idea until she got pregnant.'

We reached the beach and removed our shoes and outer clothes, stuffing them into a gap in the rocks. Taking each others hand again, we walked slowly toward the water. The tide was out and I was grateful to feel the wind all over my body. The cottage had felt stuffy this evening, suffocating even. Or was that just how I felt? The weight of my infertility was pulling me down again recently. The less I thought about the loss of

Emmy, the more I thought about the loss of my family's future.

'What's wrong?' Morgan said as our feet reached the water. 'You look sad?'

I kept moving forward, wading deeper into the water. I shook my head.

'Nothing,' I lied. 'I just really need a swim.'

I dived into the water before he had a chance to reply, swimming as fast as I could away from the shallow water. Morgan kept up with me easily at first, but he soon fell behind. I stopped about a mile out, waiting for him to catch up. He finally did and shaking his head at me, he pointed upward toward the surface. I smiled, shaking my head no and heading straight back the way we had came.

Once again I set off at speed, not even giving Morgan a chance to catch his breath. By the time I reached the buoy, Morgan was nowhere to be seen, so I made my way to the surface and held on whilst I waited for him. Ten minutes passed and I was almost beginning to worry until I felt his hands on my ankles. His hands slowly made their way up my legs and body until his head emerged from the water in front of me. His hair was flattened against his forehead, his eyes glistened in the moonlight. He held onto the buoy behind me, his eyes staring into my own. He touched his forehead to mine and our noses rubbed together. I closed my eyes and then felt the softness of his lips touch mine. He pulled away and as I opened my eyes again, he was once again staring at me, so intently, it almost made me feel embarrassed.

'What?' I said defensively.

'I spoke to Debbie today.' He cocked his head to one side, gauging my reaction, but all I could do was look away. 'She told me she saw you' he continued. 'She said how she told you she's waiting on those babies.' He used his forefinger to lift my chin, forcing me to look him in the eye again. 'I know that that's what's upsetting you right now.'

I breathed in and out deeply before letting out my next words.

'It's just hard sometimes Morgan. If no one mentioned it I'd be fine, but ever since we got married it's all I get asked about everywhere I go. At the aquarium, by people in the village. Everyone is waiting for the newlyweds to announce they are expecting. No one seems to consider that there may be a reason that we've not announced a pregnancy yet. That we can't physically have children of our own. I don't want to lie and say that we don't want children, because that would just feel awful coming out of my mouth, but I don't know what else I can do. I just wish everyone would shut up about it.'

'I know you do Vivienne and I do too, but people are people and they don't realise what they're doing when they say stuff like that. Especially old, nosey ones like Debbie.'

He smiled, searching for a response in my face. I couldn't help smiling back. This must be hard for Morgan too, but as always, he was trying to make me feel better.

'I know and I'm sorry, I don't mean to be a downer about it.'

'You can be whatever you want about it, as long as you always tell me how you're feeling.'

Did he always have to do this? Be so good about everything? Always know the right thing to say? I wrapped my arms and legs around him as he held onto the buoy. I kissed him now, softly at first, until the excitement rose up inside me. I broke my kiss away from him and took his face in my hands.

'Are you ready to head back?' I said, raising an eyebrow.

He shook his head slowly, then letting go of the buoy, he let us sink slowly down beneath the surface once more.

5.

I groaned to myself as Morgan's alarm chirped from the other side of the bed. Rolling over, I nudged him in the back until he raised an arm, thumping the snooze button. It was four thirty in the morning.

'Remind me again why you are getting up so early?'

He rolled over to face me, pulling me into his arms.

'I told you. We have a health and safety inspection today.'

I groaned.

'I don't have to be there do I?'

Morgan laughed.

'No not at all, in fact it's probably better if you stay home to be honest. You are literally the clumsiest staff member I've ever had.' He squeezed me tightly as I jokingly tried to push him away. 'Besides, Sereia's all sad about Adam going home for a few weeks isn't she?

You should keep her company today, go and do something girly perhaps, take her mind off it.'

I pushed Morgan hard by the shoulders, rolling him onto his back and sat astride him.

'But I'd much rather we both stayed here' I said.

I leaned in close to his face, bringing my mouth next to his ear.

'Don't you want to stay here with me today?'

I nuzzled his neck with my face, hoping I could get him to change his mind.

'You know that I really do want to stay with you in bed right now and any other day you wouldn't be able to stop me but…'

I ran my lips along his neck. I desperately wanted to kiss him, but I was also desperately aware of my awful morning breath.

'But…?' I said in return.

'But,' he said, pushing my shoulders up until I was sat up straight on top of him. 'But I really do have to go to work and Sereia is really down about Adam not coming back for Valentines Day next week. She really needs you to cheer her up.'

'Fine' I said.

I swung my leg around and hopped off the bed, heading for the bathroom.

'But you better be back in that bed by the time I get home.'

I stayed in bed until long after Morgan had left for the day. By the time I'd decided to get out of bed and have a cup of tea, the dark early morning sky had lightened with the dawn. I headed outside toward The Cove. The weather was dull and miserable today. Icy rain came at me sideways whilst I stripped off into my red, sporty two piece. Morgan had chosen it for me for Christmas and I was happy to have something a bit more colourful in my collection. I wrapped my clothes and shoes in a carrier bag and stuffed it in the rocks as far back as I could.

Jogging toward the water, I scanned the horizon and could see a boat in the far distance. It was a large fishing trawler and I couldn't quite tell if it was moving or if it had anchored where it was. The water was choppy enough that I doubted they would be able to see me, but I decided I would swim along the coast toward St. Ives, instead of straight out as I normally did, just to be safe.

Into the water I went, smiling as the cold water embraced my head and body. I had forgotten to tie my hair up and it flowed behind me, almost reaching my bum. I let my body twist and turn as I made my way through the shallower waters surrounding the cliff edges, every once in a while I would have to swim out further to avoid barnacle covered rocks that spread out from the bottom of the cliffs.

I knew I'd nearly reached St. Ives after I'd been swimming non stop for nearly an hour. I had a much higher chance of being seen here and decided it was time to turn around and head back. Pushing myself away from some rocks, I swam as fast as I could, pushing every muscle in my body. It felt good to swim with maximum effort, my heart was beating faster and faster with every metre. When I finally reached The Cove again my shoulders felt like they were burning and my legs ached. I swam out toward the buoy and lay myself on the floor of the seabed, staring up at the silhouette of the buoy. I closed my eyes for a moment and tried not to think about Emmy or babies, or the fact that Morgan wouldn't be waiting for me at home because of a stupid Health and Safety inspection.

At least I would get to spend some alone time with Sereia today, even if she was probably going to be miserable and sulking because of Adam's prolonged absence this month. I'm sure I could find a way to cheer her up. Maybe we would head to the pub for lunch, she always loved some day time drinking. Or perhaps a drive into St. Ives, we could do some touristy things.

Whatever we did, hopefully Morgan would be home by the time we were done. A low rumble interrupted my thoughts. Opening my eyes, I searched the surface above me. There was nothing directly above me, but then something to my left caught my eye, a dark shadow moving closer. It was a boat and it was big. What do I do? Do I stay here and wait until it moves on or do I make a dash for the beach and hope I can get out before I'm noticed, make it look like a normal human person taking herself out for a swim… in the freezing cold sea?

The boat slowed above me, the engine still churning over as it came to a stop next to the buoy. I held on to the chain that secured the buoy to the sand below. Why had they stopped? Would it be better to go now? Before I could make up my mind, the engine roared loudly and the boat began to move off away from the buoy, away from me. I felt my body relax with relief. That was a close call. What were they doing though? Boats that big didn't come into The Cove. I looked up, noticing that the boat's silhouette had slowed again.

Suddenly, a criss cross of ropes plunged through the surface. It was a net. Shit. Were they actually trying to catch me? They must think I'm a basking shark or something. I pushed away from the chain of the buoy toward the beach but I wasn't quick enough. The net was huge and it was weighted all around. It sank down in front of me before I had a chance to get out from underneath it and it was quickly pulling together underneath me.

I desperately tried to lift it up, tried to get out from underneath it but it was no use, it was being pulled together like a draw string, closing in on all sides. I was trapped inside it. Shit. Shit. Shit. What would I tell them? I would just have to say I was using a hand held oxygen tank and I dropped my gear when they pulled me in. Surely they will believe me? How could they believe me at this time of year, it was freezing and I was in a bloody two piece.

I felt my self being pulled upward, the net tightly wrapped around me, folding my body into a foetal position. I exhaled all the water from my lungs. I'd have to make sure I made a show of needing air once they got me out of the water.

As the net got me clear of the water, I could hear the chug of the chains on the pully system. I spluttered and coughed as loud as I could. I heard male voices shouting instructions over each other as the net swung inwards across the side of the boat and was lowered down onto the deck. I found the top of the net with my hands and pushed my arms, head and top half of my body through it. Two men in full orange trawler man gear stood above me, looking down.

'I'm so sorry, I was down there snorkelling and I got stuck in your net.'

I continued to wrestle with the thick rope of the net, trying desperately to free my legs. Why weren't they helping me? Harsh footsteps made me look up. Another two men, this time in dark suits and light rain coats, were crossing the deck toward me. One had a vaguely familiar face, with shiny skin and slicked back hair. The other one was…

'Adam?'

I frantically scrambled with the net, pushing my legs out, trying to get free.

'Adam, what are you doing here?' I looked from his face to the other man. 'What's going on?'

Adam turned toward the familiar man, giving a slight nod of his head.

'That's her' he said.

The other man's eyes bore into mine. Without breaking eye contact, he motioned toward me with his chin. The trawler man to his left stepped forward and raised his right hand. I realised too late that he held in it a heavy metal wrench, which he swung directly at my head.

6.

Una

They kept the lights on all day and all night. I think that was the worst part. I could sleep with them on, that wasn't a problem. I could sleep whenever I wanted to, but I never really knew if it was night time or day time. There were no windows, no skylights in the ceiling high above. There was nearly always someone in here doing something and we were watched by little cameras on the walls and above the doors with their little red lights, blinking, all day, every day.

Until today, I had thought that the only way in or out was through the double doors to the left hand side of our tanks, which they operated by swiping a key card at the side of it. But as I had seen for the first time today, there was another way in through the wall at the other end of the building. The whole side of the building had risen up, like a some sort of garage door. I had never seen it happen before, not until they brought her in. A buzzer had sounded and the entire wall creaked to life, rising slowly until it was high enough for the van waiting outside to reverse in. The dark sky outside let me know that it was night time. It was the first time I had really known whether it was night or day since I had been brought here.

She was sleeping still. She looked so peaceful lying down on her side, curled up in a ball. Her long, dark hair hung around her face in the water, covering her pale skin. She still had on the red swimming stuff they had brought her in wearing. They hadn't changed her yet. The rest of us had been made to change into black t-shirts and shorts before being put in the tanks.

Jordan had resisted. That's why his tank was always kept quite hot, it was keeping him tired. Stopped him trying to force the bars at the top of his tank, stopped him talking to me. Now he just sat in the corner of his tank all the time, knees up to his chest, arms holding them in place and his head bowed low. He looked up briefly when she was brought in, but he wouldn't look at me anymore.

I couldn't say exactly how long we'd been here, but it felt like a really long time. It could have just been months, it could have been years. Jordan's hair had grown so much that I think it was the latter.

She was much older than us, the new person. She was a grown up, she even had a wedding ring on. She would have a husband somewhere that missed her, if he wasn't already dead. It had only been three of us for such a long time before she came. There were more when I first got here, so many more, but nearly all of the twenty or so tanks were empty now.

The youngest ones always died quite soon after coming here. Their small, slightly more fragile bodies couldn't take the regular procedures of blood and bone marrow removal. At least once a week we were each taken out of our tank and led to the other side of the large room. There was a stand alone room there with a double door that didn't lock, it could be pushed open from either side and then the doors would swing back and forth. We would be taken inside and stripped of our wet clothes, bright florescent lights illuminating every part of us. A woman in green doctors scrubs would towel us down and brush our hair, before redressing us in a gown that left our backs uncovered.

The room was clinical and smelt strongly of bleach, with lots of stainless steel cupboards that had lots of medical instruments inside. We would have to lie face down on a table in the middle of the room. If we struggled, our arms and legs were tied down. People with their hair and faces covered would gather around us, their gloved hands held up in front of them. When we are lying still enough, a long, thick needle is put into our lower back and another in each arm. After they have taken what they want, we are dressed again in black t-shirts and shorts and led back to our tank, where we sleep for a long time.

Jordan was taken for procedures much more often than I was. I had overheard the people talk about him during one of my own procedures, about how well he rejuvenated, that must be why they did it to him much more often. No one that works here really talks *to* us though. None of them ask us if we are okay. They never ask us how much it hurts. I wonder what she's here for. It won't be for bone marrow. I've heard them say it's not as good from older Asrai. They only like using children for that.

Kendra had been the oldest one still here. She looked like a teenager, but she couldn't remember exactly how old she was. They had taken her from Norway. She had been living with her father, just the two of them for as far back as she could remember. She didn't know what had happened to him. She still cried about it sometimes, I could hear her when her tank was emptied. That's how it worked here, we were always in the tanks unless we were having a procedure. If we needed the toilet, we had to go right there in the tank. Then we would press a large red button on the inside just above the surface of the water and the water would quickly drain out through a small bowl sized hole that would open up at the bottom, right in the middle. The tank would immediately refill from huge hose like taps as soon as the old water had completely drained.

We were fed often enough. They would place the food on trays on top of our bars and if you held on, there was enough room for your head between the water and the bars. Holding yourself up with one hand, we would use the other to reach up and grab whatever they had given us for that meal. It was normally sandwiches of some kind, but every now and again we would get fish, or chicken with dry roasted potatoes.

Those days were always a little better than the others, but it made me miss my mother's cooking. Her spicy stews, or freshly caught fish, grilled and dipped in a creamy sauce. I missed everything about my mother, her smile, her smell, her goodnight hugs.

Kendra had been watching the new arrival intently since she had gotten here. I could tell she was willing her to wake up, itching to ask her questions. We always found out new information when someone else came, it helped us work out how long we'd been here. But we hadn't had anyone new for a long, long time. Even Kendra had lost count of the weeks since the last one. There were two tanks between Kendra and I, but we pulled ourselves up underneath the bars and talked whenever there was no one else around to hear.

They did other things to Kendra, things she wouldn't talk to me about. They were giving her something, something that was new and it was changing her. Her light brown skin had started to turn blue and pink in patches on her legs and arms. She had long hair that curled tightly and I could see it falling out in clumps in her tank. Whatever else they were doing to her, her body did not like it and it showed. She looked thinner too, no longer showing muscle definition in her legs and arms and her face was gaunt. Her dark brown eyes had a constant sleepiness about them. Maybe they had turned the temperature up in her tank too.

My tank was always kept cold. I always did what I was told, never caused a fuss, never objected to anything. I never resisted. I wished Jordan had just done the same, but every time they turned the heat in his tank down, he would go straight back to kicking at the bars, knocking his meal trays off the top of the tank. Anything to cause a problem. I pleaded with him to stop, told him we may have a chance of being freed if we just did what they wanted for a while. But we both knew that that wasn't a possibility. The only way you got out of here was in a large black bag.

I had watched nearly twenty children die one by one. Their bodies would go completely limp and they would tend to float upward a little, arms and legs hanging lifeless. Then their tanks would be emptied and their bodies would be taken to the procedure room. That's if they died in the tank. Sometimes we would hear panicked voices from the procedure room, the doors would swing open and people would rush in and out. We would hear beeping from the machines in there until eventually, quiet would settle in the room. The dead bodies would not leave the procedure room in the black bags for many hours. I don't know what they were doing with the bodies in there, but Kendra was sure they were harvesting the rest of their bone marrow. Taking all their blood and probably all their organs too.

Kendra seemed to think they took our blood and bone marrow to help sick people. But not just any sick people, only really rich *humans* that were sick. She said our blood and bone marrow, even our skin had super healing qualities that humans didn't have and that people paid a lot of money for it when they were ill. I once asked her how she knew and she said she would hear them talking when she was in the procedure room, or even in the tank room when they thought we were all asleep. She said she would pretend to sleep near the top of the tank and listen with one ear sticking out of the water.

I often thought about leaving in one of the big black bags. I would wonder when it would be my turn. Whether I would die in my tank or if something would go wrong during one of my procedures. I think I had come close to dying once. The machines in the procedure room began to beep differently and I found it harder and harder to breath. I didn't panic, but the people in the room seemed to. I had just wanted to go to sleep and I did, I felt myself slowly drift off. The next thing I remember was my eyes and mouth suddenly opening wide. I was now lying on my back, with 3 or 4 masked faces staring down at me and a large syringe sticking right out of my chest in front of me.

Then I'm back in my tank, Jordan shouting my name through his bars. He thought I had died in the procedure room, he still thought I was dying. He had called my name for hours, begging me to wake up, but I *had* been awake. I could hear every word he said, I just couldn't move. He eventually stopped, I think they must have turned his tank temperature up really high that time. That was the last time he had really spoken to me. It would be procedure day for us again tomorrow. I didn't know whether it would it be our last or not.

There had been a lot of movement in the lab since the woman had been brought in. After the truck she had been brought in had gone, other trucks had soon arrived. New machines had been unloaded and wheeled into place in the lab. There seemed to be a few more people than there normally were, sitting at computers, or bringing in boxes and taking them into the procedure room. Why would they need all this new equipment just for her? The people seemed to be talking more to each other, huddled over desks, looking at her tank. They looked so happy, so excited about her being here.

7.

I didn't remember falling asleep, but I was awoken by the muffled sound of raised voices. I knew immediately it was Jordan. He was resisting again, refusing to come out of his tank for a procedure. I hung onto the bars and pulled my head out of the water. He turned toward me and caught my eye. He looked so scared, but he seemed to relax once he saw me, or just giving up the fight maybe.

He let himself be lifted out of the tank by two large men. The lady in the green scrubs wrapped a towel around him and steered him toward the procedure room. His legs would buckle every few steps or so and she would have to sink down with him before taking his weight and standing him back up. His head was bowed down low as she walked him past my tank, her hands squeezing each of his shoulders. I watched as they disappeared through the double doors of the procedure room and kept watching as the doors swung back and forth.

I finally let go of the bars above me, letting myself sink back to the bottom of my tank. I noticed Kendra had been watching too. She also clung to her bars, her eyes and forehead the only thing above the water in her tank. It reminded me of a wildlife programme we had watched once on our small television. It was a crocodile, or maybe an alligator and it would only have its eyes and nose sticking out of the water, where the other animals couldn't see it. Like the alligator, Kendra sunk back down with only the tiniest of ripples. Under the water, she turned herself around to face the tank of the woman. She was still sleeping, still curled up in a ball, her hair still floating around her face. I pulled myself back up again, trying to get a better look at her, when the shrill beep of the door made me turn around. The woman doctor was back. I didn't know what type of doctor she actually was, but she wore a white coat, so that's what I called her in my head, among other things.

There used to be lots of other people here in white coats too, but once she came things started changing.

There were more procedures. There were more deaths. I don't know if that's what made the others stop coming, but it definitely seemed like they didn't agree with her being here. I didn't recognise the person with her. He hadn't been here before, not that I had seen at least. He wasn't wearing a white coat, only a suit. He looked much older and had his hair slicked back away from his face. His face was almost as shiny as his hair. He didn't look like he was very nice and I sunk back into the water a little as they walked past me, straight to her tank.

The doctor held the sort of small, flat television in her hands that she always had with her and tapped at it as she spoke.

'She's still unconscious, but the wound to her head should have healed by now, so we can start phase one very soon.'

'Good' the man nodded. 'Where are we with the formula for phase one?'

She tapped on the screen in front of her again.

'Subject F265 has provided us with enough data to make further changes to the formula and I believe it is now ready for un-pure testing again. We will need to administer an increasing dose each day for two weeks until the full course has been administered.'

'Why can't we do it all at once?'

'It has been tried in the past, but nearly all subjects could not tolerate the high dosage in one go. It proved fatal in most cases.'

'That was at site B wasn't it? They weren't under your care and supervision were they?'

She nodded.

'That's true, things will certainly be better now that I can control the administering of the formula and monitor the subject more closely, however I still would rather not risk it. With what we know about her being pregnant before, she really is an anomaly. I have never seen a case of pregnancy, even a failed one, in any un-pure Asrai. We've taken preliminary samples from her already and the team downstairs have run initial DNA comparisons with other un-pure samples and the preliminary results really are quite interesting.'

They came to a stop in front of her tank. The man leaned forwarded and peered in.

'How so?'

'The structure of her DNA is different. There's something else there. Unlike other hybrids who are infertile due to a mismatched number of chromosomes, she has an even number.'

'Is there any way she could be a pure Asrai?'

'No, definitely not. She has human DNA in her, that's one thing I know for sure. She just has something else on top of it. Is this what meant she could get pregnant? Is she truly a one off, or is it something we can artificially replicate in others? And if the formula works on her and we can actually get her pregnant and carry to term, we could soon have a drug that could cure infertility in our species. We could have it ready for mass production within three years.'

'You really have impressed me Dr Ayers. When I brought you onto this project I had no idea how far along you would bring the research and how quickly.'

'Don't thank me yet Lyle. Thank me when we have the cure and please… call me Brooke.'

8.

Vivienne

I was in water. I could tell that much before I opened my eyes. What was I doing in water? What was the last thing I remembered? The net, the boat.

Adam.

I slowly opened my eyes, recalling the last thing I saw, the huge wrench being swung at my head. My head didn't seem to hurt, but the bright light stung my eyes. How long had I been unconscious for? I focused my eyes as best I could, looking around. I sat up and felt the ground around me. It was glass. I was in some sort of tank. What the hell was this? Where was I? I felt my heart pound faster as panic rose inside of me. Looking beyond the tank I could see more tanks, all a few feet off the ground, but there were also desks, computers, big machines.

I was in some sort of laboratory. Looking above me I could see bars stretching across the top of the tank I was in. I pushed myself up and grabbed hold of them with both hands. I was able to pull my head out of the water. Looking straight up I could see the ceilings rose up really high. This couldn't be the same laboratory that Abraham had near London. That one was nowhere near this high, it was underground. This seemed like it could be an air craft hangar. It was huge, with no windows and there was a garage type door at the end, which would definitely fit a plane through.

I looked around a bit more, there were two other doors, one on the wall to my left and the other on the opposite side of the room. That one led into a smaller room built within the hangar, with its own ceiling, almost like a porta cabin had been added, but it was flush to the ground. I couldn't see any people. I tried to shout, my voice a harsh whisper at first.

'Hey' I had to clear my throat before it came out any louder. 'Hey, someone let me out of this thing.' I shook against the bars as hard as I could, they were completely immovable. 'Hey... heeeeeey. Is anybody here?'

'They won't come.'

I spun my head around looking for the source of the voice. There was no one I could see in the laboratory, it must be coming from one of the tanks. The ones behind me looked empty, I was in one of a row of five. To my immediate right was an empty tank, but I could see through that tank to the one on the other side of it. A girl had herself pulled up against the bars in that one. She held on with two hands as I did.

'They won't come if you shout' she repeated. 'Even when they are in here working, or working on us, they ignore us.'

She readjusted her hands, pulling her face closer to the bars. I could see from her gaunt face that she had light brown skin, but one of her hands looked like it was completely blue, the other looked gold and pink.

'What do you mean working on us? What is this place? Who are you?' I pulled myself closer to the side of the tank closest to her, 'how do we get out?'

'We can't get out. No one gets out of here. Not alive anyway.'

'What? You can't be serious? What is happening here?'

'They take stuff from our bodies. They make medicine from it I think.'

'Is that what's happened to your hands, how did they do that to you?'

She looked up at her hands clutching the bars and shook her head.

'They do other things to me. They've been testing something on me. I don't know what it is and I don't know what it's for. All I know is that is makes me feel awful sick, my hair falls out and my skin has started changing colour.' She let go of the bars with one hand and held it in front of her face, turning it from front to back. 'It's spreading pretty quick now.'

'Does it hurt you? What they do to you?'
She nodded.

'Yes, the procedures hurt a lot. I don't think that's what you're here for though, they're not going to sell parts of you. I've heard them say that it's best from the children, the stuff they take from us.'

'What do they take from you?'

'It's our blood and our bone marrow. I think the medicines they make are for humans, to cure them of diseases that we don't get.'

Could that really be true? This must be the place that I saw on the computer screens at Abraham's lab last year, he had been watching them, the children that were here in these tanks. But nearly all the tanks were empty now. Where had they all gone?

'Whats your name?' I asked her.

She readjusted her hands on the bars again. Was it difficult for her to hold herself up like that? From what I could tell, she was practically skin and bone.

'Kendra. What's your name?'

'I'm Vivienne. Were there more of you here Kendra?'

She nodded slowly.

'There used to be. We used to get a new person as soon as a tank was empty, but you're the first new person we've had here in a long time. What day was it… when you were taken?'

'It was a Tuesday, the fifth I think.'

'What month?'

'It's February. How long have you been here?'

'That makes it over five years now I think.'

'Five years? Surely your parents or someone must be looking for you?'

She shook her head.

'They killed my dad when they took me. My mum died a long time ago.'

'There must be someone who would be looking for you? Someone would have noticed you were gone? Noticed that your dad was dead?'

She shook her head again.

'We lived by ourselves, it was just the two of us in a little cabin near the sea, in Norway. Everyone who comes here has the same story. They only take us from remote places, where children live alone or with one parent. They don't leave anyone behind alive. There is never anyone left to come looking for you.'

'How many have there been?'

'Since I've been here?   Over a hundred I think, maybe two hundred. I lost count after a while.'

'And what about now?   How many others are here?'

'It's just me, Una and Jordan at the moment. They're in the tanks on the other side of you. They've both had procedures today, so they'll be sleeping for a little while yet. That's why they keep us in tanks, so that we get better quicker. Our bodies grow back what they take much faster if we are in water all the time.'

I turned around and in the tank to my left, I could make out the outline of a little figure, curled up in the opposite corner of the tank, long blonde hair floating around her head.   Beyond that tank and into the next one, I could just about see another dark figure, huddled down low at the bottom.

'How old are they?'

'Una and Jordan?   They're brother and sister. Jordan is older, he looks like he's about twelve, but he said he's a bit older. Una looks much younger, could pass for seven or eight, but I imagine she's a little bit older too.'

'And how old are you? You don't look much older than twelve yourself.'

She smiled.

'Thanks. Time does seem to have stood still for me since I got here. But no I'm not that young. I grew up in the water, I'm twenty now.'

I heard movement in the water behind me and turned to see a small, blonde haired head poking out of the water in the tank next to me. She had the lightest blue eyes, just like Morgan did and her blonde hair was almost white. She kept her lightly freckled nose and rosy pink lips under the water and blinked rapidly, as if her eyes were adjusting to the light.

'Hello' I said. 'Are you okay?'

Her eyes focused on something behind me. I turned in time to see Kendra give a nod of approval. The little girl pulled herself further out of the water. She nodded.

'Is your brother okay?'

She turned around, looking toward his tank, then turned back to me, shrugging her shoulders slightly with a tiny shake of her head. I pulled myself back toward Kendra's tank.

'We have to get you all out of here. We must be able to break out of these tanks somehow, there must be a way.'

'We've tried to force them' Kendra said. 'They don't seem to be too thick, but no amount of kicking seems to work.'

'Where do you kick? They're more likely to give at the sides I think.'

I put my shoulders against the back of my tank and pushed my feet outward onto the front of the tank. I felt the tiniest bit of give as I straightened my legs and pushed all my weight into it. I then tried to kick with my heel as hard as I could, but the water slowed me down.

'It may be easier when your tank is emptied.' Kendra signalled to a large button next to the bars. 'We press this after we've been to the toilet and it empties out and refills the water.'

'After you've been to the toilet?' I looked at her aghast. 'You mean you actually have to go in the tanks?'

She nodded with a grimace. I looked from her and back to the button.

'That is so… so gross. We have to get out of here now.'

I hit the button and felt a slight pull on my body as the water began to drain out. As soon as it was half way gone I put one foot on the bottom of the tank and, keeping my back against one side, began to kick as hard as I could into the front of the tank with the underside of my heel. It hurt like hell, but I kept going.

I could feel the glass giving just a little each time, I just needed to kick it hard enough. My tank was completely empty and now water began to pour in from the other side. I kicked faster, bracing myself against the back of the tank. My heel was in agony, but I kept kicking, each time harder than the last. Somewhere, a buzzer sounded and all three of us turned toward the door as the orange light above it flashed.

Three people entered, two large men in green hospital type clothing and one woman. She wore a lab coat, with smart clothing underneath. Her heels clicked against the hard floor and her long, brown hair flowed in waves over her shoulders. They walked toward my tank, with the water still refilling, it was now up to my knees. Kendra and Una had sunk down beneath the surface of the water in their own tanks. The three people got closer, the woman looking down at a tablet device in her hands. They stopped a few feet in front of my tank, she looked up and smiled. I recognised her. I had met this woman before.

'Hello Vivienne' she said. 'I can see you're going to need twenty four hour supervision to begin with. Trying to break out already? Such undesirable behaviour.'

'Brooke?'

Could it really be her? Morgan's ex girlfriend. I'd met her briefly one evening when I first moved to Zennor, but he'd broken up with her a short while later. She had wanted him to move to Scotland with her and he had refused.

'It's Dr Ayers here Vivienne, but yes. How very lovely it is to see you again.'

'Brooke what the hell? What have you been doing to these children? To hundreds of children? How could you do this, to anyone? Did Morgan know about this?'

She looked down at the tablet, tapping a few buttons.

'Vivienne, I'm sure I don't need to explain to you the dire situation we are in as a species. With the amount of un-pure being born every year, we face extinction within the next century. The time to take action is now and thankfully, you are going to help me with that.'

'I don't know what you think I am capable of Brooke, but I very much doubt that. But forgetting about the fact that you have *abducted* me for a moment, what on earth does taking bone marrow and blood from *children* have to do with saving Asrai?'

She used a hand to motion around the room.

'We need to fund our research somehow Vivienne, the equipment that fills this room is by no means cheap. Fortunately for us there are a lot of humans who will pay obscene amounts of money for secret miracle cures for various ailments. But do you see many children here right now? No, you don't. We only take what there is demand for and we have enough stores to see us through for a while. We're not complete monsters.'

She said the last words with a sweet smile. Her face made me feel sick. How could she be so blasé about what she was doing here, what she was doing to innocent children? I shook my head, the water in my tank had now filled to my waist.

'What makes you think I can help you anyway? I didn't have a baby, I'm still infertile, I still can't have children.'

'That may be so Vivienne, but you did *get* pregnant. Even though you didn't carry to term, it was a complete anomaly. There has never been a recorded case of an un-pure Asrai conceiving before. Life will find a way Vivienne and it looks like you are the first step in our evolution.'

'Did you… did you really just quote Jurassic Park at me?'

She laughed and took another step closer to the tank.

'We will find a way Vivienne. Even if that means keeping you here for the rest of your life. *I* will find a way.'

The water in my tank was up to my chest now and using both of my hands, I splashed water as hard as I could, sending it up and over the side of the tank, right into her face and onto her tablet. She jumped backwards, arms held out to the sides, dripping wet, her mouth open in shock.

'Fuck you Brooke.'

She shook her hands and after putting the tablet down on the desk behind her, she removed her lab coat and threw it to the floor. She turned and walked quickly toward the procedure room.

'Get her out' she shouted.

The florescent lights were brighter in the procedure room. The ceiling was much lower, plus there were large, movable lights above the table in the middle of the room. The two large men had pulled me from the tank and frog marched me to the room. I couldn't have resisted even if I had tried, with their fingers digging tightly into my arms, they weren't giving me an inch. Two more women in scrubs entered the room and whilst the two men loomed near by, they stripped and towel dried me. I didn't even bother to try to cover my modesty. I couldn't let her see how invasive this was for me, how exposed I felt. I just couldn't let her have that. I stood there proudly, shoulders back with my hands by my sides as they finished drying me off. Whatever they were going to do to me, it was going to happen one way or the other.

If I was compliant, they may let their guard down and that would make finding a way out of here easier. One of the women began to forcefully tie back my hair as the other held a hospital gown out in front of me. I held out my arms and let her slide it on and tie it behind my neck and back. After being weighed and measured, I was directed to the table in the middle of the room and instructed to sit down on the end of it. I was asked to open my mouth whilst they swabbed the inside of my cheeks, then one of them cut strands of my hair from the nape of my neck. All the while, Brooke sat at a desk in the corner, tapping away at a computer. One of the women told me they needed to take blood. I held out my arm in silence. There was no point in struggling, they were going to take it regardless.

I stayed silent whilst they measured my blood pressure and then tied a tourniquet around the top of my arm. My skin was cleaned with an anti-septic wipe and then a needle was forced into the vein. Several syringes of blood were taken before they taped cotton wool over the tiny wound. As I held it in place, the other end of the table was adjusted and angled upward, so that the table became more of a high backed chair.

'Right' Brooke said as she stood from the desk and walked toward me, pulling plastic gloves on as she did. 'If you could just lean back for me.' As she said this, stirrups were lifted from underneath the table by one of the other women. 'And pop your legs up in those for me.'

I looked around the room at each face. They were waiting. Waiting for me to resist, waiting to restrain me the moment I refused. I wouldn't give them the satisfaction. I slowly leaned myself back and one at a time, lifted each leg into one of the stirrups. Brooke sat down on a small stool with wheels and pushed herself between my legs. A tray of instruments was placed on a moveable table next to her and one of the men swivelled the adjustable light around behind her, until it was pointing right between my legs. His gaze lingered for a moment, until he realised I was staring right back at him and he sheepishly shuffled away to the other side of the room.

'Now this won't hurt but I will need to insert this speculum in order to take some samples, then we'll do a quick ultra sound and I'll have a quick feel of your cervix to make sure everything is as it should be' she said, smiling a sickly, sweet smile.

After lubricating and inserting the large metal speculum, she took her time inserting tiny plastic brushes one after the other to take samples. After the speculum was removed, an ultrasound machine was wheeled over. She took a wand type attachment and placed a clear plastic cover over it, then slid it inside of me as she looked at the screen of the ultrasound machine. A grey, grainy picture formed on the screen as she pressed buttons and highlighted different sections of the picture. She removed the wand and handed it to one of the women.

'Okay, just one last thing and then you're done.'

She said it in such a sweet voice, it was almost as if she truly believed I was here voluntarily and this was just some routine appointment. With her hands still gloved, she held up two fingers on her right hand and one of the woman squeezed more lubricant from a tube onto them. Brooke rubbed her fingers and thumb together, spreading it around, all the while looking me directly in the eye. I kept my face neutral, trying not to let her see how tightly my jaw was clenched together, desperately trying not to scream at her, kick out at her. My hospital gown was pulled up on my thighs and she reached over it with her left hand and pressed down on my lower abdomen, inserting her gloved fingers into me. She dropped her gaze, seemingly concentrating on what she was doing.

'Hm' she appeared to talk to herself. 'It would appear that she is ovulating. Make sure to take a urine sample before she goes back in the tank.'

The nurse next to her nodded, then crossed the room to a bank of cupboards, opening doors until she found rows of small pots with yellow lids. The other woman had come closer and lent in to talk to Brooke.

'Do you want me to prepare a specimen? Do you think we should carry out insemination now?'

Insemination? What the hell? Brooke shook her head.

'No, not today. It will be a waste until she's had the full course of the formula. I'm assuming she has an active sex life with her new husband and if sperm alone was enough to conceive, it would have already happened.' She shook her head again. 'No, just prepare the formula please.'

She removed her fingers and pulled the gloves off one by one, then pushed herself out from between my legs.

'Clean her up.'

One of the woman ripped tissue from a long roll and stepped toward me and with gloved hands, wiped the tissue between my legs. One of the men stepped back into view. His gaze once again lingering where it should not once the woman had moved away.

'You may close your legs now Vivienne.'

I quickly lifted each leg from the stirrups and sat up straight again on the table.

'What do you mean by insemination?'

Brooke spun around on her stool to face me again.

'Artificial insemination Vivienne. How else would you expect me to get you pregnant? Did you believe I could do that without sperm? Now if you could just hop off the table and bend over it please. We need to give you a quick injection.'

She was serious. They were actually going to attempt to impregnate me with some random sperm. I did as instructed and slid off the table, then leant across it, supporting my weight on my elbows.

'You're actually trying to get me pregnant with some stranger's baby? Brooke you are insane.'

The woman passed her a large needled syringe and she lifted the gown up, exposing one side of my naked backside.

'Oh I don't think we can really call him a stranger can we Vivienne.' I felt a sharp prick as she pushed the needle into my rear. 'It's someone who was really dedicated to the cause, even if his methods were a tad extreme. But I mustn't speak ill of the dead.'

Speak ill of the dead? Who was she talking about? It couldn't be, could it?

'Actually I believe you knew him quite well, in fact I heard that you were rather close.' She removed the needle and returned to her desk. 'He knew your parents too. Our generous sperm donor is Abraham Lean.'

9.

That process was repeated every day for the next four weeks. The same tests would be carried out, followed by an injection in my rear end. Every twenty four hours, like clock work, I was removed from my tank, stripped, dried off and put in a hospital gown. Whatever they were injecting me with left me feeling tired and nauseous for hours after. I knew I had to do what they wanted, stay compliant. I needed them to drop their guard. No one was coming to save me this time, no one knew where I was. They would have no leads, no clues about who had taken me. The boat would have been long gone by the time Morgan came to the beach to look for me. I could be anywhere in the world right now. No one was coming.

The only thing I had control over was what I said and for the last two weeks it had been nothing. Not when anyone that worked here was around, least of all Brooke. I had gotten to know Kendra and Una well over the last two weeks, about where they had grown up and their lives before they were taken. Jordan still hadn't spoken since I had been here. I could see how much it was hurting Una, that he barely talked to her. He was all she had left in this world and he had given up. This only added to my hatred of Brooke and what she was doing. How anyone could be this cruel to children was completely beyond my comprehension. But I had stopped asking questions, stopped talking to Brooke altogether. It was bothering her, me not talking, not saying a word and every day she tried a different angle to get a rise out of me. Today it was working, today I broke my silence.

'So Vivienne, how does it feel knowing that you'll be having Abraham's baby instead of Morgan's?'

I took a deep breath in and let out a long, heavy sigh.

'I won't be having anyones baby Brooke. I'm infertile, because I'm half human. I know it, you know it.' I motioned around the room. 'They know it. There's nothing special about my reproductive capabilities and there's nothing you or anyone else can do to change that.'

She suppressed a smile.

'Oh I wouldn't be so sure about that if I were you Vivienne. Your body is reacting perfectly to phase one. I think insemination could actually be successful with that on its own, there may be no need for phase two.'

'Reacting perfectly how? What even is all this phase one crap you keep talking about?'

'Phase one of your fertility treatment Vivienne. The injection we have been giving you, did you not wonder what it was for? It is slowly altering the way your body produces eggs and a whole load of other things that goes on inside your uterus.' She was tapping away at her computer in the corner whilst two women redressed me once again. 'And by the way things felt and looked today, you are almost completely ripe.'

'Ripe? I'm not a banana.'

She frowned at her computer screen.

'I am aware of that Vivienne, but nonetheless, you are near enough at the perfect stage for insemination. We'll schedule the first one for this afternoon and the next one for twenty four hours later.' She nodded toward the woman who had finished dressing me.

'Can you get the samples ready please.'

The woman nodded and left the room.

'How do you think Morgan will feel Vivienne? When you have Abraham's baby I mean. Do you think he'll be happy to raise it as his own?   Well, that's assuming that Mr Calder ever lets you and the baby leave here, which is *very* unlikely.'

She almost sang the last few words. Was she honestly serious?

'Why the fuck are you using his sperm?'

She smiled that smile again, which I so desperately wanted to smack right off her face.

'Why Abraham?' she replied. 'He believed he was purer than everyone else and this whole project was his idea.   He put everything he had into it… literally everything.' She grimaced to herself slightly. 'I'll admit I had my objections at first. I would much rather have used a much more recent Colony descendant, but your friend Mathew disappeared before we ever got a chance to get samples. Though I doubt he would have given them as willingly as Abraham did.'

Was she really going to artificially inseminate me with Abraham's sperm? The man who murdered my entire family. What if she was right and these drugs were working? What if she had, in some way, miraculously cured my infertility? Could I really get pregnant with his baby, *give birth* to his baby? What would Morgan say? How would he feel? Would he still love me, knowing I was having someone else's baby?

But she was right about one thing, what reason would they have to let me go? So I could go running back to Moses and rest of The Council and tell them all about what was going on here? If I was going to get out of here, it certainly wasn't going to be because they chose to let me go.

A few hours later I was back in the procedure room, back in a hospital gown. The table in the middle of the room was laid down flat, the stirrups already in place.

'Lay down on the table now Vivienne, legs in the usual position please.'

I stayed where I was, not moving, not saying anything. She turned around slowly.

'In position please Vivienne.'

'No.'

'No?' she repeated it back to me as a question. 'I don't think you really have a choice Vivienne. Get on the table.'

I shook my head. The woman that was stood closest to me put a gentle hand on my arm, trying to steer me in the direction of the table.

'I said NO.'

The word suddenly came screaming out of my mouth and I turned toward the woman and shoved her with both hands as hard as I could. She crashed into the units behind her, sending equipment clattering to the ground around her as she put her arms out, trying to steady herself on something. Before I could make another move, one of the men had grabbed me from behind, his arms encircled me and crossed over my chest. He lifted me up and I kicked out as the other male came toward me.

'Get her on the table, tie her down' Brooke said.

I continued to kick out, not letting him get a good hold of my legs. I was carried toward the table and dropped unceremoniously on top of it. I scrambled to get back off, but he leant forward, leaning with his elbows across my chest. Someone then pulled thick straps from underneath the table and he removed one of his arms from me to reach around for the other one. At the same time, I lunged forward and bit onto his cheek as hard as I could. He shouted in pain, tried to pull away. I clamped my teeth down harder, squeezing my jaw together as hard as I could. I felt his hands on my shoulders, pushing himself away from me, but all it did was stretch the flesh of his cheek.

I tasted blood in my mouth, but he continued to pull. I felt more hands on my arms and body until he suddenly sprang backwards, a gaping hole spurting blood from his cheek. He stumbled away from me, putting his hand up, covering his damaged cheek. At the same time, straps had been clicked together across my body and pulled tight. I could feel the flesh from his face still on my tongue and I spat it out as hard as I could onto the floor beside me, spraying blood on everyone around me as I did so. The three of them flinched, twisting their faces out of the way.

'Shall I give her a sedative? Knock her out even?'

It was the woman that I had pushed away from me.

'No' Brooke was standing at the bottom of the table, attaching straps to the stirrups. 'No medication, we can't give her anything that could affect the formula. Just strap her down, tight as you can. Get her legs in the stirrups. You...' she pointed at the man with part of his face missing. 'Get down stairs, send someone else up and get your self cleaned up for goodness sake, don't just stand there dripping blood everywhere.'

He took two steps toward me then bent down and scooped his torn flesh up from the floor. With one last look at me, he turned and all but ran out of the doors, sending them swinging back and forth. The remaining man was wrestling with my leg, trying to get it into one of the stirrups. I kicked out repeatedly with my leg until I connected with his face.

'Get her legs in' Brooke said through gritted teeth, she and one of the woman took hold of my other leg. 'Quickly, strap her down.'

Despite my constant kicks and struggles, one by one, they got my legs strapped into the stirrups. A tray of instruments was pushed up next to Brooke as she took a seat in between my legs. I felt her gloved hands applying lubricant and in went the cold speculum.

'Bring me the sample'.

One of the women left my side and I watched her hurry to a stainless steel, circular storage device. She lifted the lid and removed a small vial, then returning to the table, carefully handed it to Brooke. Brooke held the vial up against the light behind her, giving it a shake. She removed the lid and placed it upright in a tray designed to hold six vials. Her hand then moved to a large, plastic syringe, which she used to draw the liquid from the vial.

'Right' she said. 'Here we go.'

She smiled as she attached a long, thin tube to the end of the syringe, then, pulling the light down further behind her, she bowed her head right down between my legs. I couldn't feel the thin tube as she inserted it inside me, through the speculum, but I pushed my muscles down there together as if going to the toilet in protest. I felt as the speculum began to slide outward. Brooke tutted, lifting her gaze to meet mine.

'Would you rather we did this the old fashioned way? Abraham may no longer be here, but there are plenty of other pure Asrai out there who would be more than willing to oblige.'

We stared each other down for a few moments, until I finally relented. I closed my eyes and put my head back, willing the tears burning the inside of my eyelids to stay where they were. I could not give her the satisfaction of seeing me cry. I felt as she pushed the speculum back inside me and presumably continued with her task of syringing sperm into me. A few moments passed and I heard her place the syringe back on the metal tray beside her. Was that all it took? Just a few seconds for me to be artificially inseminated against my will?

'Angle her groin upward please.'

I opened my eyes, the two women were either side of the table, adjusting something on each side. Eventually, I felt the table tip backwards until my legs were up higher than my head. Brooke removed the speculum and after wiping the lubricant from between my legs with tissues, she pulled my hospital gown down between my legs, covering my modesty.

'Leave her up for a couple of hours, just to be on the safe side.'

She pulled off her gloves and dropped them in the bin next to her computer.

'We have to repeat this process again tomorrow Vivienne. I do hope you won't give us as much trouble then. I would hate to have to do away with all these instruments and have one of my team insert themselves manually.'

The threat was clear. It was this way or be physically raped. She had won, I had no choice but to give in and let this happen.

10.

Una

Vivienne hadn't spoken to us for days. She just sat in the corner of her tank, legs pulled up in front of her. She normally talked to us whenever there was no one else in the laboratory, telling us about the aquarium where she worked, about her friends and her home. Now she just reminded me of Jordan. There was a word for it I think, catatonic maybe?

She got out when they told her to, went where they told her to. Kendra had tried to talk to her, asked her what had happened, but she wouldn't speak. She wouldn't come out of the water, not even for food. Even when her tank emptied and refilled, she just sat in the corner, chin on her knees. Whatever they had done, she had put up a good fight at first. We had heard crashes and screams and then one of the men had ran out with a hand covering his face, blood dripping everywhere, all over his clothing. That had made me smile, seeing one of them hurt like that, seeing him hurt like they hurt us every day.

He hadn't been back since. Someone new had taken his place, but they were all the same. They were all just as bad as each other. She had been taken back to the procedure room the day after she had fought with them, but she didn't fight that time, she didn't make a sound. I don't know what they had done to her to get the fight out of her so quickly. Kendra said it had been a week since then and they hadn't taken Vivienne to the procedure room again since. What were they waiting for?

Jordan was at the top of his tank, eating the sandwiches that had been laid out for him. I didn't feel like eating yet. I knew it was procedure day. Extra people were in and out of the procedure room setting it up, getting it ready to steal parts of our bodies. They would just keep on going until there was nothing left of us. They came for me first today. As I was lifted out of the tank by one of the men, his hands underneath my arms, I stared into his eyes. I wondered if he knew that I wanted to kill him. That maybe I would try if I ever got the chance.

He stood me on the floor in front of my tank and one of the women wrapped a towel around me as they always did. I was directed toward the procedure room, past Vivienne's tank. She raised her head for a moment and her back straightened as she realised I was out of my tank. She moved to the front of the tank, her hands on the glass following me with her head. She looked worried, worried for me. As I was led away, I turned to see her head was out of the water as she clung to her bars.

11.

Vivienne

Had it been two weeks already? Two weeks since Abraham Lean's sperm was forcibly inseminated into my body. There was absolutely nothing I could do about it apart from hope that I wasn't actually pregnant. Hope and pray that their miracle formula hadn't really worked. They had told me some hours ago not to urinate again, as they needed my morning sample in order to test for pregnancy. In the week that followed the inseminations, I hadn't known what to do with myself. I couldn't sleep, I couldn't eat. I was just completely numb, feeling so completely powerless over my own body.

Then I had watched as they had taken Una, taken her to that room to do who knows what to her. The look of defiance on her face reminded me that I needed to stay strong. I had to be ready at all times, ready to seize any opportunity that I could to get these children out of here. I had to eat, I had to rest, I had to stay strong.

Brooke entered the lab with two men and whilst she headed straight for the procedure room, they got me out of the tank. One of them visibly flinched when I turned my head toward him. I hoped that I scared them. Biting off another man's cheek had no doubt made them wary of me. Was that a bad move on my part? Having them always alert did not bode well for any escape attempt. From this point on I had to comply with every request, make them see me as cooperative, make them believe I was not a risk, that I wouldn't try to escape. One of the men draped a towel around my shoulders.

'Thank you' I murmured, pulling it tight around me.

It was the first words I had spoken in days. I hadn't responded when the people here came and had given me instructions and Kendra had given up asking me what they had done to me. She had watched as I had eaten food properly again for the first time in a week after Una had been taken for a procedure, but she hadn't tried talking to me again yet. Maybe she thought I was fragile. That one wrong word from her would send me back to the corner of the tank. Back to not eating and not sleeping. To be honest I just didn't think I could say it out loud, say what had been done to me in that room, not once, but twice.

They had repeated the insemination twenty four hours after the first one. I had not resisted, I had not struggled in any way. They had strapped me down regardless, but I had not said a word, not moved a muscle. I had just laid there, eyes closed and fists clenched as Brooke had once again inseminated me. She had remained quiet too for once. It briefly crossed my mind that maybe she actually felt bad for what she was doing. Maybe she knew how much of a monster she was. Not just to me, but to these children too. To all the children that had been here. All the children whose eyes had closed here for the last time.

A curtain was pulled around me in the corner of the procedure room whilst I undressed and squatted over a bed pan. Dry clothes had been laid out for me and I dressed in silence. The bed pan was taken to a desk and I watched as Brooke dipped little white pieces of card into it, then looked at her watch on her wrist.

'Fuck' she said under her breath and slammed her hands against the desk.

The corner of my mouth twitched and I tried desperately to suppress my smile. Hopefully this meant what I thought it meant. I wasn't pregnant this time. She had failed. Her formula did not work and this had all been for nothing. She paced the room for a moment, then sat back at her desk, clicking the mouse at the computer.

'Administer a double dose of the phase one formula. Add seventy five grams of Clomiphene Citrate and HCG. She will need it every day until the egg retrieval.'

Brooke stormed from the room, throwing the double doors open forcibly with both hands. The remaining staff members looked at each other silently, clearly used to Brooke's wrath. I was led to the table in the centre of the room and instructed to bend over. The woman pulled down the top of my shorts and administered a notably longer injection.

'What did she mean by egg retrieval?'

I asked when she had finished and pulled my shorts up. The woman took a few steps back from me, discarding the syringe into a sharps bin and began tapping at a computer next to it.

'Um…' she looked toward one of the men, who took a small step toward me. 'The artificial insemination didn't work. You're not pregnant.'

'Well, I kind of figured that out all ready. What will happen now?'

'I think it's probably best that Dr Ayers explain the next stage to you.' She said as she continued to type at the computer.

'I'd rather not speak to her unless it's absolutely unavoidable. Just tell me what's going to happen next. Please.'

She looked nervously at the man before turning back to me.

'We um…' she looked at him again, he gave the slightest of nods. 'We have to double the dose of the formula so we can stimulate ovulation and increase your egg production. Then Dr Ayers will carry out an egg retrieval procedure so that she can fertilise the eggs in the laboratory. Then we...' she stopped herself and cleared her throat. 'Then *she* will transfer the fertilised eggs back to you.'

She swallowed hard, waiting for my reaction. I considered her words for a moment. What she was describing was IVF. Whatever I had been given had failed to cure my infertility so far and therefore the insemination had failed. Would I be as lucky a second time or would the IVF be successful?

'Do you think it will work, the IVF?' I asked her.

She gave a slight shake of her head.

'It's always very hard to tell. Your body's reaction to the formula was very promising, your markers improved every day. Dr Ayers was quite confident that you would fall pregnant from the artificial insemination. But with a stronger dose and the added medication for egg stimulation, who knows.'

'And do you think that all of this is okay? What she's doing to me? What she's doing to those children out there?'

My question caught her off guard, taking the conversation in a completely different direction. Her body tensed and the man took another step toward me.

'It's really not my place to say, I've said too much already.'

She cleared her throat and turned back to the computer. I felt a large hand on my arm as I slowly stepped toward her and leaned in.

'It's really not your place to be doing any of this.'

The words almost sounded like a hiss through my gritted teeth. She turned her face away from me as I stepped toward the door, shaking the hand off me.

12.

I spent the next two weeks being taken to the procedure room every single day. Every day I would have samples taken from nearly every part of my body. The amount of injections had increased and I was now given tablets to swallow as well. After each day I felt sicker and sicker. My hair had started to fall out on one side of my head and I would watch it float around my tank as I felt the smooth, bald patch on my scalp behind my ear. The constant nausea made it almost impossible to eat and my skin was painful to the touch, especially out of the water. I hated feeling their hands on me and flinched every time they had to hold my arm to take blood samples or when they roughly towel dried me.

'Please, just let me do it,' I almost begged the woman as she lifted a towel up in front of me on the eighth day. I pressed the towel gently against the skin on my face and then my arms, being careful not to rub the towel against myself. We entered the procedure room and the woman began to remove my clothing, pulling my top off over my head.

'Oh' she said. 'Just stay there a moment, I just need to quickly take some pictures of your back.'

My back? What could she need to take pictures of my back for? I turned to see her plug a large camera into the side of a computer.

'Just face back that way please, roll the top of your shorts down slightly. Then keep your arms and shoulders relaxed.'

I did as she asked and turned away, listening to the camera click several times until she was done. The other woman finished undressing me and I stepped into the hospital gown that was held out in front of me and turned around to allow her to tie it. As I did so, I caught sight of the computer that the camera had been connected to, the woman tapped away at the keyboard still. There was a picture on the screen, a picture of a back and the top of bum cheeks, which must have been me. My shoulder bones jutted out and you could see every part of my spine, each bone poking out. My rear end was covered in dark bruises, which must have been from the daily injections and the skin on my upper back… the skin was blue and gold, almost scaly. It was like the skin on Kendra's hands. So this what they had been testing on her, these fertility drugs. The woman turned and caught my gaze, then quickly cleared the picture from the screen.

'It's nothing to worry about' she said. 'It's just side effects from the treatments you've been receiving. It will disappear within a few weeks once you've stopped having the formula.'

She came toward me and helped me up onto the table.

'And when will that be?' I said, holding her gaze.

She turned away, unable to look me in the eye for long.

'If it works this time, then only a few more days.'

I held my arm out and flinched slightly as she tied the tourniquet around the top of it to take a blood sample.

'And what if it doesn't work this time?'

She stopped what she was doing and looked at me again.

'Then Dr Ayers will start the process again, with a higher dosage of the formula.' She returned to her task of taking my blood samples. 'So your best bet is to hope that it works this time, because she won't stop.' She pulled the syringe out of my arm and held a cotton pad over the place it had been. 'You need to prepare yourself for that Vivienne, because she won't stop until you give her a viable pregnancy.'

13.

'Vivienne, Vivienne are you okay?'

Kendra had pulled herself up to the bars of her tank. We had just had food placed on the tops of our tanks and this was the first time in a while that I had felt able to try eating something. I had received six more doses of drugs and had six more samples taken since I had seen the picture of my back. The nausea had subsided slightly today and I had summoned enough strength to hold myself up at the bars and to eat something. I nodded at her.

'What are they doing to you in there? You don't look like you're okay Vivienne.'

I struggled to swallow what was in my mouth before I could answer her.

'They are trying to get me pregnant.'

'Is it working?' she asked.

I shook my head.

'I don't know. I just know that I feel like absolute shit.'

She smiled at me.

'I'm sorry to tell you Vivienne, but you look it too.'

I laughed with her then. Despite all of this, these two girls who had been through so much, still managed to make me smile.

'I'm just glad my husband isn't here to see me like this.'

'What's he like, your husband? Can you tell us more about him.'

Us? I turned around to see Una pulled up to the top of her tank, listening intently. The laboratory was empty, so I spent the next hour telling them about Morgan and how we had fallen in love. They loved the story about him getting ridiculously drunk at the wedding, where we nearly kissed for the first time. Kendra all but swooned when I told her about our actual first kiss and she practically squealed with delight when I recounted how he had proposed. Talking about him like this almost made me forget that we had been apart for so long. It had been nearly two months now since I had been taken.

'What about you Kendra, what's your story?' I said.

'There's not much to tell really.' She adjusted her hands on the bars. 'I grew up in the ocean, never really staying in one place for long. I remember it just being the three of us all the time, we were always together. Sometimes we would spend a few weeks on a deserted island. My dad would teach me how to build things, how to catch animals for us to eat, all that sort of thing. But when my mum died we settled in Norway. We built the cabin and that's where we stayed until... until they came for me.'

She averted her gaze, a shadow of sadness had fallen across her face. I couldn't bring myself to ask her about how her mother had died, so I stayed silent for a moment.

'Why did they take you?' Kendra eventually asked. 'They only take people who won't be missed, but you have such an incredible life where you live, so many people to miss you.'

'They think I can help them cure infertility. I'm half human, but I was pregnant once. Not for long, but I was pregnant.'

'So you're special then?'

Una's small voice made me turn to face her.

'They seem to think so. I'm not so sure really.'

'Will you show us where you live? If we ever get out of here I mean. Will you take us to The Cove?'

Una looked at me with wide and hopeful eyes.

I nodded.

'Of course I will and we *will* get out of here, we have to.'

'They haven't come to take you yet today' said Kendra. 'You're normally in the procedure room by now.'

'They have something different planned for me today I think.'

Yesterday one of the women had told me that today was my egg retrieval day. It was a simple surgery she had said. I would be sedated, to stop me feeling any pain as the needle was inserted via a catheter and the eggs were removed. They would need as many as possible and my ultrasound yesterday had showed that I had fifteen viable eggs that had fully matured. So today was the day.

'How are we going to get out?'

I turned at the sound of Una's voice. I shook my head.

'I don't know. There's nearly always someone here and there'll be no getting out without one of those key cards. Plus there's the CCTV, I imagine it's always being monitored. Brooke knew that I had been kicking at the tank when I first woke up. Someone must have been watching somewhere. We just need the right opportunity, when we're in the procedure room or something and they're distracted or there's not as many of them. I don't know. Do they ever have more than one of you out of the tanks at the same time? One could distract them and the other steal a key card?'

Kendra shook her head.

'No, never' she said. 'It's only ever one at a time.'

'Plus we don't even know where we are' I continued. 'It's got to be somewhere remote to hide what they're doing here. We'd have no way of getting home. We can't call the police and even if we did, I've got no idea what would happen to the three of you. We could try and flag someone down, persuade them to help us without calling the police, but it could end up being someone from here. I don't know, there's just too many what ifs, too many things that could go wrong.'

All three of us spun and faced the door as we heard the buzzer sound. Brooke strode in, her heels clicking on the hard floor, tablet computer in hand. The bottom of her lab coat flapped in the wind she created as she walked, just like her long flowing hair. It still amazed me that someone so beautiful could be so evil. Every time I looked at her, all I saw were the dead bodies of children. The hundreds of children that she had used for experiments, the children she had continuously harvested for money. She was flanked by two men and two women, who came toward my tank whilst Brooke headed straight for the procedure room. One of the men was pushing a wheelchair, which had what looked like a large fluffy blanket draped over it. My tank was opened by a key card and the bars were pushed away.

'Careful now' one of the men said as he reached in for me.

I soon had four pairs of hands on me, gently lifting me out of the tank. I was clearly getting some sort of special treatment today. I stood in front of the wheelchair and the fluffy blanket was held out in front of me, but it wasn't a fluffy blanket, it was a big soft dressing gown. I turned around and slipped each arm in and pulled it together in front of me. The wheelchair was pushed closer behind me and then I was able to lower myself down onto it.

Kendra's eyes followed me as I was pushed toward the procedure room and through the double doors. Brooke was checking instruments on a tray as I was wheeled to the other side of the room. I was held up whilst the women removed the dressing gown and my wet clothes. They dried me gently, taking great care on my back. I was put in a hospital gown and helped to the table. I struggled to get on and eventually had to be lifted up.

'I'm going to give you a sedative Vivienne.'

Brooke was setting up an IV drip next to me.

'You don't need much because of your weight loss, but do tell me if you can feel anything once the procedure starts and we can increase it.'

I held out my hand and after cleansing the back of it, she pushed the needle in and taped it down. She attached the tube from the IV drip to it and I watched the liquid come down slowly. As it disappeared into my hand, I immediately felt a wave of calm wash over me, almost making me smile, making me happy to be sitting on that table at that very moment.

'Why are you being so nice to me today Brooke?'

I hadn't meant to say the words out loud, but somehow my thoughts were tumbling straight out of my mouth. I felt my head lol from one side to another as I tried to keep looking at her. She had a surgical gown on now and one of the women was stood in front of her, holding out a glove for her to put on.

'The person who is ultimately responsible for this facility is quite concerned for your welfare it would seem. We've been reviewing the results of your samples and the side effects you are experiencing… and there are some concerns that have been raised.'

'So, what you mean is,' I blinked slowly, struggling to keep my eyes focused on her. 'Your boss is pissed off with you because the infertility cure guinea pig isn't doing too well. Are they worried that I might die and you'll all lose your only chance at saving all the un-pure from extinction?'

My words were almost slurred and still unable to focus my eyes, I lay my head back and stared blankly at the ceiling. I felt my legs being put into the stirrups.

'It would definitely not be in anyones best interests if you were to die Vivienne, no. So we are going to do all we can to look after you today, starting with this procedure.'

Her voice sounded like it had moved, she was sat in between my legs now. I meant to say my next thought in my head, but once again it just came out.

'I think I'd prefer it if you did just let me die.'

14.

For the next few days, Brooke was busy with petri dishes and microscopes at the far end of the laboratory. I would watch her through the glass of my tank as she carefully handled samples and instruments. If she looked my way I would turn away, I couldn't bear to look her in the eye. How could a woman do this to another woman? I know she must have a dislike for me, as the wife of her ex partner, it was completely understandable, but did she actually enjoy torturing me like this? Because that's what it felt like, absolute torture.

She was currently fertilising my eggs with sperm from the man who had murdered my whole family, with the aim of getting me pregnant with his child, which I was expected to carry to term. I couldn't fathom how I would feel if she succeeded. How would I look at my child? How would I love my child, knowing how they had came to be? And what about Morgan, I couldn't expect Morgan to love me after this, expect him to love my child.

Unless I got out of here right now, those eggs were being put back inside me very soon. I watched as Brooke stepped away from her microscope and walked toward me. She could see I was looking in her direction, so I couldn't pretend that I didn't see her coming. I pushed myself to the top of the tank and held on to the bars.

'Your embryos are ready Vivienne. I will be transferring them into you today. It's a painless procedure and I'd rather not sedate you if I don't have to. Will you cooperate?'

I looked away from her for a moment. I would much rather be sedated. Did I even have the strength to remain calm whilst she was putting *him* inside of me?

'Did you love him?' I said.

Brooke looked taken aback for a moment.

'Abraham? I barely knew him Vivienne' she said, shaking her head.

'No not Abraham. Morgan. You were together for a long time. Did you love him?'

She seemed to frown for a moment, considering her response.

'Of course I loved him. I wanted to be with him... always. I begged him to come here with me, but I would have stayed there if it had meant we could stay together. I told him I would stay, the night he ended things, but it was too late. He had already fallen for you. So yes... yes I loved him.'

'So how can you do this to him? You're not just doing this to me, you're hurting him too. You do understand that don't you? He probably thinks I'm dead right now. He would have found my stuff on the beach and assumed that something had happened to me out in the water. He'll be grieving for me, he'll be heartbroken.'

'You don't think that I know that?' Her voice was raised a little, but then softened once more. 'Do you know when I knew it was over? It was the day I met you Vivienne. I just knew. I could tell by the way he was looking at you, before he saw that I was there. The way his eyes were, his smile. He'd never looked at me like that, not really. Then the way he talked about you when we got home that night. He was trying to play it down, I could tell, but he was so happy that you had spent the day together. I could just see it in him, that glow of happiness that you have when you're falling in love with someone.' She shook her head and looked away from me. 'I don't think he ever loved me, not like that, not like the way he loves you.'

She stopped talking but her eyes stayed on me, her jaw clenched tightly together. Her eyes glistened under the florescent lights around us and she blinked rapidly for a moment as if holding back tears. I thought she may say something else, but instead, she turned and walked back to her desk, not saying anything more.

I couldn't have put up much of a fight even if I had wanted to. I felt so weak still, my arms and legs felt too heavy to lift on my own once I was out of the water. I was again helped into a dressing gown and lowered into a wheelchair, before being wheeled to the procedure room. I had to be held up whilst I was undressed and dried, then draped in a hospital gown. One of the men lifted me in his arms and laid me down on the table in the middle of the room. My legs were lifted into the stirrups with care and one of the women smoothed my hair out of my face.

I closed my eyes tightly, trying to stop the tears from falling, but they fell anyway. There was no need for restraints today. They knew it, I knew it. I was physically unable to fight, I was completely helpless against what they were about to do to me, what they were about to put inside me. I wanted to scream, I wanted to shout no, but it would make no difference. This was happening now no matter what I did.

Morgan had no idea where I was. No one had any idea where I was. There would be no rescue at the eleventh hour, no one would come for me here. I felt gloved hands on me as the procedure started. I refused to look and instead, kept my eyes closed with my head leaned back toward the ceiling whilst the tears silently fell.

I was given a good meal that afternoon, roast chicken with golden roasted potatoes. Perhaps that was their token of compensation for what they had done to me.   Was I being treated better now so that my body would behave, so that a baby could live inside of me? I had to eat, I had to get better, get stronger so that I could get us out of here. I had no idea how long would I be like this. I couldn't really ask them how long it would take for the side effects of the drugs they had given me to wear off.   Not without arousing some sort of suspicion. Kendra was looking much better now though, how long had it been since she had been given the drugs? I pulled myself over to the side of my tank that was closest to her. She was eating too and like me, had been given the good stuff today.

'Kendra?'

She turned toward me, still holding a chicken leg to her mouth.

'Hmm?' She mumbled through her meat.

'Kendra, what have you been going to the procedure room for? Are they still giving you drugs?'

She shook her head and placed the chicken leg back on the plate on top of her bars.

'No, not since before you got here. They just take blood and bone marrow from me again now, like Una and Jordan.'

'How do you feel now?'

'Still pretty awful. The bone marrow removal really takes it out of you, but my hair has stopped falling out and my skin feels better. I can stand to be touched again now at least, so it doesn't hurt as much when they dry me off anymore.'

'Well you look a lot better' I said.

And she really did look better. She had more weight around her middle and slightly more muscle definition in her arms and legs again.

'I wish I could say the same about you. They've stopped giving you the formula now though haven't they? Hopefully you'll get better soon too.'

'I hope so Kendra.'

15.

Una

She had slept a lot these past few days. She would come to the surface of her tank whenever they brought us food, but other than that she just slept. I was watching her from the top of my tank, holding onto the bars. I think it had been a week since she last went into the procedure room. The lady doctor would come to her tank sometimes and look at her, just watch her as she was sleeping. Then she would go back to one of the desks and look at things on a computer or through a microscope. She didn't talk to her. I don't think she had spoken to her since they had talked about her husband. Vivienne had said he would think she was dead. I don't think there could be any greater pain than that. The pain you feel when someone you love dies. When your family is gone.

I still thought about Mama nearly every second of every day. I tried not to think about the last time I saw her face, lying lifeless on the floor of our cabin. I also tried not to think about how her face looked as she pushed us out of the cabin that night, screaming at us to run. I'll never forget the terror in her face, but I tried not to think about it when I thought of her. When I thought of her, I tried to remember the last time I saw her smiling and laughing.

It was when she had been calling us in for dinner that evening. We had giggled, hiding behind rocks as she pretended not to know where we were. Or I thought about the time before that, when we had all been in the water earlier that day. She had chased us through the seaweed, grabbing at our toes, tickling our feet. Her face creased into her beautiful smile as we squealed in delight, trying to get away from her. I really missed that too, the freedom of the sea. This glass prison had been all I had known for so long now. I almost couldn't imagine being free of it now.

'Una?'

I heard Jordan's voice behind me, the first time in months. I turned to see him pulled up at the side of his tank. I was so happy to hear him say my name I could have cried.

'Jordan! Jordan, are you okay?'

I pulled myself over to the other side of my tank, getting as close to him as possible. He shook his head.

'I love you Una' he said.

'I love you too Jordan. We're going to be okay Jordan, I know it. We're going to find a way out of here.'

He shook his head again, his face a painful frown.

'We'll never get out of here Una. We're going to die in here, just like everyone else. I just want you to know that I love you and… and I'm sorry I couldn't save you. I'm sorry I couldn't keep you safe.'

'No Jordan, this is not your fault. You didn't do this to me, you didn't do this to us. But we can survive this, we don't have to end up like the others.'

'I'm sorry Una.'

He let go of the bars above him and slid back under the water, turning his back on me.

'Jordan no! Jordan please, please Jordan, come back. Just talk to me, please.'

Tears fell from my eyes. It was pointless, he had given up. He had resigned himself to die here just like the hundreds of other children before us. I had to get us out of here, there must be a way.

Before I could get my thoughts under control, the alarm sounded and the door opened. I stayed where I was at the bars and watched as a man and a woman walked toward my tank. It was time for my procedure. They stopped at a desk not far from my tank. The man bent over the keyboard and tapped at the keys.

'See, look at this' he said to the woman, pointing at the screen. 'The CCTV is out again. Security told me it's been shorting out intermittently since that storm last week. He reckons the camera units need replacing. He's having to reboot the entire security system every few days.'

I looked up at the security cameras, which were mounted above the doors and at various points on the walls around the room. There were no red lights blinking. The man picked up a phone from the desk and hit a few buttons.

'Yes hello, it's the lab. The cameras are out again… yes… yeah if you could, thank you.'

He put down the phone again.

'How long does a reset take?' Said the woman.

'Sometimes fifteen minutes, sometimes hours.'

'Wow. Dr Ayrers is going to be pissed. I take it she doesn't know yet?'

'I doubt it. I haven't heard her screaming at anyone about it yet, so lets hope it stays that way until it's fixed.'

They looked up from the computer as I sank below the surface of the water. They walked toward my tank, still talking to each other, not realising that I had heard them.

I felt weaker than usual after my procedure today. It had taken much longer than it normally did, like they were taking more of everything from me. I could hardly stand and had to be carried back to my tank by the man. It was hard to keep my eyes open, but as he walked through the double doors of the procedure room, I could see the CCTV camera above the door. The red light was blinking again. They were working again. He stepped gently up the steps at the side of my tank and placed me on my back into the water, watching me as I sunk down.

For a moment I just lay there, staring back at his face, until he backed away and I was blinded for a second by the fluorescent lights high above me. The man went straight to Jordan's tank and I sat up and watched as he was pulled out and place on the ground. I could barely watch as he was held up on his legs, which continuously gave way beneath him. The man eventually gave up and hooked his arm under Jordan's knees, carrying him the way he had carried me, straight through the doors of the procedure room.

16.

Vivienne

Something made me jump awake. A siren? No an alarm, perhaps a fire alarm? I rolled myself over in my tank to face the front. A light flashed from inside the procedure room as the doors swung open and a woman rushed out from it, sprinting toward the other doors. She swiped herself out and disappeared. I felt like I could hear screaming, muffled or far away. I came to the surface of my tank and the minute my ears were clear of the water, I heard a piercing cry.

'No, Jordan, no please.' Una was at her bars, an arm outstretched toward the procedure room. 'JORDAN, JORDAN!'

Her screams got longer and louder, her face screwed up in agony. Her feet kicking hard against the glass of her tank. I could hear raised voices from the procedure room, not quite knowing what they were shouting.

The woman returned, followed closely by more people in hospital scrubs and lab coats. Each one ran to the procedure room and joined in the shouting. Una continued to scream for her brother, she knew what was happening, she knew what this meant. The alarm stopped and the voices from inside subsided. Una's screams quietened to forceful sobs, her arm went slack against the bars, her head bowed down and shook from side to side. I turned away and saw Kendra up at her bars.

'He's gone now' she said.

Turning back to Una, I tried to speak gently.

'Una?'

She didn't answer me. What was I really expecting to be able to say that would comfort her anyway? There was nothing anyone could say or do that would ease her pain in any way whatsoever. She let go of the bars and sank beneath the surface of the water, pulling her knees into her face as she touched the bottom, wrapping her arms around herself.

'They'll harvest him now, take every usable part of him. We're worth almost as much to them dead you know. Lots of human lives will be saved. They can charge a lot of money for that.' Kendra turned her face back toward the procedure room. 'But at least he's free now, free of that room. Free of this pain.'

She clenched her mouth tight, but she couldn't hide the wobble of the lip, the glistening in her eyes. She pushed herself away from the bars, sinking back into the depth of her tank too. I wondered how long would it be until Kendra and Una met the same fate as Jordan. How long did any of us have?

I watched and listened for hours, I just kept my eyes on the doors, waiting for the inevitable. For Jordan's body to be removed from the room. When the doors finally opened, I was surprised by how small the black bag he was zipped into actually was. He barely took up any of the gurney he was wheeled out on. One by one the men and women followed him out. Some carrying small, white boxes, no doubt filled with pieces of him, pieces to be sold to the wealthy. Those boxes would extend their lives beyond their natural capabilities, after Jordan's was cut so short.

Each of the men and women were expressionless as they walked toward the exit. None looked toward the tanks, none noticed myself, Kendra and Una all watching from our watery prisons. Una's tiny hands pressed up against the glass, a look of utter grief upon her face.

17

I had lost count of the days since Jordan had died, but Una had finally started eating again. She hadn't been taken for any procedures since the day he had died. They must have been waiting for her to eat again, because they came for her soon after she had done so. Is that what had caused Jordan to die? Was he not eating enough to sustain his body and replenish what they were taking from him, or did they all die eventually? Could their tiny bodies simply not withstand the constant removal of bone marrow and blood? Although we knew that Asrai biology meant that we healed quickly in comparison to humans, was it fast enough for this?

Una seemed calm as the man took his key card from his pocket and swiped it on the pad next to her bars before lifting them open. He helped her out of the tank and placed a towel around her shoulders. Before he had a chance to do anything else, she started walking toward the procedure room. I held her gaze as she caught my eye, her face no longer looked sad as it had done since her brother had died, it looked defiant. Her jaw was clenched together and her eyes narrowed as she turned to face the doors of the procedure room and entered.

The hours passed and I waited at my bars, praying not to hear the sound of the alarm or to see the flashing of the lights that had signalled Jordan's imminent demise. Eventually the doors swung open and Una stepped out, followed closely by one of the men with his hands on her shoulders. She batted his arms away with her own.

'I can walk by myself' she said firmly. 'Don't touch me.'

She seemed angry. I would feel the same way too. I wouldn't want anyone who had had a part in the death of my family laying a hand on me. She took a few more steps and her legs began to buckle, then she fell to the floor in a crumpled heap. The man knelt down beside her, pulling her face toward him, checking if she was conscious.

'Leave… me… alone' she mumbled.

He pulled her onto her back and hooked his arms under her knees and back. Her head lolled from side to side and her arm swung over his, completely floppy. I watched as he began to stand up, then saw as her tiny hand slipped into his pocket and pulled out the key card. Once he was standing up straight, he carried her back to her tank, where the bars had remained open since he had removed her from it earlier.

He lowered her inside and I watched as she quickly drew her hands into her chest and rolled to the bottom of the tank, curling up into a tight ball in the corner. He pulled the bars back across the top of the tank and I heard the click as they locked into place once more. He stepped down from the tank and I watched him as he returned to the procedure room. Surely he would notice his key card was missing? As soon as he needed to leave he would realise he didn't have it.

Una stayed where she was, not moving a muscle. I felt my body tense as the people in the procedure room came out one by one. The man that Una had stolen the key card from was carrying white boxes in his hands, boxes that would have been full of Una's bone marrow and blood. That meant he would need to be let out, he wouldn't need his key card. I watched them walk across the lab in single file and held my breath as the woman at the front of the line swiped her key card in the door. The buzzer sounded and she pushed the door open, then stood holding it open as one by one, each person left the lab. The doors clicked shut behind them and I turned to face Una's tank. She was no longer curled up in the corner, now she was up at her bars, looking at me.

'Are you ready?' she whispered. 'We can go, we can leave right now.'

She lifted the key card out of the water and holding onto her bars with one hand, lifted it up through the bars with the other.

'Una no, wait. We need to think about this for a moment, we need a plan.'

'She's right Una.' A loud whisper came from Kendra's tank. 'We can't go now anyway, we need to go at night time, when there will be fewer people on the other side of that door.'

Una shook her head and whispered back.

'But we don't even know what time it is, we never know when it's nighttime and there's always a doctor or someone in the building somewhere, they never go home.'

'Yes, that's true Una' I said in a low voice. 'But Kendra is right. We need to go at nighttime, it's our best chance of getting away from this place without anyone seeing us.'

Before I could say another word, Brooke pushed open the doors of the procedure room. Una quickly slid back beneath the water, curling back into a tight ball, keeping the key card out of sight. Kendra slunk away too, but kept herself closer to the surface. Brooke walked across the lab, pressing fingers to her hand held device and took a seat at one of the computers nearest to my tank.

'Brooke?' She looked up at me, her face almost seemed friendly with a faint smile. 'How long until you know… until you know if it's worked?'

She pursed her lips together and looked down at her lap. Did she actually feel bad about it, about what she had done to me?

'I'll be testing your blood tomorrow for HCG levels. That's when we will know.'

'Tomorrow?' She nodded. 'What time is it now?'

She lifted her wrist out in front of her, consulting her watch.

'It's just after seven pm now. You'll have to give a urine sample first thing in the morning and then I'll be taking your blood at about midday tomorrow.'

I nodded. Tomorrow I would find out if I have his life growing inside of me. I didn't want to know. She opened her mouth as if to say something more, but I pushed myself away from the bars. I watched as her gaze lingered on me for a while, before she turned back to her computer.

After what seemed like an eternity, Brooke finally left the lab. Una and Kendra were both at their bars before the doors had even closed completely. Una held up the key card and I nodded in agreement. It was time.

'What about the CCTV?' Kendra said. 'They'll see us getting out of the tanks.'

'It's okay' Una said. 'It's not working. I heard them talking about it, it keeps turning off. See, look.' She pointed to one of the cameras. 'The light isn't blinking. We have to go now, before they reset them.'

Holding onto her bars with one hand, she put her other arm through the bars and awkwardly twisted it until she was in the right position to swipe the key card. It took her a few attempts, but eventually we heard the familiar beep and a light on the keypad turned green. She clenched the key card between her teeth and began to push the bars upward. She couldn't get out of the water enough to push them right up and over and instead, let the bars rest on her arms as she threaded her leg through the gap she had created between the bars and the glass of the thank.

Using both hands, she pulled her body over the lip of the glass, before finally swinging her other leg around, until she was completely out of the tank. She lowered herself down onto the steps in front of the tank and let the bars of the tank click shut again.

Keeping herself low, she made her way to my tank, where she climbed the steps and swiped the key card. I heard the beep and saw the green light straight away and whilst I got myself out of the tank in the same way Una had done, she crept across to Kendra's tank and unlocked her bars too. As Kendra got herself out of her tank, I stepped toward a bank of computers, my legs shaking with the effort. The monitors were locked, but had the time showing in the bottom corner. It was just after midnight. Kendra was right, there would be fewer people out there now and with the cover of darkness, if we did manage to get out of this building without being caught, we stood a much better chance of getting away.

'The procedure room, quick' Kendra almost shouted, before striding over and pushing through the double doors.

'Kendra, what is it?'

Una and I followed after her, pushing through the still swinging doors. Kendra was at a cabinet, opening doors and drawers.

'What are you looking for?'

'Scalpels, knives, I don't know. Just something that can help us.'

Una and I quickly rushed to other cabinets and started rifling through them ourselves.

'I've found them, they're over here' Una said.

Kendra and I rushed to where she was standing, a drawer full of packaged scalpels open in front of her. Una handed me the key card and began ripping at the packages, passing each of us a scalpel.

'Come on' Kendra said. 'Let's go.'

We followed her out of the procedure room. Would this be the last time I saw the inside of this room, we were getting out now. We had to get out now, or would I be giving birth to a baby in here in nine months time. But I couldn't think about that now, couldn't think about what I may have growing inside of me. We had to get out of here, I had to get these children out of this place, I couldn't let anyone else die here.

We kept low and made our way toward the exit. I held the key card in one hand and a scalpel in the other. There were no windows in the door, so there was no way to know who or what was on the other side. It could be packed with people, there could only be one way out and it could be heavily guarded, we simply had no way of knowing. As I lifted the key card up to the pad on the side of the door, the door buzzer suddenly sounded.

All three of us leapt back against the wall in unison as the door swung open. Brooke stepped into the lab, not noticing us behind the door as she looked down at a device in her hands. I leapt up behind her and put my arm around her neck, lifting her chin upward. She dropped the device and it smashed on the ground, the glass top breaking into several pieces. With my other hand, I pushed the metal blade of the scalpel against the cold skin of her throat. I was weak, but I definitely had the upper hand and Brooke knew it. I felt her body tense beneath my arms.

'Don't make a sound' I hissed into her ear.

I nodded at Kendra in the direction of the procedure room and the four of us walked slowly across the lab. I looked up at the camera, still no blinking light. I could feel Brooke taking long, controlled breaths. Once in the procedure room, Brooke resisted slightly, trying not to get close to the operating table as I pushed her into the middle of the room. I pressed the blade harder against her skin.

'You will get on that table or I will slash your throat Brooke, do you understand?'

I felt the tiniest nod from her head. Slowly, I let my arm go from around her neck, but kept the other hand and the blade pressed tightly where it was. As instructed, she slowly slid herself up onto the table.

'Strap her in.'

Una dived under the table and retrieved the body straps, pulling them across Brooke's arms and body and clipping them in place, pulling them in tightly. Kendra lifted out the stirrups and put Brooke's legs into each one, then fixed each strap in place. I finally stepped back from her and took the scalpel away from her neck.

'What's on the other side of that door?' I said.

'You'll never get out of here' she said shaking her head.

I stepped toward her, pushing the blade against her neck once more.

'Tell me what's on the other side of that door or I will kill you Brooke, I mean it.'

She flinched away from me, squeezing her eyes shut at the site of the blade.

'Okay, okay, I'll tell you.' I pulled the blade away from her again and she relaxed again. 'There are some offices and a staff room down stairs.'

'Whose offices? How many?'

'I don't know' she shook her head. 'Ten, maybe fifteen. All the doctors have one. I have one and there's a security office on this level at the front of the building.'

'How do we get out?' Kendra said angrily, stepping closer to her. Brooke flinched again.

'Through the front door, that's the only way in or out other than the big roller door at the end of the lab.'

'Do we need the key cards for the front door?' I said.

'No' she replied. 'They're only for the doors to the offices and the lab. The security guard controls the front entrance. Everyone has to be let in and out of the front door.'

Kendra and I exchanged a glance. We would have to hurt him to get past him, we couldn't let him notify anyone else.

'How many people are out there now?' I said.

'Just the security guard. Every one else left hours ago. But it doesn't matter, you won't get past the security office, he controls the door.'

'We won't need to. We'll get out another way.' I looked at Kendra, before turning back to Brooke. 'Do you have a car?' Brooke paused for a moment, before nodding yes. 'Where are the keys?'

'They're in my office.' She looked at me, her eyes seemed almost pleading. 'Please Vivienne, please don't leave. I need to know, we have to know the outcome, if it's worked or not.'

I scowled at her.

'Why would I do anything you ask me to Brooke? After everything you've done here, all the children you've murdered. We don't owe you a single thing. Now, where is your key card?'

Kendra checked the pockets on Brooke's lab coat and soon produced another key card.

'You two, stay here with her. Make sure she stays quiet. If I'm not back in fifteen minutes, use her as a hostage to get out of here okay?'

'Where are you going?' Una said, looking worried.

'I'll be right back, I'm going to get her car keys and then we are leaving out that back door.'

On the other side of the lab door was a long corridor. To my left about a hundred feet away, there was a door at the very end of the corridor, with a green exit sign above it. That must be where the front door was. At the other end of the corridor, to my right, was a metal staircase going down below the lab. I headed to the end of the corridor and down the stairs as fast as I could, my feet slipping on the cold metal every few steps. The stairs led to another empty corridor, with a row of doors along one side. These would have been directly beneath the lab up above. Each door had a plaque to the side of it, showing various names and titles.

I followed the corridor to the very end, until I came to a plaque with her name on. Dr B Ayers, Location Director. She really was in charge of this place. I swiped her key card in the door and pushed down on the handle, making the door open silently. Her office was neat and tidy, with a desk and chairs. On the desk was a laptop, a small printer and a handbag. I grabbed the handbag, searching inside for her car keys. Relief surged through me as my fingers clasped the rings of a key chain and I pulled them out. As I set the bag back on the desk, I saw her mobile telephone. It must have been underneath the bag. I picked it up and tried to unlock it. A pass code was required. I hit 1, 2, 3, 4. Nothing. 0, 0, 0, 0. Still nothing. I would never be able to guess her pass code, I knew nothing about her. Underneath the numbers, it said 'emergency'.

I clicked on it and it opened a medical ID screen. There was no information on that, but underneath it showed emergency contacts. Morgan. His name and his mobile number were right there. She must have never got around to changing it. I clicked on it, my hands shaking, then held it up to my ear. Tears burned my eyes as it rang and rang until the voicemail kicked in.

'You've reached Morgan, please leave a message and I'll get back to you.'

It beeped in my ear and for a moment I couldn't say anything, the words just wouldn't come. I took a deep breath, forcing the tears back.

'Morgan. It's me, Vivienne. I'm… I'm alive. I was taken by people, taken to Brooke. They've kept me here, but… but I have no idea where *here* is. They take children, they've killed hundreds of children Morgan. We're trying to escape, tonight, the last of us. I don't know where we are, but I'll get back to you Morgan, I promise, I will get home to you. I love you.'

I ended the call. I didn't have time to keep trying him. He would get the message. He would at least know that I was alive.

It was still clear on the other side of the office door and I made it back to the lab without seeing any movement from any of the other doors. Back in the lab, I tried to run toward the procedure room, but my weakened legs now struggled under the weight of me. The surge of adrenalin that had been giving me strength was waining and I was almost completely out of breath as I pushed through the double doors. Una and Kendra stood either side of Brooke as she lay there, still strapped to the table, scalpels in their outstretched hands.

'It's okay, it's me, it's me.' I walked in, arms out in front of me. 'I've got the keys, let's go, come on.'

I motioned for them to follow me out of the procedure room and turned toward the doors.

'Wait' Una almost shouted. 'We can't leave her like this.'

'Una it's fine, someone will find her in the morning, come on, let's go.'

I took a step toward her and held out my hand, holding everything else in the other.

'No' she said, more firmly this time. 'We can't leave her alive. We need to kill her. She needs to pay for everything she has done.'

Una turned back to Brooke and stepped up close to the table. She reached out the hand holding the scalpel and pushed the blade against Brooke's throat.

'She killed my brother. She made them kill our families so that we would be taken. Why should she get to live after everything she's done, everything she's taken from us? Everything she's taken from *me*?'

Brooke's face showed true fear. As her chin shook, her eyes shone with tears. She knew what she had done, she knew that Una was right. Anyone of us would be justified in killing her.

'Please Una…'

Brooke's voice was a quiet whisper.

'Shut up' Una said, stepping closer and pushing the blade down harder.

I reached out to Una, putting my hand underneath her chin and turning her face toward me.

'Una, you don't have to do this' I said softly. 'You don't *want* to do this, not really. Killing her won't bring Jordan back. It won't bring any of them back. It won't erase what she's done to you, it will only make you feel worse. You're not a murderer Una, you're not like any of these people. You're better than all of this, we all are.'

I took my hand away from Una's face. Brooke's body continued to shake as Una turned her head back toward her, her gaze bearing down upon her. The rage and determination in Una's face slowly began to subside and she took the scalpel away from Brooke's throat, but then I watched in horror as a look of pure hatred suddenly spread across Una's face again and she raised the blade high above her head.

'Una no!' I shouted.

I reached my arms out to stop her, but I was too late. Una slammed the blade down into the operating table, right next to Brooke's ear. A terrified scream escaped Brooke's mouth as I sighed with relief. Not because I didn't want to see Brooke hurt, but because I didn't want to see Una become that person, a person who inflicted pain out of revenge. She stepped away from the table and looked from me to Kendra. Then she put her small hand in mine and we made our way out of the procedure room toward the back of the lab.

'Find the keypad thing' I shouted to Kendra as we both reached the large, rolling door.

Please, just let it be operated by the key card was all I could think to myself. If we couldn't get out this way we had no other option but to use the front door. I looked up at one of the cameras. Still no flashing light.

'It's here, it's here! I've found it, come over this side.'

Kendra beckoned me toward her. On the right hand side of the door was a keypad with a place to swipe a card. I let go of Una's hand and with shaking hand, I fumbled with the things I was holding until I got hold of one of the key cards. I gripped it tightly, my hands still shaking so much I thought I would drop it, until eventually I managed to hold it up the right way and swipe it downward through the keypad.

A loud siren sounded as the door slowly creaked into life. It was alarmed. Shit. Brooke knew it would be. The door began to open and as it cleared a couple of inches the siren seemed to wail louder and an orange light above the other door began to flash. The security guard would now know what was happening, someone was coming for us. We all got down on the ground, willing the door to open faster. Kendra used her hands to pull at it. The gap was big enough for Una to fit her head through.

'Go Una go, go now. If we don't follow, just run, keep running until you get to water.'

I looked behind me, someone had entered the lab through the double doors, it was the security guard. I could hear shouting in the distance, it was Brooke, screaming.

'Stop her, stop the woman… don't let her get out.'

Kendra was sliding her body out underneath the door and then she was gone.

'Vivienne, hurry up!'

The man was running toward me now. A hand shot back underneath the door.

'Come on Vivienne, take my hand.'

I dropped everything except the keys and grabbed hold of her, laying myself flat on the ground. She yanked me hard and I felt myself slide under the door, then she and Una were pulling me up onto my feet. We had done it, we were outside. Where were the cars? Where should we go?

Kendra pulled me along at a run as fast as I could go. Adrenalin surged through me once again and I managed to keep pace without falling over. She held onto Una with her other hand and as we ran around the side of the building, we found rows of parked cars. We all stopped and I fumbled with the car keys, pressing the unlock button, hoping for any sign that Brooke's car was here somewhere. I could hear running footsteps near by, but before I had time to react, Kendra pulled us down behind a car.

'We need to find her car' she said. 'Keep low, keep pressing that button.'

We shuffled around a car, crouching low behind a larger vehicle as someone sprinted past.

'Keep going' Kendra whispered.

We shuffled between the rows of cars as I frantically pressed the unlock button of the car keys. Eventually I saw the flash of orange lights as a car unlocked on the other side of the car park.

'It's over there' I whispered. 'The black one. Come on.'

We kept low as we made our way across the car park, then each got in the car as quietly as we could. Kendra and Una sat in the back.

'Put your seat belts on' I said whilst pulling mine across my body and clicking it into place.

I looked around me at the controls and hit the button for locking all the doors. I turned on the ignition and watched as the car park in front of me lit up. I put the car into gear, my bare feet struggling with the peddles. As I pulled slowly out of the space, Brooke came running into view at the other end of the car park, a phone pressed to her ear. I put my foot down as hard as I could and sped toward the exit of the car park. As we got closer, I could see the security guard attempting to block the way out. I pushed my foot down harder on the accelerator. I really didn't want to hurt anyone, but I had to get us out of here, I had to save these girls. I got closer and closer and was just about to hit the brake when he jumped out of the way.

I looked in the rear view mirror. Brooke had caught up to him and they stood there together, watching us leave. It wouldn't be long before they had someone looking for us. I pulled out onto a two lane road and headed right. I had no idea where we were or which way we should go. I hit the satellite navigation on the cars touch screen. The screen changed to a map.

'Kendra, get in the front, come look at the map, tell me where we are.'

She released her seat belt and climbed into the front seat. Our position was marked on the map by a little arrow.

'B...Bal... Ba-li-van-iche?' she said slowly, not sure of the pronunciation.

'Where the hell is that?' I said. 'Zoom out on the map, that button down there on the left.'

I pointed to the little magnifying glass at the bottom of the screen. I looked from the road to the screen and back again as she pressed the button, over and over again until I could see we were on an island.

'We're in Scotland' she said. 'An island at the top of Scotland. It's really small, it won't take them long to find us.'

Shit. This meant we couldn't just drive away from here. I looked from the map to the steering wheel and back again. This island was so small. There were only be two ways off this island, plane or boat. We must have been at the airport and there was no way we could go back there. Plus we had no money, no dry clothes, no way of getting on a plane to anywhere. We would have to swim, *I* would have to swim. I had no idea if I could or not. My strength was leaving me quickly. I felt so weak, my arms could barely keep hold of the steering wheel. But I would have to, I had to do it to save us, to save these girls.

We drove for a while, not seeing any other cars on the road. We passed houses here and there, some with a light on, but most of them dark. The road initially followed the coast of the island, but eventually moved us further in land. We had been driving for nearly an hour when I caught sight of headlights behind us in the distance.

'Shit.'

'What is it?' Kendra looked behind us too. 'Oh no, they've caught up with us. What are we going to do?'

The map on the screen showed we were approaching the most southern point of the island.

'We have to get to the water' I said. 'Before they catch up with us, we need to get in the water.'

'Then where will we go?' Una's voice came from the backseat, sounding as scared as I felt.

'The Colony' Kendra almost shouted the words. 'We can go to The Colony, we will be safe there, they can protect us.'

'Nobody knows how to get there Kendra, we have to get to a phone, call for help.'

'I know how to get there, I know the way.'

I looked at Kendra, my eyes wide, before turning back to the road.

'You know how to get to The Colony? How? Only Keepers know and they can't tell anyone.'

'My dad knew someone years ago that told him, they showed him a map, hidden in some kind of mirror. He's been there, he went to The Colony a long time before I was born. He told me how to get there.'

This couldn't be real, this young girl knew how to get to The Colony. We could rally go there, we could be safe and protected from all of this. It was almost too much to think about right now.

'No, we can't.' I shook my head. 'I can't. I have to get home to my husband. We need to stay together, we're safer together Kendra. Come with me, to my home and we will think about The Colony once we are safe.'

She pursed her lips together, but eventually nodded. The lights behind us were getting closer, they were gaining ground quickly, but we were almost back at the coast, only half a mile away. I put my foot down, the speedometer soon swung up to eighty miles an hour. I unlocked my seat belt and use the buttons next to me to put the front windows down.

'Kendra, get in the back. Then both of you, put your windows all the way down, take your seat belt off Una and both of you, get down behind the front seats.'

They quickly did as I instructed.

'Why are we doing this? What are you going to do?' Kendra sunk down behind my seat.

'We won't have time to get out and make a run for it, we can't risk it, they're too close to us. I'm going to drive us off the road and into the water, it's not high, but it will probably still hurt. As soon as the car is fully under, we get out through the windows and swim as hard as we can, do you hear me?'

I looked behind the passenger seat where Una was crouched down, nodding her head.

'What about you?' Kendra said.

'I'll be okay, just make sure you stay down there until after we hit the water.' I gripped the steering wheel as tightly as I could. 'Are you ready?'

I pressed my foot down all the way on the accelerator, making the engine roar even louder. The car following us was only a few meters away now. The road started to curve to the left, but I kept heading straight forward, leaving the road and violently bumping across the grass. I kept my foot pressed down as hard as I could and then braced myself as the car flew into the air and the ground disappeared from beneath us. The water twinkled ahead of us in the moonlight and time almost stood still for a moment as the car seemed to pause in the air, before everything sped up again and we crashed nose first into the dark water beneath us.

18.

Una

I hadn't really felt the impact, I just heard the sound of Vivienne screaming before she hit the wind shield, then the ringing in my ears. Maybe I had gone into shock. The car was full of water in seconds and the tyres touched down on the floor under the water within a minute. Vivienne's body floated under the roof of the car, Kendra was pulling herself out from behind the seat, then she was reaching for Vivienne. She grabbed hold of her shoulders and shook her, but Vivienne's eyes had stayed closed. She looked like she was dead. Had we gone through all of that just for her to die, right after she had saved us?

Kendra looked at me, motioning me to follow whilst she took hold of Vivienne's hand and began to pull her through the open window. I followed close behind, pushing on Vivienne's legs until she was completely clear of the car. I copied Kendra and hooked my arm under Vivienne's and then we started to swim.

That had been hours ago. I don't know how long exactly we had swam for, but there was now brilliant blue sky above us. Kendra returned from the surface of the water and said she could see land again, a small island with no buildings. She couldn't see any boats, or anything else to suggest that Brooke or anyone else was close by. We would rest on the island, try to get Vivienne to wake up. I felt my stomach grumble, hopefully we would find something to eat too. We got to our feet once the waters were shallow enough and dragged Vivienne up the shore and onto dry land. We laid her on soft grass behind some bushes.

'Look around for dry twigs and branches, dried leaves too if you see any' Kendra said. 'Stay near her though, I'll be right back. If you see anything, any boats, anyone in the water, make a run for it okay?'

Kendra ran off back toward the water before I could reply. I felt around underneath bushes and gathered as many sticks and dry leaves as I could, piling them up near Vivienne. She looked so peaceful lying there. If it wasn't for the black and blue bruises on her forehead, you wouldn't think she had been hurt at all. It made me think of my mother again and how she had looked the last time I had saw her, she had looked so peaceful too. I watched as Vivienne's chest rose up and down slowly. I shuffled closer to her and moved the wet hair from her face. She had saved us. She said she would get us out and she had and now it was our turn to save her.

Kendra returned after a while with four small fish clasped tightly in her hands.

'Best I could do I'm afraid.'

She dumped them on the grass next to me and walked back toward the water, returning in a few minutes with a large rock, which she put down next to the piles of sticks and leaves I had made. She turned around and scanned the horizon.

'Have you seen anything?'

I shook my head. Kendra knelt down in front of me and made a hole in the middle of the pile of dried leaves I had made. She then took the two biggest sticks I had found and started rubbing them together in the hole. It took a long time for wisps of smoke to appear, eventually followed by a flicker of orange flame. She leaned in close to the pile of leaves and began to softly blow until the flames got bigger. She piled up some smaller twigs and sticks on top of it, then put a stick in the mouth of each fish, pushing them down as far as they would go. She held two out to me.

'Hold those over the fire' she said. 'Like this.'

She picked up the remaining fish and held them above the flames.

'Make sure you turn them over every now and again.'

We sat there for a while, slowly turning the fish on the sticks.

'Jordan was really good at catching fish' I said. 'He had this cool knife that Mama got him that he would use. He would attach it to a long stick and use it like a spear. He got some really big ones sometimes. He was going to teach me how to do it. How to catch the big ones I mean. I could only ever really catch the small ones.'

Kendra smiled at me.

'I'm sure I can teach you how to catch the big ones. I'm quite good with a knife too you know.'

'Really?'

She nodded.

'Really. You have to know how to catch fish if you want to make it to The Colony. That's what my dad always told me.'

'Do you really know how to get there?'

'If I remember what my dad told me right, then yeah I do.'

'I hope I get to see it one day.'

Kendra turned the fish she was holding around a few more times.

'Me too Una.'

Kendra put one of the fish down on the rock she had placed by the fire and held the other up to her face.

'Should be done now' she said and gently blew on the fish before biting into it.

I copied and did the same. It felt amazing biting into the soft, fresh meat. It had been so long since I had eaten something so fresh. Kendra chewed loudly.

'You know' she said between bites. 'I honestly thought I would never eat nice food again. I thought we'd be stuck in that place forever.'

Within minutes we had each finished the first fish and had started on the next ones. I looked over at Vivienne, still lying peacefully where we had left her.

'Don't worry' said Kendra. 'I'll get more as soon as she wakes up. We all need our strength.'

She finished her fish and lifted the rock onto the fire.

'We don't want anything giving away where we are. You never know, they may try looking for us. I doubt it though, we could have gone in any direction, they wouldn't know where to start.'

I wondered if she really believed that. I was scared waiting here on this tiny island. We could easily be found if they were looking for us.

'How long until she wakes up do you think?'

Kendra shrugged her shoulders.

'No idea. She hit her head pretty hard. It probably would have killed a human. It will take a while to heal.'

'What will we do until then?'

'All we can do is wait I guess. If she's not awake by tomorrow we can try swimming with her again, see how far we can get.'

I nodded. Kendra stood up and looked out toward the water.

'Come on' she said, holding out a hand to me. 'Let's teach you how to catch a fish.'

It had been amazing swimming free with Kendra, chasing after fish, chasing each other. After so long in the tank, the freezing water felt magical. Kendra swam in circles around me, her tight curls spreading out into long waves. We swam around for hours, with Kendra going back to shore every now and then to see if Vivienne was awake.

By the time the sky began to get darker, I still hadn't managed to perfect the technique of catching a fish with my hands, but Kendra had caught enough for us to eat well again. I watched as she made the fire once more and we sat in silence as we cooked our fish and ate until we were full. I looked at Kendra's hands, noticing where the skin had turned blue and pink.

'Do you think your skin will go back to normal?' She opened up one of her hands and turned it over and back again.

'I don't know. Everything else seems to be going back to normal so far, except this.'

'Well I like it. I think it looks really pretty. Like a mermaid from the story books.'

She leaned toward me and tapped my nose gently with her finger.

'We are the mermaids from the story books Una' she said with a smile. 'Now come on, eat up. We need to get some rest.'

19.

Vivienne

I could feel a cold breeze on my face and as I tried opening my eyes slowly, I remembered the car, remembered being chased, driving off the road and into the water. I finally opened my eyes fully and found a nest of blonde hair in front of my face. Una had her back to me, her legs curled up in front of her. Had she slept like that all night? Cuddled up against my stomach. I sat up slowly, my forehead suddenly pounding.

'Ow' I couldn't help but say it out loud as I rubbed my head.

Una sat up suddenly.

'Vivienne! You're okay.'

She turned toward me and wrapped her arms tightly around my neck, our faces squeezing together.

'Yes I'm fine' I said.

I put my arms around her tiny waist and squeezed her right back.

'Are you okay?' I asked. 'Were you hurt? Where's Kendra.'

'I'm okay, we both are. Kendra's probably off getting some more fish to eat.' Una let go of me and sat back on her heels. 'She's been catching fresh fish for us to eat, it's delicious. I can't wait for you to try some. I better get the stuff ready for the fire.'

She stood up and began rummaging in the bushes behind me.

'A fire? Una, I don't know if that will be safe. What if we've been followed?'

She came back and knelt down in front of me, then started crunching leaves and twigs into a pile on the floor. She shook her head.

'We've been here for a day now, there hasn't been any sign of anyone. Kendra says they wouldn't have come after us yet, they would have no idea which direction we went, so there was no point.'

I hoped Kendra right about that. I didn't know if that would really have stopped them coming after us.

Just the fact that we could have gone anywhere. I wasn't so sure. I stood up and stretched out my legs and back. The weakness in my legs felt less than before, they felt stronger than they had in a long time. Maybe that was because the drugs I had been pumped full of were finally wearing off, or had the fresh salt water healed me? Whatever the reason, I was glad to feel more like myself again.

'How far did we swim? Or how far did you and Kendra swim I should say. Sorry that you had to do it with my added weight.'

'Oh it wasn't hard at all, don't worry' Una said matter of factly. 'It took us a while. The sun had come up by the time we got here.'

'Which direction did we come from?'

Una stood up and the wind picked her hair up from around her face. She looked to her right, lifted up her arm and pointed.

'We came from that side. Kendra said that judging by the map on the screen on the car, the mainland should be that way.'

She turned and pointed in the other direction. She crouched back down and continued piling leaves and branches up together. I walked a few steps inwards, away from where I'd woken up. We were on a small, rocky island, with patches of grass and shrubbery here and there. It couldn't have been more than a few hundred metres across and I could see larger islands in the direction Una thought the mainland was. Everywhere was so remote up here. I needed a phone, I needed to speak to Morgan.

He knew I was alive now, but would he know where to start looking? I had called him from Brooke's phone. He knew Brooke was in Scotland, but she had moved to Edinburgh when they had broken up. That was miles away, we were up in the North West of Scotland. There was no way he would know where to look for us. I had to get to a phone somehow. We were going to have to swim a long way before finding anywhere that would have a public phone. I didn't really want to risk finding people and asking to use a phone. There would always be a possibility that they were one of them, one of the people from the lab. But we would have to risk it, unless we could swim four hundred miles back to Cornwall. I looked out toward the bigger islands I could see in the horizon. There had to be a phone over there somewhere.

Kendra returned from the water not long after I had woken up. In her hands, she held three large fish by the tails.

'How on earth did you catch those?' I said.

'These?' She lifted them up slightly. 'I had to go further out to find them this size. Sorry it took so long, the small ones just weren't enough for me any more.'

She smiled and held out the fish in front of her. Una practically skipped over and gently took the catch from Kendra's hands. She returned to the fire she had managed to get going and laid them on the grass beside it.

'Wow, you girls have been pretty resourceful haven't you.'

I watched as they set about spearing the fish with thin sticks and held them over the fire.

'How do you feel Vivienne?   Are you up for travelling yet? We need to move on soon. These fires could draw attention to us.'

'I feel okay and you're right, we need to move on from here as soon as possible. I need to get to a phone. If I can let Morgan know where we are he can send someone to get us. We'll be safe then.'

She nodded and turned the sticks of fish she was holding over in her hands, letting the flames brush against the silver skin.

'So what do you want to do?'

'I'm not sure. It's so remote out here. It would take us days to get to a town. We'd have to swim to the main land, then walk in land until we found a town. We would certainly draw a lot of attention seeing as we are barely clothed.'

'What's the alternative?'

'We check out some of these larger islands. There may be houses on one of them, but there's the risk of the people in them being linked to where we have just escaped from. What do you think?'

'I say we risk it. If we get picked up by authorities in a town, what do you think they will do with me and Una? We're just kids to them. There's no way to guarantee they will let us stay with you, even if they believe us when we tell them what happened. Which we can't tell them anyway, not without saying what we really are.'

'No, you're right Kendra. Okay, we swim to the next island over and see what's there.'

Kendra nodded, then held up a stick of fish to me. I watched as Una bit into the one she had been holding over the flames. Taking it from Kendra's hand, I sat down next to her and held it up to my face. It smelt delicious and my mouth watered instantly. I was going to enjoy this.

The water had done its job of invigorating me, every part of me had felt instantly stronger and more energised, but fatigue was now setting in again. By the time we reached the next island, I felt like I could sleep again. Although it was quite overcast above our heads, it seemed as though the sun was higher in the sky. We climbed up onto the rocky shore and walked inwards toward the middle of the island. This one was much bigger than the one we had been on, but I could still see a fair way across it. From where we were stood, it was nearly all rock. We hiked inland for a while, covering a few miles at least. But there was nothing here.

'What now?' Una said?

'We keep going' I shrugged. 'Try the next one.'

'But what if they're all like this?'

'Then we will think of something else.' I took her tiny hand in mine. 'Don't worry Una, I will get us somewhere safe. I promise.'

The three of us turned and headed back toward the water. The sea was choppier now. The clouds above had grown darker and rain threatened. Waves crashed against the rocks and we struggled to get down into the water as the waves pushed us back unmercifully into the rocks. We held onto each other as we forced our way under the water, the waves still pushing us back in the shallows.

Kendra managed to push off ahead, whilst Una clung to my arm and I tried my best to pull myself along the rocks under the water. Then, out of nowhere came a familiar clicking sound. I clung onto the jagged rock I was being slammed against and looked around me. A few metres out, just in front of Kendra, I could see one, a dolphin. Then from the side of me came two more. They swam right up in front of us and then went back and forth. I nodded to Una and pushed her out in front of me. She grabbed hold of one of the dolphin's dorsal fins and I managed to do the same on the other. As soon as we were holding on, off they went.

As we rushed past Kendra, she quickly followed suit and grabbed hold of the dolphin next to her. They stayed near the surface at first and we were soon joined by more dolphins. Could these be the same ones from The Cove? It would be crazy to think that they remembered me and that they were here, right when I had needed help.

Once the water got deeper, each dolphin took us lower down, only returning to the surface every few minutes. I had no idea where would they take us or how far. Before I had time to fully consider what the dolphins were doing, we were in sight of another island.

Slightly smaller than the last one, but as the dolphins swam along the curve of the land, each time the dolphin pushed through the surface, I could see the masts of small sailing boats. Next I saw a stone wall that curved out into the water, like a jetty almost.

The dolphins pulled us in close to the end of the jetty, which we took as our cue to let go. The high concrete end of the jetty had a built in ladder, which we each held onto. The water was still rough and we were pulled in and out with each wave. We watched as the dolphins disappeared into the dark water.

'Wait here' I said to the girls.

I pulled myself up the ladder rung by rung, bracing myself each time a wave hit, trying not to let it slam me any harder against the concrete wall. I reached the top of the ladder and peered over the top. The jetty had a small cabin built upon it, a few hundred feet away from where I held on tightly to the ladder. I had to squint to make out the sign on its side. Eigg Ferry Terminal. I'd never heard of it, but at least I knew where we were. In the distance behind it, I could make out other buildings. There must be a phone up there somewhere. Climbing back down the ladder, I lowered myself back into the water with Kendra and Una.

'We'll wait here until it's a bit darker, then I'll go up on land and see if I can find a phone. I don't know if there will be many people about, but it's safer if they can't see me.'

I could see in their eyes that both Una and Kendra were exhausted. We needed to find somewhere for them to rest. The wind was howling loudly and the rain battered the sides of our faces. With no let up from the rain and waves, I knew we couldn't wait it out where we were.

'Let's swim around out the way a bit, find something to hold onto down low, maybe get some rest?'

They both nodded, almost eager to get out of way of the waves battering them against the wall. We pushed ourselves below and swam away from the jetty. The current was strong and it took nearly all of my strength to even swim a few meters. The water below was dark and murky, making it difficult to see where we were even going. I took hold of Una's hand and pulled her up next to me.

We swam outward and further away from the jetty and I scanned the bottom of the water. Below us I saw some plastic crates, tied together with ropes. They looked worn and covered with seaweed and barnacles, like they had been there for while. Whether abandoned fishing equipment or something that had fallen off a boat, right now I didn't care. We could huddle up against them together and rest. I pointed downward and the girls followed me toward the crates. The crates were formed in the shape of a horse shoe and we positioned ourselves in the middle, each pulling our knees in tight around us.

Una cuddled into me and I put my arm around her as she closed her eyes. Everything seemed still for a moment until I noticed Kendra looking upward and then all around her, her eyes squinting with concern. Then I heard it too, a low rumble, a boat. I looked out away from the direction of the shore and sure enough in the distance, I could see the bow of a large boat pushing its way through the water. It was some distance away and we were hidden out of sight, but it looked as though it wasn't quite low enough to reach us. We would be fine, these crates had obviously been here for a long time and were undisturbed.

Una was now looking out toward the boat. It was big, very big. She looked at me, her face was worried. I shook my head and shuffled myself down, so our heads were beneath the top of the crates. I pulled Kendra by the arm, trying to get her to do the same, but she was pushing herself upward, away from where were hidden.

I held onto her arm, trying to pull her back down toward us. She looked down at me, shaking her head. She was scared, she was panicking, trying to get out of the way of the boat. It was closer now, the rumble of the engines was so much louder. It was big, it was too late to get out of its way, we had to stay here, hunker down out of the way, why couldn't she see that? We would be okay. I held onto her tightly, with both hands, willing her to stop, trying to pull her into me.

I got her down low as the boat was almost upon us, her face twisted in fear and she opened her mouth as if screaming. The sound that came from her vibrated through me and my grip on her loosened. She pulled away from me, her hair wrapping around her face as she brought her arms up above her head, trying to swim away from the boat, I managed to grab hold of her leg, but it was too late.

The front of the boat plowed into Kendra, striking her shoulder and head from the side. I screamed silently as the water around her filled with dark, red blood. The rest of the boat kept coming and I pulled Kendra back down toward me and held on as tight as I could as the boat passed over us. I had to get Kendra down low, the back of the boat would have propellers, huge propellers. I couldn't let us get sucked in. I pulled Kendra and Una into me tightly, I was on my knees, leaning over, my head almost touching the ground. I held Una under one arm and Kendra under the other, holding them onto the seabed. I could hear the thud of the propellers overhead as I held on tighter to the girls, blood still filling the water around us.

I looked up, the boat had passed over us, the pull of the water had subsided. I let go of Una and pushed her away from where we were, we needed to get back to the shore. She swam ahead of me while I pulled Kendra behind me. Una took my hand and I kicked my legs as hard and as fast as I could. We didn't stop until we were close enough to land for me to put my feet down on the seabed. I let go of Una and we stood in the water up to my waist. I held Kendra in my arms and pulled her face toward me. Her eyes stared blankly ahead, her mouth slack.

No, no no. This can't be it, she can't be dead. I turned her head to the side and saw the left hand side of her head was completely caved in. I turned her head back toward me quickly, trying to keep Una from seeing the wound, but it was too late. Her face was already scrunched up in pain. I felt my face heat up as tears welled in my eyes. I stroked Kendra's face. Her face was clean, the blood having been completely washed away in the water. How could I have let this happen? I pulled Kendra into my chest, wrapping my arms around her head. I gulped in the fresh air, trying to hold back the tears. I didn't want Una to see me crying. I had to stay strong for her.

I looked around, we had to get out of the open like this. I could see the jetty and the boat that had hit Kendra, a huge ferry carrying cars and foot passengers had now lowered its ramp and cars were driving off one by one. I pulled Kendra's body ashore, trying my best not to drag her along the rocks, eventually managing to get up onto a grass verge. We were so exposed here, we had to keep moving, but I couldn't keep dragging Kendra everywhere. I would have to hide her somehow. I scoured the shoreline behind us. There were some small trees and shrubs a few metres away, where the ground looked uneven.

'This way Una, come on. We have to get out of the water, get out of sight.'

I lifted Kendra's body up under her arms and legs. She felt so light, I easily carried her across the grass toward the trees. Behind the bushes, the grass banked downward and Una and I quickly got ourselves down and out of view of the jetty. I laid Kendra's body down gently, then softly used my fingers to close her eyes. Una knelt down beside us and moved the wet hair from Kendra's face.

'She won't heal will she?' She said.

I shook my head.

'No Una. No one could heal from this.'

We sat together silently for a while. Una reached out and held onto my hand as I squeezed my eyes shut, trying even harder to stop the tears from falling. I heard a sob escape from Una and pulling her in close, I rocked her back and forth whilst she cried into my shoulder.

We had stayed that way for a while. Una's tears flowed and flowed. I knew she wasn't just crying for Kendra. She cried now for the last few years of pain she had experienced. The loss of her mother, the months, if not years of abuse whilst imprisoned in the laboratory, the death of her brother. This tiny little girl had experienced so much trauma in her short life. Something took hold of me as I thought this, a resolve so strong I could almost feel it strengthen my muscles. I would protect Una with every fibre of my being. I had to make sure she was safe, I couldn't let anything happen to her ever again. She had already been through too much. I pulled away from her gently and cupped her tiny face in my hands.

'Una, I need to find a telephone, I have to call for help.' She blinked quickly, then nodded slightly. 'You have to stay here, it's not safe for us both to go. Can you do that for me? Can you wait here until I get back?' She nodded again. 'Okay, good. If anyone comes, just get in the water and swim around to the other side of the island. I will find you okay?'

She nodded again and I pulled her back in tightly, squeezing her with both arms. I felt her little arms around my waist, squeezing back.

'Stay out of sight okay? I'll be back soon.'

I got up and crawled to the top of the bank we were hiding behind. The ferry had now gone and the jetty was empty, no cars and no people. I pulled myself up and over the top of the bank and got to my feet. I ran slowly across the soft grass, looking from left to right for any sign of other people. As I neared the jetty, I could see buildings in the distance behind it. My feet hit the concrete of the road leading to the end of the jetty and I let my feet move faster and faster as I headed toward the small wooden structure at the end of it. A clock on the side of it told me it was now after five. I checked the printed timetable that had been mounted on the side underneath the clock, that ferry had been the last arrival.

There were no more ferries tonight, hopefully that meant there would be no more people around.

I peered in the window and tried the door handle. It was locked. I would have to try the buildings further inland. I ran back across the jetty, reaching the main road within a few minutes. There was still no one around, the small convenience type store looked like it was closed, with no lights shining from beyond the door or windows. As I neared, my stomach flipped with relief as I saw a pay phone at the side of the building. I grabbed the receiver and my hands shook as I dialled the operator number.

'*Hello operator, how can I help?*'

'Can I make a reverse charge call please?'

'*Please type the number you wish to call into the keypad and state your name clearly.*'

I punched Morgan's mobile number in as quickly as I could.

'Vivienne.'

There was a moment of silence before the ringing started.

'Hello?'

Oh thank god, he had picked up this time.

'Will you accept a reverse charge call from Vivienne?'

'Yes, yes I accept, I accept. Put her through right now.'

There was a soft clicking sound as the operator transferred me over and ended her side of the call.

'Morgan?'

'Vivienne, fuck I can't believe it, I can't believe it's really your voice I'm hearing. Where are you? Are you okay?'

'I'm fine, I'm okay for now. We need help, we need someone to come get us.'

'I'm close Vivienne. Moses had the call traced, we were able to see which cell tower Brooke's phone last pinged from, we know you're on an island in Scotland, I'm on my way there now.'

'We escaped from the island. We're on a different one now. It's called egg or something. I don't know how it's pronounced, but it's E. I. G. G, we are hiding near the jetty where a ferry comes in and out of.'

I could hear paper rustling in the background.

'Flatten it out Martin, can you see Eigg? E. I. G. G?'

'Martin? Who are you with Morgan? Where are you?'

'I'm with Martin, Bill Flett's son. We're on his boat, we're close Vivienne.'

I heard a muffled voice in the background.

'We'll be there in an hour, just stay hidden.'

'We will Morgan. But wait, what does Martin know? What have you been telling people while I've been gone? Did you go to the police or just Moses?'

'Martin just knows that you're in trouble Vivienne. Everyone around here thinks you've gone away on conservation work. We haven't involved the police, Moses and his people were investigating your disappearance. When I got your message though, I didn't want to wait, Martin had a boat ready, I couldn't wait for Moses.'

'Morgan, one of the girls I escaped with, she died, she was hit by a boat. I can't just leave her here, we have to take her back with us.'

'Shit.' Morgan was quiet for a moment. 'Okay, don't worry Vivienne. We can trust Martin. He won't say anything to anyone about any of this, don't worry.'

'Okay.' I took a deep breath.

'How many others are there?' He said.

'It was just the three of us that escaped, me and the two girls.'

'Okay good. Be ready.'

'I'll see you in an hour.' I said.

'I'll be there Vivienne. I love you.'

'I love you too Morgan.'

I put down the receiver and looked around me, making sure the coast was clear before heading back to where I had left Una. It didn't take long to reach our hiding place and I found Una, still crouched next to Kendra's body when I got back to her. She visibly relaxed when she saw me.

'He's coming, he was already on his way for us. He won't be long.'

She stood up, but kept her eyes on the body at her feet.

'What about Kendra?'

'We will take her. We can't risk anyone else finding her.'

Una stepped forward and put her tiny hand in one of mine.

'Where will he take us Vivienne' she said, staring up at me.

'Home Una. He'll take us all home.'

After what must have been well over an hour later, the rain had stopped and the clouds above had begun to disappear. I searched the horizon again and after seeing nothing, turned and slumped back onto the grassy bank. Where was he? He said he'd be an hour, it felt like it had been much longer than that.

'Vivienne,' Una's tiny hand was shaking my shoulder. 'Vivienne look.' She was up on her knees pointing to the other side of the jetty. 'There's a boat coming from over there.'

I got back up onto my knees and craned my neck to see around the bushes to the right of us. She was right, a boat was coming from the right hand side of the island, the same way we would have come with the dolphins. I recognised the boat once it got closer, big enough for a large crew, with red and white painted sides. It was the boat Bill Flett's son Martin still took Bill out on when he could. I'd often seen them set off from the harbour back in Zennor. I looked around, there was still no one to be seen on the jetty.

'Quick Una, go now.'

I pushed her up over the top of the bank, then slid myself back down to get Kendra. I picked up her body again and moved as fast as I could toward the jetty. When I got out of the bushes, Una was already running along the jetty toward the boat as it came in. I caught up with her where she stood on the end of the jetty, just as the boat pulled up along side, Morgan stood tall on the bow. As soon as it was close enough he jumped off and without hesitation, he grabbed Una and practically threw her on the onto the deck of the boat.

'Quick Vivienne.'

He helped me onto the boat with Kendra's body still in my arms. As soon as both my feet were on deck, he took her from me, carrying her below deck without a word. I looked up to see Martin looking down from the helm of the boat.   He smiled at me, then began to quickly manoeuvre the boat away from the jetty. I stood still and watched as we got further and further away from the shore, the island getting smaller and smaller in the distance. I was finally going home.

20.

Una

It had been so long since I had slept in a soft bed, I had almost forgotten how good it felt. For the first time in so long I had woken up with my head on a soft pillow and a blanket covering me. Vivienne and I had slept in bunks below deck, reminding me of the bunk beds I used to share with Jordan. Last night, Morgan had made us hot soup and we had eaten our fill of bread, dunking it in the soup and mopping the bowls with it after. I couldn't remember the last time I had eaten soup. Mama used to make the most delicious soup. I slipped out of the bed and stood on my tiptoes to check the bunk above me. Vivienne was sleeping still. Her eyes still looked red.

She had cried for hours last night. I had heard Morgan trying to ask her why, begging her to tell him what had happened, but she said she couldn't yet. She just needed to cry about it for a while and then she could deal with it, deal with telling him what had happened. They didn't know I was listening, they had thought I was asleep already. I felt bad for being able to hear, but I didn't want to disturb them. I wondered what would happen to them, if what the doctor had done to her had really worked and she was going to have a baby.

It was windy up on deck and my hair blew around my face and neck. I climbed the steps to where the owner of the boat was controlling the steering wheel, Martin I think Vivienne had said his name was. He was a human and she wasn't sure what he knew about us, about Asrai, so it was best not to say anything about what had happened at the laboratory in front of him. He turned around as the last step of the stairs creaked to life underneath me.

'Oh, hey there. Una is it? Come on up, come have a look around.'

I shuffled further into the room, then stood on my tip toes to peer over the control panel and out of the window. The sea ahead looked rougher than it felt on the boat.

'You want to have a go at steering for a while?'

He stood to one side and took one hand off the wheel. Looking up at him and then back at the wheel, I stepped in front of it. Once both my hands were holding on tightly, he let go completely. I could feel a strong tug on the wheel once he had let go, but it was easy enough to keep under control.

'Wow, you're really good at that. Someone as tiny as you shouldn't be able to hold it steady like that, not in these conditions.'

I couldn't hide my smile. I was so happy to have impressed him and for the first time in a very long time, I was excited to be doing something that another person thought was good. He looked down at me, his smile just as huge as mine.

'How on earth are you so strong?'

I gave my shoulders a small shrug and looked out toward the horizon.

'It won't be long now. We should get back to Zennor just after lunch. They can get you some clean clothes.'

I looked down at what I was wearing. Morgan had brought clothes for Vivienne, and I was wearing one of her t-shirts over my vest and shorts. I wouldn't have any clothes where we were going. I wondered what they would do about it, what they would do about me even. I looked out ahead of me again as I gripped the steering wheel tighter. I wished Jordan could be here. He would have loved this, an adventure on a boat.

'Would you like to sound the horn?'

He pointed to a large button next to the wheel. Without hesitating, I slammed my hand down on it as hard as I could and held it there as the sound of the horn blared out around us. A tiny scream escaped my mouth as I laughed with excitement. Martin laughed too, his eyes wide.

'Woah there, that was a long one. Let's not wake up the rest of the boat.' He moved closer and took the wheel in his hands once more. 'Why don't you head back down stairs and help yourself to breakfast. You can have anything you want down there.'

I let go of the wheel and nodded as I smiled up at him. He reached out and ruffled the hair on the top of my head.

'See you later sailor' he said.

I turned away and made my way back down below deck, passing Morgan as he stood up on deck, sipping from a mug. In the kitchen below, I found milk and cereal and helped myself to a large bowl full. The fresh milk was so delicious and cold on the crunchy cereal, but then I realised that everything was going to taste amazing after so long in the tank, eating the same boring food every day.

After my third bowl of cereal, I looked up at the clock. It was nearly nine in the morning. Vivienne would probably be awake by now, I should see if she wanted some breakfast. I walked down the hallway toward the room with the bunks in, but the light was on in the shower room as I passed, the door slightly open. I could hear the sound of someone crying on the other side of the door. I put my hand up against it and pushed gently, slowly peering inside.

'Vivienne? Are you okay?'

As the door opened, I could see Vivienne in front of the sink, bent slightly over herself, wiping her legs with a wash cloth. The water in the sink was a dull pink colour and she had streaks of red water running down the inside of her thighs.

'Una' she said in surprise. 'It's okay, I'm fine, I'm fine. It's just my um, it's nothing, I'm fine.'

She looked me in the eye and I watched as her face scrunched in on itself, the corners of her mouth pulling down on each side. She went back to wiping her legs with the wash cloth, more frantically now.

'I'll be out in a minute, I'm fine, honestly.'

As she said the words, her knees bent forward and she sunk to the floor. She sat with her back against the wall and pulled her knees into her chest, burying her face in her arms. I watched as her back shook and she cried loudly into her knees. I pushed the door closed and knelt down beside her. Then I stroked her hair until the sobbing stopped. Eventually she looked up at me, her face red with tears. I tried to gently wipe them away with my hands.

'Is everything okay now Vivienne?'

She sniffed loudly and nodded.

'Yes Una' she said. 'Everything is fine now, everything is going to be okay.' I smiled as she pulled me in close and hugged me tightly. 'We're all going to be just fine.'

She was probably the most beautiful Asrai I had ever seen. Her red hair sparkled in the sunlight that shone through the window. Her eyes looked like they were made from cloudy water and when she smiled, her whole face seemed to glow. When we had arrived at Vivienne and Morgan's home, I had showered in their big, clean bathroom and now Sereia was showing me all the clothes she had bought for me, all hung in wardrobes and folded neatly in the drawers of this huge bedroom.

'Now' she said. 'Morgan told me what size to get you when he called me from the boat, so if any of it isn't a good fit, just let me know and we'll take it back and change it okay?'

She picked up a hairbrush and walked toward me. I was sitting on a little padded stool in front of a small dressing table with a mirror on top. I turned around to face the mirror as she began to softly brush the tangles out of my hair.

'Also, if you don't like any of it for whatever reason, we can still change it. I didn't know what sort of things you would like, so I just got what I thought looked good you know? Next time we get you clothes, you'll be there with us, so you can tell us exactly what you like and what you don't like.'

I smiled as she got the last of the tangles out of my hair.

'Okay,' she said, placing the brush down. 'I'll let you pick out what you want to wear, you can get yourself dressed and maybe I can plait your hair for you? I haven't done a french braid in a while, but I'm sure I'll get the hang of it again soon.'

She headed for the door, but before she left, she turned and smiled, her head tilting to one side.

'I'm so glad you're here with us Una.'

As she left the room, I looked back at my reflection in the mirror. I was glad to be here with them too.

Sereia had made us all curried chicken, chips and rice for dinner. I don't think I'd ever eaten that much food in one go in my life. It all tasted so good, especially as they had let me have fizzy drink with it, just as a treat they had said. I had really liked all the clothes that Sereia had picked out for me. Morgan had guessed my size pretty well, so everything fit me perfectly, even the shoes. After dinner, Vivienne had sat with me in the living room whilst Sereia and Morgan tidied things away in the kitchen. Vivienne searched the menu on the television and selected a film for us to watch and sat back with her arm around me.

'Are we safe here Vivienne?'

Vivienne seemed to take a deep breath and sighed a little.

'We'll be safe as long as we stick together Una.'

'Will they come here looking for us? They took you from here, so they know where to find you again don't they?'

Vivienne nodded.

'They do Una, that's true. But we all know about them now, so hopefully they won't try anything like that again.'

I looked up at her.

'But what if they do, what if they get us another way?'

Vivienne pulled me in closer.

'Then we fight back Una, we are strong, we won't let them beat us.'

A bad feeling rolled through my tummy.

'But I'm not strong, not like you. I'm small, I can't hurt them.'

'You can't?' She said. 'I know that that isn't true Una. I know that you are strong, you are so much stronger than you think. I've seen it in you. You got us out of that place Una, you did that.'

'I'm still so scared. I don't ever want to go back there.'

'And you won't Una, I promise you.'

'But I can't stop someone from hurting me. We couldn't stop the men that took us from our home. They were so big and so much stronger than us, we couldn't get away.'

'You don't need to be big to be able to defend yourself. If you ever find yourself in a situation that you can't get out of, remember that you have teeth and you have nails. If you bite or pinch someone hard enough, they will let you go and then you run and you swim. You run and swim faster than you've ever done before.'

The film eventually came to an end and the sky outside had grown darker. Vivienne was scrolling through the television menu again when there was a knock on the door.

'I'll get it' I heard Sereia shout from the hallway.

She opened the door and I could hear a muffled voice from outside, but it soon became clearer as whoever it was stepped inside the house.

'Where have you been? I've been calling you.'

'Oh Adam, I'm so sorry, I completely forgot you were coming down from London today. I'm sorry babe, now's not really a good time. Vivienne literally just got back from her um… work trip.'

'Vivienne's back?'

Before Sereia could answer again, Vivienne shot up and ran out the door. I stood up and watched through the doorway as she lunged at whoever it was that Sereia was speaking to. All of a sudden, she had him pinned to the wall, her hand around his neck, her face in front of him, shielding him from my view. But I knew his voice. This man was no stranger to me. Vivienne's voice came out in a loud shout.

'Did you know? Did you know what they were going to do to me?' She banged his head against the wall and he cried out in pain. 'Tell me now. Did you know what they would do to me? Did you know what they were doing to the children?'

Morgan was now in the hall, staring at Vivienne in disbelief along with Sereia.

'Viv, Vivienne please, I swear, I didn't know. All I knew is that they needed me to confirm who you were, that's it. I had no idea they would take you.'

'You were involved in this?' Sereia raised her hands to the side of her face. 'What the fuck Adam?'

Vivienne loosened her grip on him and he relaxed against the wall.

'You're lying.' I didn't realise I had said it out loud until Vivienne, Sereia and Morgan all turned to look at me. 'You knew where they would take her. That's where you took me and my brother.'

He craned his neck to peer past Vivienne and I could see a look of recognition pass across his face as he remembered who I was. There wasn't a day that had gone by that I hadn't pictured his face, his cold eyes looking at me and Jordan as we stepped outside our house. I would never forget his face, his eyes, his scar. Vivienne looked between him and me, her anger rising again.

'You took her too? How many? How many children did you deliver to that place? Do you know that every single one of them, except for her, is dead? They are fucking dead Adam, did you know that?' Vivienne turned toward me. 'Is he the one? Did he take you from your home? Did he kill your mother?'

I watched his eyes widen as I nodded. Before anyone could react, he bolted for the door. Morgan ran quickly after him and we watched from the hallway as he quickly caught up to Adam and tackled him to the floor, pushing his face hard into the gravel. Adam continued to struggle for a moment, before finally giving up. Morgan pulled each of Adam's arms behind his back and held them together, his knees resting on his back. Sereia now ran out of the house behind them, followed by Vivienne. I stood in the doorway of the house, not knowing what to do next.

'You did this?' Sereia was almost screaming the words as she stood over Adam. 'You're not a human? You're Asrai? You were lying to me this whole time? Our whole relationship has been fake, a fucking lie? I trusted you Adam. You tricked me. You tricked me into loving you.'

Her voice broke as she said the last few words. I watched as tears fell from her eyes. The sound of a mobile phone ringing cut through the silence her words had left. Adam began to jerk and struggle again. I watched as Vivienne stepped in front of Sereia, crouching down next to Morgan and Adam. She reached under Morgan's leg where it was on Adam's back and pulled a mobile phone from Adam's back pocket.

'It's a withheld number' she said.

She tapped at the screen. Before she had a chance to say anything, a male voice echoed from the phone.

'Adam, we have a problem. The laboratory has been compromised and the assets have escaped. I need you to return to Zennor and let me know if and when she returns. Don't engage until you receive further instructions. Do you understand?'

'I understand perfectly well' she said.

Vivienne tapped the screen again, ending the call. She turned to face Sereia, her face expressionless.

'Call Moses' was all she said, before handing Sereia Adam's phone and taking me by the hand, pulling me back into the house.

21.

Vivienne

As I stood atop the cliff above The Cove, I wondered if I would ever be able to get in that water by myself again. All I could think about was that we would always be in danger here in one way or another. Did my parents have the right idea disappearing away to another country, far away from the water? Moses stood silently beside me. He had arrived just before midnight last night and Adam had been taken away.

I had spent the next few hours telling Morgan, Sereia and Moses exactly what had happened to me and what I had seen and heard at the laboratory. Morgan had contacted Moses after I had called him from Brooke's phone, so they were already searching the Scottish Isles for the laboratory we had been held in before Morgan had picked us up. Once we were on the boat, I had managed to tell Morgan that the location on the on screen map in the car had said we were in Balivanich and that we were at an airport of some kind. He had relayed this to Moses and so they had known exactly where to look.

'It was abandoned by the time we got there, as we knew it probably would be' Moses said.

'So she's still out there somewhere then?'

Moses nodded.

'We will find her Vivienne.'

'And in the meantime?'

'I will make sure you and your family are kept safe Vivienne.'

'How worried do I need to be about this Lyle person? She said once that it was down to him whether I ever got to leave or not. I'm assuming that that's who called Adam to let him know I'd escaped.'

'Yes, Lyle Calder. He's been on our radar for a long time. He's half human, which has fuelled his desire to cure infertility in others like him. He's also a promoter, but for different reasons. He thinks that if we are out in the open, it will be easier to find each other, make connections, find a mate of our own kind as it were.   Meaning there would be fewer Asrai/human pairings and fewer infertile offspring being born every year.'

'Would you have chosen not to marry your wife if you had known more Asrai women?'

He turned to face me, his eyebrows furrowed.

'You and I both know that fanatics stop being able to think in any rational way Vivienne. What we really need to be worrying about is what his plan B is, now that his tests for curing infertility have failed.'

'Have you searched the laboratory?   Seized his research?'

He turned back toward the water, staring intently at the horizon once more.

'When we got there, it was all gone, the place was empty. It was a small set up they had there and an efficient one at that. A tiny airport, lots of private light aircraft coming and going, they could easily get people and equipment in and out. It didn't take them long to empty the laboratory, nearly all the equipment was gone, all the computers taken, no paper files left. Everything gone, except for one thing.'

'And what was that?'

'Your file.'

'Why would they have left that behind?'

'I think they wanted me to see it.'

'Why? What does it say? Do they think I'm cured? Because I already told you, I'm not pregnant, it didn't work on me.'

'I know' he nodded again. 'But there was something else very interesting in your file. Your DNA, it's not the same as other Asrai, human hybrids. You're not half human.'

I was confused. For nearly the past two years I had been told I was half human, an un-pure Asrai. Now he was going to tell me I was a pure Asrai? This couldn't be happening.

'So I'm not half human? I'm just like the rest of you? Only not as stoically good looking and tall?'

'No,' Moses smiled to himself. 'You have near human DNA in you, you're not a pure Asrai, but there is something else in you too. Something I don't think we've seen before.'

'And this was all they left out of all their research? How can you be sure it's genuine.'

'I can't Vivienne. So I was hoping, that before I return to London, you would let me take some samples from you?'

His words sent a shiver through my whole body. He had asked me once before and I had declined, not wanting to know what the answers would be, not wanting to be a human guinea pig, but if what he was saying was true... could I really be something else? I nodded slowly.

'Fine. Take whatever you want.'

Moses looked at me, his eyebrows raised in surprise.

'Thank you Vivienne. After what you've been through I would have completely understood if you had told me where to go, so I appreciate your cooperation.'

'It's not going to help you though. I'm still infertile, nothing they did to me worked, they couldn't get me pregnant.'

'That's not the reason I want to study you.'

'It isn't? Then why?'

'VIVIENNE!' We both turned to see Una running toward us. 'Vivienne, breakfast is ready.'

I waved an acknowledgement and she turned and ran back toward the house and Moses and I began walking back.

'What's going to happen to her?' I said, deeply regretting it as soon as I did. I didn't want to know what they would do with her, now that her family had been taken from her. 'Where will she have to go?'

'Well that's up to her really. I spoke with her this morning and she seems very keen to stay here, with you.'

'She does?'

Moses nodded and I felt butterflies in the pit of my stomach.

'She does. In fact I think I would have a hard time trying to convince her to go anywhere else. So, are you happy for her to stay here, with you and Morgan?'

'Yes, of course.'

I realised then that from the moment I had met Una, I knew that this is what I was meant to do and I would love and protect her as any mother loves and protects their child. It was never going to be my choice, because Una had chosen us.

22.

Una

I was eight years old. If anyone asked me, that's what I had to say. I'd never been to school before. Mama had taught me and Jordan to read and write and she read to us from books to teach us about history and all the people and places in the world. But mostly she would tell us stories about The Colonies, stories about the ancient Asrai.

I was not to talk about any of that today, or any other day at school. I was still so excited to go though. Vivienne had told me that I would make lots of friends and learn lots and lots of new things. I couldn't wait to meet my new teacher, Miss Ball. Vivienne had taken me into the nearby town to get my very own school uniform. I had to wear a pinafore over a white t-shirt with a collar and a red cardigan. I held on tightly to Vivienne's hand as we walked together along a stone path toward a small building.

'There's only about thirty other students here. You'll know every body's name in no time. You're eight years old remember, so you're in the junior class, but you may have to do some lessons with the infant class until you're all caught up. Have you memorised your birthday, the year you were born?'

I nodded as Vivienne crouched down in front of me, her hands on each of my shoulders.

'Are you ready for this?'

I nodded, smiling at the concern in her face.

'Are you sure? It's only been a month since... well since the laboratory. You don't have to do this if you don't want to.'

'I want to Vivienne' she said, 'I really want to.'

'Okay' she said, giving my shoulders a squeeze. 'If you're sure you're ready, then I guess you're ready.'

'I'm ready Vivienne, but are you ready?'

I couldn't help saying it with a laugh. She definitely seemed more nervous than I did. She smiled and leaned in to me, kissing me on my forehead.

'Everyone is going to love you so much Una.'

She gently brushed some hair away from my face with the tip of her fingers. She stood up and took my hand again, leading me to the door.

The day passed almost too quickly and I couldn't wait to tell Vivienne and Morgan all about it. As we drove home, I told her all the names of all the teachers and children that I could remember. She asked about what I'd learned and what I'd had for lunch and I told her every single detail. I couldn't wait to go back tomorrow and do it all over again.

'I just have to nip in to see Sereia on the way home Una' Vivienne said. 'I haven't seen her for a few days so we'll see if she wants to come over for dinner.'

I wanted to get home as quickly as possible so that we could go to The Cove with Morgan.

'Can't you just call her and invite her?'

'I've tried calling, she's not answering. She must have misplaced her phone or something. We'll just pop in quickly, I promise it won't take long.'

It wasn't long before we pulled into the driveway of the cottage Sereia lived in. It had been where Morgan had lived before he and Vivienne were married. I had been here before with Vivienne and I jumped out of the car as soon as it stopped and ran across the driveway to the front door. I pulled at the knocker on the door continuously before Vivienne caught up to me, laughing.

'I'm sure she heard it the first time Una.'

She pulled down on the handle and pushed the door inwards.

'Sereia' she called out. 'It's me, Vivienne.'

She stepped through the door and I followed close behind. The house was dark inside, all the curtains were closed.

'Hmmm' said Vivienne. 'Maybe she had a late night and isn't up yet.'

She made her way around the open kitchen and living room area and started yanking curtains open. I walked right through and pushed open the door to the hallway. It was dark here too and I fumbled on the wall for the light switch. I flicked it on and the hallway lit up, so I could now see Sereia's bedroom door, which was half way open. I looked in through the gap and could see Sereia where she lay in bed, her back to the door. The light from the hallway lit up her room just enough for me to be able to see that there were two empty wine bottles on her bedside cabinet, along with an empty glass. I heard a sniffle from her bed and watched as her shoulders shook slightly. She was crying. I turned to see Vivienne behind me, looking into the bedroom too.

'Oh, um Una sweetie, could you just uh… just go wait in the living room for a moment.'

I stepped back from the doorway and Vivienne pushed open the door and stepped through, closing it behind her slightly, but not quite closing it completely. I stayed where I was for a moment. I knew I shouldn't listen in on what was happening, but I felt so bad for Sereia, I just wanted to know what was wrong with her.

'Sereia?'

Vivienne's voice was soft as she said it. I peered through the small gap that remained in the door and watched as Vivienne sat down on the edge of the bed next to Sereia, her hand on her shoulder.

'Sereia, are you okay?'

I could see Sereia move her head from side to side and heard her sniff tears away.

'Sereia, tell me what you're feeling, please.'

Sereia sniffed again as she raised an arm, it looked like she was wiping her eyes.

'I just can't… I just can't stop thinking about him, about what he did. What he did to you, it's my fault.'

'No Sereia, no… it's not your fault. He was here to find me, he never needed you for that.'

'He used me to get closer to you though. None of it was real. I thought it was real, I really did and I loved him more than I ever thought it was possible to love someone.'

They were quiet for a moment.

'And I hate that I feel this way Vivienne. I am heartbroken over a… over a murderer. He has killed people. He helped deliver hundreds of children to that place and they all died and I'm here crying because all I can think about is how much I loved him and how that it's all gone. So many people have been hurt and I'm sat here feeling sorry for myself, crying because my relationship with him is over.'

I watched as Vivienne stroked a hand across Sereia's head, smoothing her hair away from her forehead. Vivienne nodded slowly.

'It's okay for you to feel that way Sereia. You didn't know who he really was. The Adam you fell in love with isn't the same person who did all those things. You didn't fall in love with the Adam who worked for Brooke. The Adam you fell in love with was never real. So you cry and you grieve for him all you need to Sereia. You grieve and you heal.'

'I just want to go… I want to go home now. But I'll never be able to do that, Olivia is never coming back.'

Olivia was Sereia's keeper. Vivienne had told me all about how Sereia's older brother Mathew had left last year with Olivia and returned to The Last Colony. Sereia had no way to get back unless Olivia returned for her.

'I should have gone with them. I was going to go with them, but I didn't, because I met him. I had a reason to stay here. I had him. I wanted to be here *with him*. That was all a lie and now I don't have him and I don't have a way to get home anymore.'

'I'll get you home one day Sereia' Vivienne said. 'I promise.'

23.

Vivienne

Una had settled into school so well over these past few months. Moses Cain had delivered us some very official looking adoption papers and the school had fully accepted my story of her being a distant relative whose mother had recently died. She was fitting in well with the other children and was almost sad at the thought of the end of term next week and the six weeks she would have to have off school for the summer. I hadn't lied about her coming from a remote place in Greenland and having little schooling, so the school were prepared to have to teach her the basics, but she was really excelling herself and had picked everything up so quickly. She was already reading at the same level as other children in her year group and she had picked up maths incredibly quickly, already matching the skill level of children older than her perceived years.

The school had fortnightly swimming lessons at the nearest swimming pool and we had had to remind her not to swim underwater for too long around her teachers and class mates. Every afternoon after school, Morgan and I would take Una down to The Cove and swim together. Sereia would often join us and the four of us would explore the coast around our home. I hadn't yet swum alone. I wanted to, I missed swimming as fast as I could for miles at a time, especially as the effects of the drugs I had been pumped with had seemed to have worn off completely now and I was back to my old self, feeling strong and full of energy.

I had walked down to The Cove early in the morning a few times, but I just couldn't get in the water by myself, my chest felt like it was caving in on itself, like I couldn't breathe. Morgan was more than happy for me not to swim alone. Although Adam was in custody, neither Brooke nor Lyle Calder had been found yet. Morgan was always ready to accompany me on long swims, whilst Sereia watched over Una. Moses assured me I was safe, he had people looking for them and he had no doubt that they would be apprehended eventually. I hoped he was right.

'Moses, hello. Is everything okay?' I was surprised to see him stood at the door. 'Come in, come in. Have you found Brooke? Lyle?'

I directed him through to the living room. I had just got home from the aquarium for lunch before picking Una up from school.

'I'm afraid not Vivienne, but I can assure you that I am doing my utmost to apprehend them.'

I nodded, the excitement I had felt at the thought of hearing good news swiftly left me.

'Please take a seat, can I get you a drink? Tea, coffee?'

He sat down on the sofa.

'No, I'm fine thank you.'

I took a seat in the armchair opposite him, searching his face for a clue as to why he was here if he was no closer to capturing Brooke or Lyle Calder.

'You must be wondering why I'm here.' He let out a long sigh, considering his next words. 'Vivienne, many years ago, not long after you were born, someone came to your parents claiming to know things about you.'

My eyes narrowed questioningly.

'What do you mean claiming to know things about me? What did they say?'

'This person, Kelvin Hudson, he wasn't of sound mind, or at least we didn't think he was at the time. He made claims about your biological father, about what he was and what you are. You were very important to him. He said you needed to be saved, he needed to keep you safe until you were needed. We couldn't get a full, coherent sentence out of him to be honest. He couldn't tell us exactly why you were needed, why you were so important to him. We dismissed what he was saying at the time, we thought it was just the ramblings of a lunatic. We intervened when he returned and tried to take you from your parents. He's been in Hadian ever since.'

'My parents never told me that. But as you know, there's a lot that they never told me.'

I shuffled awkwardly in my seat. My parents moving to another country was making more and more sense.

'So what does this have to do with why you're here now Moses?'

'After we arrested him, his house was searched. There were signs of a struggle and we found a body there. We assumed that Kelvin had killed that person, but when we showed him a photo of the body and asked who the person was, Kelvin was genuinely distraught. He screamed about that person being his guardian angel. He said that that person was the key to everyones future. Without him and the help of his kind, we would all be doomed. Kelvin hasn't said a word since. He's been silent for more than twenty years because of it.'

'So he didn't kill that person? Why does that have anything to do with me now? Or what he thinks I am and why he tried to take me in the first place?'

'I'm not quite sure Vivienne, but what I can tell you is this. That deceased person had neither human, nor Asrai DNA. We couldn't look into it further at the time, DNA technology was very juvenile back in the early eighties, it wasn't like it is today. We thought it was just an anomaly.' I shook my head slightly, waiting for what I knew was about to come. 'Whatever that was Vivienne, we think we've found it in you too.'

I shook my head again, harder this time.

'No, that can't be true, this can't be a thing. You're telling me there's another secret race of people that I didn't know about and that once again, I'm one of them.' I stood up and paced the room. 'Moses this is ridiculous. Are you telling me I'm some sort of alien? You can't possibly tell me that you believe this can you?'

Moses stood up and put his hands on my shoulders, his eyes stared me down.

'Vivienne, all I know for certain is that from the moment you were conceived, todays events were put in motion. You are different in more ways than one.'

He took his hands from my shoulders and crossed the room to the fire place, resting his hand on the mantle. His eyes took in the mirror and its ornate frame, the way he did every time he was in this room.

'Your DNA is the reason you can get pregnant. When we see human and Asrai offspring, they are technically a hybrid and they are infertile because of a mismatched number of chromosomes. The reason you can get pregnant is that your other half actually matches up equally to the Asrai half. Brooke and Lyle know this now.'

'So then why didn't it work? Everything they did to me? Why aren't I pregnant? Fuck, I could have been pregnant, I could have been pregnant with his baby.' I slumped down on the sofa, my hands on my face. 'What would have happened if I had been? What would I have done?'

Moses sat down next to me.

'You don't need to worry about that anymore. Their plan failed, they didn't get you pregnant. You're okay, Morgan is okay and most importantly, Una is okay.'

I nodded my head.

'I know it's just... *fuck*. This is a lot to take in you know? One minute I'm half human, the next I'm not. One minute I'm infertile and now you're telling me that I'm not. Lyle Calder and Brooke are still both out there. It's just... it's just a lot okay?'

Moses nodded this time.

'I do truly think that you are safe from them for now, but now we know that you are different and what Kelvin said about your biological father appears to be true, should we worry about the other things he claimed about you?'

'What? That I need saving? I think that past events have proven that I'm more than capable of saving myself, even if I do come across as a bit of a wimp most of the time.'

'No Vivienne, I'm not saying that.' He turned to face me again. 'What he said about you being important, you needed to be saved for a reason. A reason we don't yet know about.'

'I need to know what he thinks I'm needed for. I want to speak to him Moses.'

'Vivienne' he said, shaking his head. 'That's not possible, not even I can just take someone out of Hadian.'

'Then take me to him. I want to see him Moses. I have to find out what I am.'

We both froze at the sound of the front door, our heads whipping toward it in unison. Sereia stepped into the living room.

'Oh Moses, hi, hello. Sorry, I didn't realise you were visiting.'

She looked between us as she tucked her long red hair behind an ear and straightened the dress she was wearing.

'I thought I'd pop in for a cup of tea before we went to pick up Una.'

I nodded quickly.

'Yeah no problem Sereia. Can you stick the kettle on?'

'Yeah course.' She looked at Moses again. 'Would you like one Moses?'

The corners of his mouth raised slightly.

'If Vivienne doesn't mind, I'd love one thank you.'

Sereia beamed a wide smile before turning and leaving the room. I raised my hands to my hips.

'I thought you didn't want one?' I said, cocking my head to one side.

His smile was suddenly bigger.

'You're asking me to take you to Hadian Vivienne. I'm going to have to sit down and think about it for a moment.'

24

Morgan had been resistant, but once he knew I was going to go whether he liked it or not, he decided he would come with me. I had wanted him to stay, it would be better for Una if he stayed home with her, spent the summer holidays at the beach, the aquarium, anything for a bit of normality for her, but he insisted that Sereia stay in the cottage with Una instead. Una and Sereia were already firm friends, so I knew Una would be more than happy to spend a week or two with her new Aunt whilst Morgan and I "worked" away, but I still felt guilty. After everything she had been through, she finally had stability, she had routine and now I was disrupting that again.

'Vivienne' Una said as she curled her small arms around my neck, jumping onto my back whilst I sat on the sofa. 'Why do you look so sad? It's not for long.'

She squeezed me into a hug.

'I know darling, but I will miss you and it's your first summer here. I had lots of fun day trips planned for us.'

She swung herself around until she was hanging from the front of my neck, her bum on my lap.

'Then don't go, stay here with me and Sereia.'

She smiled sweetly, I knew she didn't really mean it, she was more than happy to have a fun few weeks with Sereia, she was trying to make me feel better, which now made me feel even worse. What had I done to deserve this kind and caring little girl in my life?

'I have to go sweetie. It's really important.'

I stroked some hair away from her face as her smile beamed at me. She pushed her face toward me and touched her nose to mine.

'You'll be back before you know it' she said. 'We can do all the day trips we want as soon as you get home.'

I heard the click of the front door opening.

'Did somebody call for an awesome babysitter?' Sereia shouted from the hallway.

Her bright red hair rolled down her shoulder as she leaned her head around the living room door.

'Where's the concierge? I have lots of bags.'

Her face wore a huge smile, she was as excited as Una, who sprung from my lap.

'I'll help you Auntie Sereia, I can show you to your room, it's right next to mine.'

She grabbed hold of Sereia's wheeled suitcase and disappeared down the hallway. Sereia looked at me and her smile softened.

'Are you okay?'

I nodded.

'I will be once I get answers.'

The journey would take a few days including some stop overs, that was as much as I knew. Morgan and I were to meet Moses at Gatwick Airport tomorrow before seven in the morning. We had packed relatively light and had our passports ready. We decided to drive to St Ives Train station for a train to Gatwick Airport. The direct train to our first change over at Reading Town was uneventful and the journey onward to Gatwick from there was easy enough. We checked into a hotel near the airport and made our way out for dinner. Morgan squeezed my hand as we walked.

'We can still back out of this you know. He may not even talk to you, he hasn't spoken for over twenty years, you said so yourself.'

'I have to try Morgan, you know I do. I've spent so much of my life not knowing.'

'I get that, I really do, but…'

'You don't though Morgan' I interrupted. 'You've always known exactly who you are, exactly where you came from. You don't know how I feel, not really.'

He stopped me where I was in the street, pulling my face into his hands.

'But I'm here, I'm here for you now, you have me.' His voice was firm, not quite angry, but a level of frustration was clear. 'You know who you are. You are Vivienne, you're a wife… you're a… you're a mother now… you…' He looked away from me. I searched his face, waiting for his next words. 'This could be dangerous.'

I put my hand on his cheek and pulled his face back toward me.

'Hadian is the most secure place in the world, we are with Moses, it's all perfectly safe.'

'Not just that Vivienne, I'm talking about what you are going there to find out. Once you've heard it, it can't be unheard. There could be nothing to what this man has said, but what if there's not, what if this is all true? Are you part of something bigger than us, bigger than you and me… and Una?'

'I don't know Morgan, but I have to know, I need find out what he thinks he knows about me.'

I put my arms around his waist and buried my face into his chest. I felt his hands move to my hair, his cheek against the top of my head. He took a deep breath in.

'If we do this Vivienne, there's no going back.'

I squeezed my arms tighter around him.

'I know Morgan.'

He pulled my face away from his body and put his hands against my cheeks again, his forehead touched mine and he held his eyes tightly closed.

'I just don't want this to change things for us, you're perfect to me and what we have is perfect. It doesn't matter what you are.'

His eyes opened and his mouth edged closer to mine. I suddenly became aware of every sound around us, the planes sounded louder, the traffic sounded closer. He brushed his lips against the skin around my mouth until our lips finally touched. He kissed me softly and I could tell he was hurting, he really didn't want me to do this. After what had happened with Abraham, could I blame him? Those events all happened because I wanted to go and find out what had happened to my parents, but had it really done me any good? Had it changed anything, did I feel any less grief for them because of it?

I couldn't admit to myself or anyone that it did, but it had changed my life in different ways. If we hadn't have been through all that with Abraham, Brooke and Lyle wouldn't have found out that I had once been pregnant and I wouldn't have been taken by them. Although what I went through in that lab was horrendous, I wouldn't have Una in our life right now if none of that had happened. So really, it had all been worth it, every single minute from the moment I had moved back to Zennor.

25.

The terminal building hummed with the sound of people. Hundreds and hundreds of people, despite the early hour. I looked at my watch, it was seventeen minutes past six in the morning. Moses had told us to meet him here at quarter past. Morgan and I held onto our cases, trying to keep out of the way of everyone, while I anxiously looked around for Moses.

'Are you sure this is the right place?' Morgan said.

I rummaged in my bag for my phone, finally finding it and checking the email.

'Yes, he definitely said the South Terminal entrance.'

'Mr and Mrs Whidden?'

A voice behind us made me jump. I turned to find a large, suited figure stood there. I recognised him, he looked young, but tall and strong. He didn't wait for us to answer.

'Follow me please' he said with a smile, before turning and walking back out of the building.

We hurriedly followed him, dragging our cases with us. He strode through the crowd, people parting around him to let him through. Women didn't hide their stares as he passed them. I realised then where I had seen him before, he was the one who opened the door to us once at Moses' London office. So did this mean that Moses never travelled without a personal bodyguard, or was there a chance that this trip could be dangerous?

He led us out to a black car, with blacked out windows. He took our cases from us one at a time and put them in the boot, before opening the front passenger door and motioning for Morgan to get inside. He then repeated the process for me with the back passenger door. Moses was already sat inside, dressed in a casual style shirt and jeans, he looked relaxed as he sat, legs crossed in the spacious backseat.

'Good morning Vivienne. I trust you slept well in the hotel?'

'Yes it was lovely' I nodded. 'Thank you again for making all the arrangements, you really didn't have to.'

'It is my pleasure.'

I looked out the window as the car pulled away.

'Where are we going? Is this not the terminal we fly from?'

'Oh it is, but we will use a private plane today. It makes the journey go much quicker.' He smiled at me. 'I hope you packed for warm weather.'

'Yes, I remember what you said in the email about it being much warmer. So where exactly are we going?'

I noticed Morgan's head in the front seat seemed to straighten, listening in.

'We fly to Mauritius today. From there, we will take a boat to an island three hundred miles to the west of Mauritius. That's where Hadian is located.'

'So you access it from the island?

'Yes, it is well hidden and heavily guarded, but not obviously so. The island is listed as uninhabited, but it is also known to be privately owned, the waters around it are restricted also, so we do not get too many intrusions. There are additional security measures in place to deter both accidental and intentional visitors.'

'What sort of measures?'

'A large population of sharks inhabit the surrounding waters. Anyone swimming to or from the island would not last more than an hour or so I imagine.'

'Sharks? Like as in real, man eating, dangerous sharks?' I looked at him in amazement. 'You can control them?'

Moses smiled widely and let out a soft laugh.

'No Vivienne' he said. 'We cannot control nature, as much as many would like to. It's just a densely shark populated area.'

I felt my cheeks flush with the heat of embarrassment. Why on earth did I actually think Asrai could control sharks, what was wrong with me? I looked up and saw the bodyguards eyes in the rear view mirror, the hint of a smile evident.

'I… I'm sorry, I don't know why I…'

Moses smiled wider and squeezed my hand.

'Don't apologise Vivienne, you of all people will be completely forgiven for assumptions like that. This is all still relatively new to you to a degree.'

'I know' I said. 'But that was quite a stretch even for me. I guess I've watched The Little Mermaid one too many times.'

Moses looked out of his window and nodded.

'Yes, one of my favourites' he said. 'A classic.'

Morgan's voice interrupted us from the front seat.

'I always preferred Splash if I'm honest.'

We laughed then and my embarrassment ebbed away. Moses nodded to himself again.

'Yes… Daryl Hannah if I remember rightly' he said.

I rolled my eyes at them both.

'Yes I'm sure you remember that film very well Morgan. So back to the sharks, why are there so many around the island?'

'Well it is helped in part by Asrai providing the occasional food source from the island, but the area itself is a breeding ground for Great Whites.'

'You feed them from the Island? Can they smell the blood? Is that what keeps them there?'

Moses shook his head.

'Contrary to popular belief, sharks can really only smell blood from about a quarter of a mile away. Sharks do however tend to stay in areas where they know they can eat, so we make a habit of providing food at certain points around the island every now and again. It keeps the waters populated enough so that we don't have to worry about anyone swimming to or indeed, *from* the island.'

'Have you had many? Escape attempts?'

'We've had one or two over the years, yes. None so far have been successful though, which is one thing we are extremely grateful for and we can confidently say that the security measures work.'

The car was slowing down and I finally looked out of the window for long enough to see that we were on a runway, with a small jet fifty or so feet away from us.

'Is that yours?'

I could barely hide the excitement in my voice. As much as I wanted to remain composed, I was about to fly on a private jet... to Mauritius. The bodyguard had already got out and before I knew it, my door had been opened and I was stepping out onto the tarmac. Another man dressed in a black suit was pulling our luggage from the boot of the car, I watched him carry them up the stairs of the plane whilst Moses and Morgan had their doors opened for them and got out of the car. Morgan was beside me now and took my hand in his.

'Are you ready for this?'

I nodded.

'Does it make me a bad person for being really, really excited about this now?'

He squeezed my hand tightly and pulled me toward the plane.

'Not at all' he said with a beaming smile. 'Because I am too.'

His eyes widened as he said the last words and we practically skipped toward the steps of the plane. The wind of the runway whipped my hair around my face and I was grateful that I hadn't worn a skirt as I climbed the stairs. I turned around to see Morgan's eyes fixed on my rear. When he looked up to see why I had stopped, we both burst into laughter. He made a shrugging motion with his hands and arms.

'What?'

I ran up the last few steps, laughing in the wind as I was greeted by a beautiful air stewardess, again dressed all in black.

'Welcome aboard' she said. 'Please come in and make yourselves comfortable.'

The interior of the plane was plush with leather seating. The neutral colours made the bright colourful flowers on each of the tables stand out. We took seats next to each other at one of the tables, Morgan mouthing the word 'wow' to me as he sat down. I nodded slowly. This was the type of thing we only saw in movies or reality shows about ridiculously rich people. I was so excited I actually felt nauseous for a moment. I took some deep breaths as I watched Moses stepping through the doorway, his mobile phone pressed to his ear. He nodded to the stewardess and she disappeared toward the front of the plane behind a curtain. He held in his other hand a large briefcase. He made his way toward us and pulled the phone away from his ear, holding it against his chest instead.

'I have quite a lot of paper work to catch up on, so I'm just going to hide in my office at the back of the plane if that's okay?   Please, ask the attendants for anything you want. There's a variety of drinks and they will tell you what hot and cold food is available when you're ready to eat.'

We nodded and he disappeared with his bodyguard close behind before we had a chance to say anything in return.

'Busy man.   That's not how I would spend my time on a private plane.'

I leaned into Morgan, cuddling my face into his shoulder.

'Well he's got a lot to deal with on a quiet day I imagine.   When he's got stuff like Lyle Calder and Brooke to handle and who knows what else, I imagine the normal stuff soon piles up.'

'Must be nice flying everywhere on this big private plane though.'

'Well he is kind of a big deal.'

I looked up at Morgan.

'What do you mean, *kind* of a big deal? I know he's important, he's one of the Council Leaders, but there's lots more of them isn't there?'

'Yeah, but he's like *the* Council Leader. He's basically the equivalent of the Prime Minister and the rest of them make up his government.'

'Wow, so he really is kind of a big deal.'

'I guess you could say that' he said, almost mockingly.

I angled my chin up toward his face, hoping for a kiss. He turned toward me with a serious, but nonetheless gentle look on his face.

'Are you sure that you're ready for this Viv?'

'I'm ready for anything when I'm with you Morgan.'

I reached my hand up to his cheek and he finally leant down and kissed me.

Despite taking nearly twelve hours, it hardly seemed like it was long enough. Morgan and I had eaten a breakfast on board of Eggs Benedict, followed by a movie on the inflight entertainment system. In the afternoon we were served sushi and champagne before we settled down on one of the large leather sofas to watch another film. I had eventually dropped off, feeling fat and full from all the food and champagne and Morgan had had to wake me so we could take our seats for landing.

Like at Gatwick Airport, we had no requirement to go through the main terminal when we arrived. A large black 4 x 4 was waiting for us on the tarmac and once again, Moses' bodyguard loaded our luggage into the back whilst we took seats in the back. Moses sat up front this time and talked quietly on his phone for the entire journey. Just over an hour later, the car pulled up in front of a beach front villa. The sun had nearly disappeared behind the horizon to our left. I took in our surroundings in awe as luggage was transferred from the car to the villa by a young man who had appeared from the front door. Moses strode past me, walking past an older woman who had stepped from inside the building. He turned back to us, dropping the phone from his ear again.

'Please, come on in. Eileen here will show you to your room. Please, help yourself to anything, freshen up if you need to. Dinner will be served in an hour.'

He turned and continued to the front door, leaving us stood in front of a smiling Eileen.

'Come' she said, 'please follow me.'

We held hands as we stepped past the sign mounted at the front of the villa. Paradise Point had to have been the most beautiful holiday home I had ever seen. Everything about it was modern and clean, yet authentic at the same time. We were shown to a simplistic bedroom, with a large double bed and minimal furniture. Our bathroom overlooked the ocean right outside the window. There was a large outside dining area, directly by the small pool surrounded by plush green grass and there were even two sun loungers on a small, private beach.

'This is ridiculous Morgan.'

I sat on the edge of the bed, looking out at the view before us. I couldn't wait to get into that water.

'Can you believe we are in a place like this. I mean I've been on holiday to nice places but this is just crazy.'

'This isn't a holiday don't forget.'

'I know, I know. But just look at it. It's literally Paradise.'

He took both my hands in his and pulled me up from where I sat on the bed, bringing me into a tight embrace.

'I imagine that's why it's called Paradise Point.'

I smiled to myself. I know he felt this was all a bad idea, but he was still here with me nonetheless. What did he really think could go wrong? I couldn't quite work out what I was more afraid of. Finding out that this man, Kelvin Hudson, and everything he said, was just crazy... or finding out that everything he claimed, was true.

We had eaten dinner with Moses at the outdoor dining table, overlooking the ocean. Soft lighting around the table made it feel even more like the exotic island it was and as a gentle breeze blew my hair around my face, Morgan reached toward me, stroking it behind my ear.

'Dinner was beautiful Moses, thank you so much' I said.

'You are most welcome Vivienne. The hospitality here is always most enjoyable. It is a rare treat for me to get to share it with someone else.'

I remembered then about his wife and his daughter. He was a widower and his daughter had disappeared many years ago in search of The Last Colony.

'Do you visit this island often Moses?' Morgan spoke as he reached for his wine. 'Do you have reason to come here other than Hadian issues?'

Moses shook his head.

'No, I'm only really here when it comes to official Hadian business. I used to come more frequently, with my family but… well you know the story there.'

I nodded in acknowledgement. Morgan shot me a wary look, as if to say I shouldn't press Moses any further, but he kept going by himself.

'I knew she was going to do it before she did you know. I could just tell by the way she spoke about Abraham and his fairytale ending if he ever found The Last Colony. How he would be able to cure us all. She was certain of it. He would cure her and she would have a baby and all would be right with the world in her eyes.'

His eyes had glassed over slightly and I couldn't quite tell if it was because of the wine he had consumed or the sadness of the memory.

'I should have done more to stop her. I should have had her followed, locked her up somehow, I don't know.'

'Moses' I said, 'it wasn't your fault, you couldn't have stopped her. It sounds like she would have found a way if it was what she really wanted to do.'

He nodded slowly and lifted his glass from the table as I continued.

'What would you do if you knew where The Last Colony was, would you go and try to look for her?'

He shook his head this time.

'I know she never made it there. If she had, Abraham would have been close behind her. If she did make it there, something must have happened to her on the way back to get Abraham. She wouldn't have gone through all of that to find it and not come back to let Abraham know now would she? Could she have let her magical cure go? I don't think so, that's not her, that's not my Cora. Once she started something, she saw it through to the end. So no, I wouldn't go there to try to find her. I know that she isn't there.'

'I'm sorry Moses, I didn't mean to…'

'Don't apologise Vivienne, you have done nothing wrong. I tend to dwell on the past a bit too much when I've had a drink. It's my own fault really.' He pursed his lips, pulling them into a small smile. 'So with that in mind, I think it is probably time for me to call it a night. Thank you for joining me for dinner. Feel free to drink or eat as much more as you please, we leave for Hadian at eight tomorrow morning.'

He rose from the table.

'Goodnight Moses'.

Morgan stood and reached out, shaking Moses' hand.

'Goodnight' Moses repeated, nodding toward me. 'Have a good nights' rest.'

'You too Moses' I said.

I watched as he disappeared into the villa. Morgan had sat back down and took my hand, pulling it onto his lap.

'Do you think he'll be okay?' I asked him.

'I don't know Vivienne. I can't imagine what it's like to go through what he's gone through. I mean, I know Una has only been in our lives for a few months, but I can't fathom my life without her now. The thought of anything bad happening to her is just… just thinking about what she's already been through before we met her… or thinking how terrible it is to lose your daughter? You would just never get over it would you? The pain he must feel every day, especially with the loss of his wife too.'

Morgan's face had a pained look across it. I squeezed his hand gently.

'You're not going to lose Una, Morgan, nor me for that matter.'

'Can you promise me that? Because I already have lost you once Vivienne and I don't think I can handle that ever again.'

He leaned in toward me and pushed his forehead gently against mine. I put my hands either side of his face and nodded.

'Yes Morgan, I can promise you that.'

I felt his hands on my thighs as our lips met and he kissed me deeply. Taking deep breaths in and out of my nose I sank deeper into his kiss, tightening my grip on his face with my hands. After a moment, I pushed him gently away and stood up.

'Where are you going?' he said.

I ignored him and stepped away from the table and walked toward the pool. At the edge, I slipped off my sandals and undid the belt tie around the waist of the flowing, summery dress I was wearing. I looked behind me to make sure he was still watching and one by one, pulled the straps of the dress off each of my shoulders. The dress fell from my body into a pile on the floor around my feet and I dived into the pool, wearing nothing but a thong.

26.

Una

'Sereia…' I shook her gently on the shoulder whilst I whispered. 'Sereia, wake up. It's time to go swimming.'

She grumbled from her pillow.

'We'll go later Una, let's just stay in bed a little while longer.'

'Sereia we can't wait any longer. The beach will get too busy, people will notice.'

It was already seven in the morning. If we left it much later we wouldn't be able to swim out very far without people noticing when we got back. The summer holidays meant lots more people on the beach all day. It was great to see my school friends and play on the beach all day, but Vivienne and Morgan had said many times, we couldn't let anyone know that I was different.

'Why can't you just watch television in the morning like normal kids?'

Sereia rolled over and opened one eye to look at me. She wasn't mad I had woken her up, she was smiling, just like she always was when we were together. I watched as her thin, sparkling necklace fell from around her neck.

'I'm about as normal as you are' I said.

I reached for the stone that hung from the end of it, turning it between my fingers. Sereia looked down and the briefest of frowns showed on her face before she smiled again. She pushed herself up until she was sat up, legs crossed.

'Fine, we'll go swimming. But go and put the kettle on. I'll need a coffee for the road.'

It was already sunny on our walk down to The Cove. There would definitely be more people on the beach today. These first few weeks of the summer holidays had gone by really quickly. I had come to The Cove every single morning with either Vivienne and Morgan or Sereia. The first week of the school holidays, it had rained everyday, so the water and the beach had been ours alone for as long as we had wanted it, but from the moment the sunshine came out again, so did the people. It was about half past seven by the time we reached the sand and luckily, the beach was still empty. Sereia drank the last of her coffee and we stuffed our clothes into her rucksack and hid it behind a rock.

'Ready?' she said.

'I'm always ready.'

I started running toward the water before she had a chance to say anything else.

'Una... wait!'

She screamed loudly after me. I looked over my shoulder to see her running after me. I laughed out loud, running faster and faster the closer I got to the water. I felt her hands on my shoulders as our feet touched the water for the first time. She was screaming with laughter as loudly as I was and once we got deep enough we dove under, then we raced as far as we could out to sea. The water was calm and we raced until our bodies ached.

We had turned around and were heading back in the direction we had come, swimming close to the seabed when a large shadow passed above us. Sereia took my hand in hers and we both stopped where we were, looking up. I froze as I saw the outline of a shark. I grabbed hold of Sereia who just looked at me and smiled. She pushed up toward the surface of the water, closer to the shark. I wanted to scream at her, tell her to stop, but she kept on going. We broke the surface a few meters from the huge monster. Sereia was laughing.

'Una don't panic, there is nothing to be scared of, its just a Basking Shark.'

She began to swim toward it leaving me treading water where I was. I watched as she swam along beside the shark and stroked her hand along its side. The shark didn't react to her, it just kept on swimming slowly along. I quickly caught up to them and ran my hand along its slippery skin. It was so much bigger up close. We swam alongside it for a while, until Sereia said it was time to go back to The Cove. We swam back down to the bottom of the seabed and made our way back, with Sereia checking once we were close enough that no one was there.   The beach had been clear, so we swam toward the shore until I could stand up with the water up to my waist.

'That was so much fun Sereia.'

I grabbed her hand and skipped over the small waves, but Sereia had stopped and was looking up at the cliff top. I stopped skipping and looked up too.

'What is it Sereia?'

'Nothing I just... I thought I saw someone watching us.'

'Who was it?'

'I don't know, I think it was a woman, but she's gone now. Probably just one of the people Moses has looking out for us I guess.'

I looked from one side of the cliff top to the other, not being able to see anyone.

'They haven't sent a girl before though have they?'

Sereia shook her head.

'I don't know Una, I've not really been paying attention to them. I'll check with Vivienne when she calls. Come on, lets get back home and get sorted. Shall we come back later with a picnic? Maybe some of your school friends will be here again today.'

27.

Vivienne

I was happy to feel a cold breeze on my face and in my hair as the we sped across the water on a small yacht. It would take us about six hours to get to Hadian Island. I longed to be in the water though, watching it crash around the sides of the boat was almost like torture. I stood at the side of the boat, looking over the railing. I felt Morgan's hands on my waist, then his cheek next to mine as his hands made their way around me. As his arms tightened, a wave of nausea passed over me.

'Oh careful Morgan, I'm feeling a bit queasy.'

He loosened his grip on me and pulled away slightly.

'Queasy? Have a bit too much to drink last night did you? Or are you going to be one of those weird Asrai that actually get seasick?'

I gripped onto the side of the boat as I breathed in deeply, waiting for it to pass.

'I've definitely just been over indulging on all this lovely food and drink since we left home. I'll be fine in a second.'

'I'm going to go below deck and get a drink, would you like one? Water? Tea?'

'A cup of tea would be good if they have it, maybe that'll help settle my stomach.'

Morgan headed off below deck and I stood there for a while, just looking out at the water, watching the waves. The nausea soon subsided.

'I know it looks really inviting, but you definitely don't want to be in there, I can assure you of that Vivienne.' I looked up to find Moses next to me. 'I know we're not close yet, but you will start to see them soon.'

I scanned the horizon. It still amazed me how vast the ocean could be.

'So how many are there? Approximately do you think? Hundreds? Thousands?'

The corners of his mouth turned downward as he thought about it.

'Not quite thousands I imagine, but there really is no way to know for sure.'

I nodded, thinking to myself that hundreds of sharks still sounded like an awful lot of sharks to me. Something in the distance caught my eye, movement of some kind that wasn't waves. It was fins, yes, I could definitely see fins in the water. I pointed in their direction.

'Is that some over there? Would they be together like that?'

Moses turned his gaze toward where I was pointing.

'No, those aren't sharks, those are dolphins.'

'Dolphins? I wouldn't have thought they would be anywhere near sharks.'

'I haven't seen any around here for a long time to be honest. Maybe something has pushed them out of their normal feeding area' he shrugged. 'They'll soon leave this part of the ocean once they know what lives here. Now, promise me you won't go jumping in?'

I smiled at him.

'I promise. How long has it been there? Hadian I mean.'

Moses folded his arms across his chest.

'Hadian has been there for a long, long time. Before it was a prison, it was believed to have been one of The Colony's. Asrai don't tend to like warmer climates like this in the long term, so it's not surprising that it evolved into what it became. Records of inmates go back to the early eighteen hundreds, but who knows how long before that it was used. It's been modernised quite a bit this century though, as you will soon see, but the main structure of the prison is as it has always been.'

I watched the waves as the dolphins continued to jump between them.

'Is it safe there? Inside I mean, amongst the prisoners.'

Moses nodded.

'Security is very tight there Vivienne. You'll see when we arrive. I can promise you, you have absolutely nothing to worry about whilst inside Hadian.'

I looked back out toward the dolphins as Moses disappeared below deck, wishing I could be out there with them. As important as this trip was to me, as much as I needed to find out what Kelvin Hudson believed I was, I longed to be back home, in the sea, just swimming with Morgan and Una. Just me and my family.

As we neared the island later that afternoon, I realised that Moses was not wrong about the sharks. We would see one every few hundred meters or so. They varied in size, but every single one of them was bigger than me. One looked as though it was as long as the boat we were on. I clung onto Morgan, the thought of getting caught in the jaws of one of those things sent shivers down my spine. I don't think even our quick healing biology could help us recover from that. I watched Moses at the front of the boat as he held binoculars up to his face, then signalled behind him to the person at the wheel. The boat began to slow. I looked up at the helm and saw the bodyguard talking into a radio. Moses turned and walked toward us.

'We should reach the island in about an hour or so. We have to take it slower from here.'

'Because of the sharks?' Morgan said.

'No, not them. We have to follow a very specific route to the island from this point onwards.' He passed the binoculars to Morgan. 'Can you see the red buoy out there? From that point on, the boat must approach the island at an angle of between fifteen and thirty degrees or there is a very high possibility that we will be blown up.'

'Blown up? By what?'

'We have mines surrounding the island. It's one of the ways we keep unauthorised Asrai boats away. Security on the island will always make radio contact with any boat that approaches. It will warn them of the danger if they fail to turn back. For non-Asrai boats, the area is a protected breeding ground for the sharks. This means we don't really get anyone stumbling across the island by accident. We get the odd expedition of shark researchers out here, but if they get too close to the island, they get warned that it's a military training ground for submarines and they're soon turned around.'

'Don't the sharks set the mines off?'

'As far as we know, they don't. We've never known any of the mines to be set off by anything other than a person or a boat. Maybe it is a little bit of that Little Mermaid magic after all.'

Moses and Morgan laughed. I pushed Morgan away from me gently, rolling my eyes.

'You lot are never going to let me live that down are you?'

I turned away from them as they laughed. I looked back out across the water, watching the gentle waves. As I scanned the surface, in the distance I saw something round disappear below the water. It had almost looked like the head of a person. I stepped away from Morgan and Moses, putting my hands on the side of the boat, trying to pin point where it had disappeared. Morgan put his hand on my shoulder.

'What is it? What are you looking at?' He said.

I shook my head.

'Nothing. I just thought I saw… something.'

'More sharks?'

I put my hand on top of his where it still was on my shoulder.

'Maybe.'

He wrapped both his arms around me and brought his face close to mine. I closed my eyes, taking in the smell of him, almost forgetting for a moment where we were. I felt the engine shudder beneath us and the boat seemed to turn gradually. Looking up again toward the horizon, I could now make out land in the distance. Morgan followed my gaze and Moses joined us where we stood at the railing.

'And there you have it' Moses said. 'Hadian Island. Home to the worst of our kind.'

The boat came to a stop along side a jetty that protruded out of the luscious, green island. We were greeted by a man dressed in all black tactical gear, with an automatic weapon held in front of his chest. He nodded at Moses as he stepped from the boat.

'Mr Cain, Sir.'

Moses nodded in return and strode past him. Morgan and I followed him off the boat, each receiving nods from the sentry as we walked past him. The three of us walked along the jetty. The island appeared to be a mass of green trees, however the closer we got, the more I could see indicating that this was more than just an uninhabited island. Although it was surrounded by golden sand a few feet from the tree line, the tree line itself was fenced in by thin wires. The gaps between would have been large enough for someone to climb through by just pushing the wires apart slightly. Moses must have known what I was thinking.

'It's electrified, the entire circumference of the island. The only way past those fences is through this gate up ahead.'

He pointed to the only structure that was visible, two small concrete buildings, no bigger than the size of a garden shed, with a huge wrought iron gate between them. More guards with guns held across their bodies stood in front of the gates. As we neared, one of them turned and unlocked a smaller door within the gate. He pushed it open and we followed Moses inside. We were in a clearing that was surrounded by trees, with no other buildings visible.

At one side of the clearing, an army style truck sat idling at the edge of a dirt road. We followed a guard across the clearing and the four of us pulled ourselves up into the back of the truck, taking seats either side. The guard sat close to the open end, his gun still in his hands. He banged against the side of the truck and we all braced ourselves as it lurched forwards, before it bounced along the dirt road. The road was bumpier than it looked and I found myself holding onto one of the ropes behind me, hanging on for dear life.

'The staff live on site in a kind of barracks near the entrance to the prison' Moses said. 'They are paid well to live here all year round, but we don't permit the staff to have visitors here or back on Mauritius, they must use their leave to return home. Prisoners aren't permitted any personal visitors whatsoever. We try to limit communication as much as possible. We will inform them of any deaths in the family, but that is as far as it goes. This ensures that the only people coming to the island are staff, or people such as myself when prisoners need to be questioned further.'

'How will it work?' I asked. 'Us visiting I mean, what is the process?'

'Half the prison is submerged under the island, whilst the other half is built up into a small mountain, which you would be able to see right now if you were sat in the front of this vehicle. There is only one way in or out and that's through an entrance at ground level. We have built a structure over the top of the entrance at the base of the mountain, which is were we process new prisoners. Once you get through the processing area, we must swim downward through a tunnel until we get to the caverns, which is where the prisoners are held. We have wet cells, which are under the water level and we have dry cells, which are above water level. Kelvin is in one of the dry cells. We have rooms inside the mountain where we can talk to him privately.'

'You mean interrogation rooms?' I said with a raised eyebrow.

Moses nodded.

'You could call them that I suppose. Don't misunderstand me Vivienne, this is an awful and lonely place to be if you are a prisoner, but we are not in the practice of torturing individuals. Maybe Kelvin would have told us more if we were, but like I said, he hasn't spoken since he arrived.'

'Do you really think I can change that?'

Moses looked me dead in the eyes, almost staring me down.

'Yes Vivienne' he said. 'I really do.'

'How big is the prison?' Morgan spoke this time.

'It's about a mile across and probably reaches about half a mile below the entry way and half a mile above. We currently house about four hundred and fifty prisoners, with room for more.'

'Do people who get sent here ever get out?'

It was my turn to ask more questions. Moses nodded.

'Yes, just like in a human court of law, Asrai are given sentences dependant on the crime. And just like in a human court, we can only convict and give a sentence if we have enough evidence. We don't follow the same process as humans with a trial and judges, but The Council will meet and review all the evidence. We will then vote on whether or not the accused should be sent here or not.'

'So you don't just vote on whether they are guilty or not?'

Moses shook his head this time.

'No we don't. If someone has already admitted to the crime, but appears genuinely remorseful, The Council may not deem it appropriate for them to come here. There are better ways to rehabilitate someone for more minor crimes.'

'So are the prisoners here mostly guilty of more serious crimes?'

'In most cases Vivienne yes. Nearly all of the inmates here were convicted of murder. Many of those against humans. Some Asrai operate under the illusion of believing we will not prosecute our own for crimes against humans. They are of course, very wrong.'

'Why are there so many murders committed against humans?'

Moses raised his eyebrows, as if he expected me to already know the answer to this question.

'Some Asrai, Promotors in particular, have a deep hatred of the human race Vivienne. If it weren't for humans, we would all live our lives freely and out in the open. To have to hide as a species is a bitter pill for some of us. Even more so for those who have been groomed by people like Abraham. Just because you have rid the world of him, doesn't mean the problem will go away. There are much more fanatical people out there Vivienne, people who would go much further than Abraham ever could have.'

His words sent a shiver down my spine. What lengths would Asrai really go to in order to be able to live the life they wanted? Hiding in plain sight would never be enough for some of them, they wanted the world to know that they were better than humans, that they should control the world instead.

Looking out the back of the truck I could see that we were now in a another clearing surrounded by trees and eventually the truck came to an abrupt halt. The guard was the first to jump out, followed by Moses and Morgan. Both men held out a hand and helped me gently down to the ground. Walking around the truck, I took in the surrounding buildings. To the left, were four ground level buildings, each one looked about as wide as a tennis court. They were fenced off and a lone guard stood idle next to an open gate.

On the opposite side of the clearing was a further building, again the length of a tennis court with only one level. This building was surrounded by a wrought iron fence that must have been more than twenty feet high, with sharp metal spikes protruding from the top. At either end of the building, turrets loomed high above the fence and within each one stood two guards, each holding weapons across their chests. Behind this building, I took in the site of the mountain Moses had described to me as small. It didn't look small from where I stood, taking in the view of luscious green trees that covered the mountain all the way to its peak.

We followed the guard, who had accompanied us in the truck, toward the building. The fence had a large gate, big enough to fit one of the trucks through, which was flanked by small shed like buildings. Each building had a guard seated inside, protected by what I am sure would have been bullet proof glass. Two more armed guards stood in front of the gate, which began to open slowly as we approached.

The inside of the building was cold, almost clinical. In a way, it reminded me of the laboratory Una and I had been held in. There were more guards inside and behind desks there were uniformed men and women, dressed more like you would imagine a prison guard to be dressed. Moses motioned around the room with his hand.

'This is where all prisoners are processed before being taken to a cell. Their general health and fitness will be assessed and we of course take finger prints, blood and DNA samples. We will use those to check human authority databases and confirm if our prisoners are linked to any other crimes. From here, we can make sure that human authority records are altered to hide any anomalies that may be flagged up.'

'You mean about our DNA being different?'

'Yes indeed. We use our resources to amend human authority records, so as not to draw attention.'

'But is that fair to the families of the victims? Never knowing who killed their relative?'

'We let the human authorities know that we have evidence proving that we know for certain who committed the crime, but that that individual is now deceased. The perpetrator is here for the rest of their life, paying for the crime they committed and the families of the victim have closure, believing the murderer to be dead.'

I nodded, trying to take it all in. There was so much that went into hiding a whole species of people, so many different ways that we could be discovered. I did not envy Moses and his position.

'Now I'm going to have to ask you to change Vivienne.'

Moses directed me to a corner of the room where two doors indicated changing facilities.

'We have provided standard underwater wear for you, issued to all staff. Morgan, we have a waiting area over there.' He gestured to the other side of the room. 'You are more than welcome to help yourself to hot and cold drinks, light refreshments if you wish.'

Morgan nodded, then turned toward me, taking my hands.

'Are you sure you want to do this alone? I can come with you.'

I shook my head.

'No Morgan it's fine, I'll be fine. He hasn't spoken for years, we have no guarantee he'll talk to me, but he doesn't know who you are at all. It could spook him into not saying anything to me.'

Moses interrupted.

'She's right Morgan. This is going to be very out of the norm for him. He's not been outside of his cell since he was originally questioned all those years ago. We gave up trying after he refused to answer anything we asked for a few months. We need to keep this visit as calm as possible if we are to get some real answers from him.'

Morgan squeezed my hands one last time before letting go.

'Okay, I know, I understand. Go and get changed.'

He let me go and Moses and I walked toward our respective changing rooms. I stepped inside the small room, where there was a toilet, sink and shower, plus fluffy towels stacked on shelves. Hanging on a clothes hook on one side of the room was a long garment that looked like a wetsuit. I felt the material with my fingers, it felt almost like lycra, but softer and smoother. As I stripped off, I caught my reflection in the long mirror above the sink. My physique had returned to normal and I could no longer see bones protruding from my ribs and back. Under this florescent lighting, my skin still looked a little bit blue in places, but it no longer looked scaly, just light and shiny. I pulled the wetsuit on and it fit snugly over my whole body. The material was very thin and left little to the imagination. I had to let Moses see me in this? I wondered with a smirk if his wetsuit would be as tight and revealing.

For my feet, I had been given some type of shoe made from the same material as the wetsuit, with extra layers on the soles. I pushed open the door and peered outside. Moses was standing outside waiting, his wetsuit also covered every part of him except his face and hands. I couldn't help looking him up and down. He had been hiding a strong physique under the clothes he normally wore. The wetsuit clung tightly to him and I could make out defined muscles all over his body.

'Are you ready?'

'I'm ready' I nodded, averting my eyes quickly so that he wouldn't notice where I had been staring.

I looked across the room to where Morgan was sitting on a small arm chair in the corner. He gave a little wave as Moses and I turned our backs on him and walked toward the door at the opposite end of the room. The door was flanked either side by armed guards, who nodded as we approached. One of the guards leaned in toward the door and waved his hand in front of some sort of keypad. There was a low beep and he took hold of the handle and pulled the door outward.

I followed Moses through the doorway into a large, low lit room, which looked almost completely empty. I heard the door click shut behind us and the low beep sounded once more, indicating that we had been locked inside. The room was much bigger than the entrance building we had just left and the ceiling reached high above us, at least the height of a five story house. I could see either side of the doors, that there were large bundles of rope tied up against the walls.

'Wow.'

I said it out loud and the sound echoed slightly around the room as I turned around slowly, taking in the huge, empty space.   'This place is huge. But how do you… how do *we* get into the actual prison.'

Moses nodded toward the middle of the room.

'We have to go down there' he said.

I turned back around to face the middle of the room. As my eyes had adjusted to the low light, I could now clearly see a round opening in the middle of the room.   There was no wall or edge surrounding it, the middle of the room quite literally, just disappeared.   I walked closer to the edge.   It was at least twenty feet across and appeared to be a perfect circle.   The inside walls of the hole looked completely smooth. I crouched down at the edge and ran my fingers along the inside.

'They're made of granite' Moses said.   'It's impossible to climb out of.'

I looked down into the darkness of the hole.   I could hear water, but not see it.

'How far does it go down? How do the staff get out?'

'It's about a hundred meters down. It's half way full at the moment, but twice a day it is nearly completely filled with water. 'The staff swim up to the top and climb out.' Moses joined me at the edge of the hole as I stood up. 'If the water isn't there, there is no way out.'

'Is this the only way in and out of the prison.'

Moses nodded.

'Are you ready to enter?'

I looked around again.

'Yes I am, but how do we…'

Moses' face softened and for a moment I thought he would smile.

'Like this' he said.

Moses turned toward the hole and before I had a chance to register what he was about to do, he pushed himself outward, chest first, arms out to the sides, before disappearing head first into the darkness.

'Moses wait…'

The shout escaped me before I could tell my brain it was absolutely pointless shouting after him. A few silent seconds passed before I heard a splash deep below me. So that was how we got in was it? Jumping head first into a hole that was one hundred meters deep and pitch black?

Brilliant.

I turned myself toward the middle of the hole and shuffled my feet to the edge. He better not have been lying when he said it was half full. I took a deep breath, exhaling slowly and closed my eyes tightly for a second. As soon as I opened them again I pushed away from the edge, throwing myself out into the void. Cold air seemed to whistle past my ears as I began to angle my head, arms and body downward in preparation for hitting the water. I tucked my head between my arms just in time before my hands sliced through the cold water.

I don't know how far down into the water I went before I was able to right myself. The water was fresh, from the mountain, not the surrounding sea. It was completely dark down here and I spun around, looking for some indication of where I should go next. Looking down below me, I could see a soft glow of light and in that glow of light, I could see a shadow moving that had to be Moses. He was coming toward me and soon I could see him clearly, motioning for me to take his hand. I grabbed hold tightly and together we swam directly downward toward the light. The closer we got to the light, the more I could see and we eventually came to a large oval door, like the kind you see in movies about submarines. The door was open, with a metal, circular handle attached to either side.

Moses guided me through the door and once through himself, pulled the door closed behind us. As soon as it shut, the handle spun around of its own accord. Looking around, I could see that we were in a small room of some kind, with one side made of clear glass. I could see guards on the other side of the glass, all dressed similar to us, but with utility belts holding some sort of baton close to their bodies. One of the guards came toward us and waved his hand in front of a small box attached to the other side of the glass. As soon as he did, I felt a slight pull on the water around me. I looked below me and could see that the bottom of this room was grated. The water was draining. I could soon stand on the bottom and my head was no longer submerged.

'How are they controlling it with their hands like that?' I said.

'The doors?' Moses said. 'Well key cards can be stolen and finger prints aren't the most reliable when you spend a lot of time in the water, so the staff here have implants under the skin. It works the same as a key card though, they just have to put it in front of the keypad and it will open.' The water continued to drain around us, and it was now at my chest. 'We can't risk any prisoners getting hold of a key card and making an escape attempt.'

'And the staff are okay with that? Being microchipped?'

The water was at our hips now.

'They wouldn't work here if they weren't. Plus, they are paid very well for their troubles.'

'Oh really? How well?'

'Ten years employment here will mean these men and women don't have to be concerned about money for a long time. Depending on how long they live for that is. The wet cell shift is the most popular among the staff and not only because it is paid at a higher rate. Most people who work here serve between twenty and thirty years and they leave looking almost exactly the same as the day they arrived.'

'How old are you exactly Moses?'

The water level reached our thighs and Moses did smile then.

'I met my wife at Dunkirk.'

'What? As in The Battle of Dunkirk?'

I could barley hide my surprise as he nodded again.

'We wanted to help, we took boats to help with the evacuation. She was a nurse with the British Army.'

'When did you tell her what you were?'

'I had to tell her the night we met. There were so many soldiers trapped in boats that had been hit. They had sunk fast. She had watched me from the boat as I kept going down, bringing back unconscious men. She did CPR on them all. There were so many of them, I couldn't get to all of them. Some had been under for too long, but we saved quite a few men between us. When she asked me how I had done it, how I managed to hold my breath for long enough to swim all that way down and get them out of the boats, I just couldn't lie to her.'

I looked down to see the water at our feet now.

'When did she die?'

'It was back in the early eighties. She was sixty five and she got sick. We could have saved her, but she wouldn't let me. She didn't want to grow any older whilst Cora and I remained practically the same. I had tried to age with her, I stopped swimming daily once we were married, but by the time she died she did look much older and deep down I knew she hated it. She feared going out with Cora in case people assumed she was her grandmother. Both Cora and I started sleeping in water again once my wife died. I suppose we both thought that if we could stop time it would stop the pain. Stop the memories of her fading away perhaps.'

'And did it?'

The water had gone. Moses turned away from me as the glass wall in front of us parted in the middle.

'You know it doesn't Vivienne.'

He stepped from the tank before I could say anything else to him. Is that what we were all doing when we swam, stopping time, holding onto memories that would otherwise fade away? Maybe that was what I was doing here and now, chasing memories of my parents. Trying to make it seem like they were still here. Moses sensed my hesitation. He stopped and turned to look at me again.

'It's not too late to change your mind Vivienne, we can go back up right now if you want to.'

I bowed my head and bit my lip, breathing deeply. I could do this. I had to do this, I had to know what I was, where I really came from. I composed myself and raised my head, staring directly at Moses. I stepped out of the room.

'I'm fine, I'm ready to do this Moses.'

He nodded his head.

'Okay then Vivienne, follow me.'

We had been briefed by the guards as we stepped out of the room. Kelvin Hudson had already been taken to one of the interview rooms. In order to get there, we had to walk through the dry cell wing and swim through the wet cell wing. The walkways through the dry cells were narrow, but the cells were fronted with reinforced glass, so we didn't have to worry about any prisoners trying to get to us. We followed the guard through a door, which he first unlocked with another wave of his hand before we stepped into a long corridor. On the left were the cells, which like the guard had said, were glass fronted. Each had a door, which looked like it was the kind that slid open and each door had a circle of small holes, which must be how the prisoners heard the guards through the glass.

The first cell was empty, so I could clearly see the bed along one side of the wall and on the other, a waist level metal wall, which presumably hid bathroom facilities. I looked up and saw row upon row of these cells stacked on top of each other. Each level had a small metal walk way running along the front of it, which were each connected by metal stairs. After closing the door behind us, the guard made his way down the corridor. At first I tried not to look directly in the cells, but out of the corner of my eye I could see that in nearly every cell, a prisoner, wearing typical bright orange clothing from head to toe, was sitting or lying on the bed. I jumped in surprise as I heard a bang on the glass behind me.

'Vivienne, Vivienne wait please, Vivienne please, come back.'

Moses and the guard both stopped abruptly and turned around, the guard not missing a beat and striding back toward the cell the voice had came from.

'Quieten down inmate' the guard almost bellowed.

I had taken a few steps back and could now see into the cell. It was Adam, Sereia's Adam. Adam who had kidnapped Una, the Adam who had taken me to Scotland, where I was held for months against my will at the hands of Brooke and Lyle. He was standing at the glass with his hands and face pushed up against it.

'Vivienne, please I'm sorry. But you have to tell them, tell them I never hurt you. I never laid a hand on you.' I walked slowly back to the cell. 'Tell them to let me go. Tell them I never hurt you, I only told them where to find you.'

His eyes were watery as if he would cry at any moment. I put my hands on the glass close to where his were on the other side.

'Do you really think you did nothing wrong Adam?'

His face crumpled and tears escaped his eyes.

'I didn't hurt you Vivienne, she promised me you would be okay, you were special. You had to be kept safe.'

I could feel my own face twist in anger.

'And what about all those children? Did you keep them safe? How many survived, Adam?'

He scrunched his eyes shut, pushing out more tears as he sobbed.

'One survived, Adam, just one. Out of all the hundreds that you took to that place, there is only one left. And how many people did you kill to get those children there?'

'That wasn't me Vivienne I swear. I just found them, tracked down the ones it would be easy to take. I was just a finder, that's all.'

'That's all?' I nearly shouted the words back at him. 'You helped them commit mass murder, Adam. Because of you, hundreds of people are dead.'

'He bowed his head down between his hands, his shoulders shuddering as he continued to cry. I pulled my hands away from the glass.

'Will he ever be released?' I said to Moses.

'He's not been officially sentenced yet. Once we have Brooke in custody, we will have a much clearer picture of the extent of his crimes and we will make a decision then.'

Adam sniffed away tears and raised his head again.

'Can you tell Sereia that I love her. She was never part of what I had to do, I love her, I really do. Tell her I'm sorry, I'm sorry for everything I put her through.'

'I hope you die in here Adam. I hope you die the way those children died. Locked up and all alone.'

'Have him moved to a wet cell' Moses said, 'on one of the lower levels. We don't want to have to hear him again when we leave.'

I felt Moses' arm on my elbow as I was pulled away from the cell. I could hear the crackle of a radio and the guard repeating Moses' instructions to whoever was listening on the other end. We continued to the end of the corridor and the door ahead of us opened before we reached it. Two guards came marching through, stomping past us. They stopped and exchanged a few words with the guard escorting us, before heading in the direction of Adam's cell.

Moses stopped in the doorway and stood aside, motioning for me to go ahead. I stepped through to find myself in a much wider, open space again. There were more staff, some sat at desks, looking at monitors. Others were in some sort of kitchen area, where metal dishes were being filled with food. There was a strong smell of fish here and I could see on a back wall hundreds of fish hanging in nets. Moses followed my gaze.

'The wet cell inmates aren't allowed out unless they are being questioned. They only get fed fish, nothing else would really work under water.'

'And what about the prisoners in the dry cells, what do they eat?'

'It's either fish, or your stereotypical prison slop for them I'm afraid. Those metal dishes get filled and passed through a flap in cell door. Like I said, no one leaves their cell here unless it's for questioning.'

'So that's where Kelvin has been, all this time? Locked in one of those cells for over twenty years?'

'He's a murderer Vivienne. He tried to kidnap you. All the evidence shows us that he is a dangerous man.'

I looked around the rest of the room. There were no other doors that I could see, apart from one that had a toilet and shower sign on it.

'Where do we go from here?'

'Follow me' said the guard from behind me.

He walked to the right of the room, there was little light there, but I soon made out another hole in the floor, this one much smaller than the one that had got us down here. The guard stepped into the hole and I realised there were stairs heading downward. Moses and I followed until we found ourselves in a small room with a single door at the other end. Next to the door sat a guard at a desk, with two monitors in front if him.

We followed our guard as he approached the door, waving his hand in front of the keypad and motioning us through as the door opened for us. We stepped out onto a large metal platform, which looked out over the surface of a wide body of water. We were in some sort of cave, with high cavernous walls. Glowing lights were spaced evenly around the edge of the cave, close to the water level. The lights gave the water an eery, yet beautiful sparkle. The metal platform was fenced off, with a long jetty protruding out into the water.

'We have to swim from here, right down to the bottom of the wet cells' Moses said. 'Just aim for the red light. That's where the entrance to the next block is. You will have to swim up as far as you swim down okay? Some people find it quite claustrophobic. The tunnel is quite narrow.'

'How do you get the prisoners up there?'

Moses looked between me and the guard, then cleared his throat.

'Inmates are heavily restrained when they are removed from cells, they don't really have a choice when we need to take them for questioning.'

'So by people, you mean the prisoners. The prisoners find it claustrophobic?'

'It's a very narrow space Vivienne, I just want you to be prepared for it.'

I don't know why I almost felt defensive for the prisoners and the fact that they got tied up and dragged around tunnels. These people were criminals, dangerous criminals who had hurt others. They deserved the way they were treated here.

'I will remain here for you' the guard said. 'There are guards in the water below, so you are perfectly safe. No other inmates are being moved from cells, so no harm will come to you Mrs Whidden. You will be met by my colleague in the next block.'

Moses nodded and began walking across the jetty. I quickly followed before he reached the end, turning to look at me.

'Remember, aim for the red light. It's on the far side of the wall, right at the very bottom.'

I nodded my understanding.

'How far down is it exactly?'

'There are ten levels of wet cells. You will need to swim down past all of them. Try not to stop, try not to look for too long okay.'

I nodded again and before I could reply, Moses turned and dived into the calm water, barely making a splash. I gave it a few moments, to make sure he was out of my way before diving in myself. Once again I was greeted by cold, fresh water. This must be some sort of underground lake. I opened my eyes and took in my surroundings. The light under here glowed a soft green and as my eyes adjusted, I could make out what seemed like hundreds of cells that were built into the walls of the cavern. A green light in each one gave everything a spectral glow.

Unlike the dry cells, the cells here were fronted by thick metal bars and every cell was completely empty apart from its lonely occupant. In almost every cell, the prisoner had come forward and now held onto the bars. I could see Moses a few feet below me and every prisoner holding onto their bars followed him with their gaze before looking toward me. I could hear a faint humming noise, it sounded like it was all around me. I stopped where I was and turned all the way around, taking in every cell in the circular structure. It was them, the prisoners were making the noise. It sounded like they could be singing, but it was the saddest song I had ever heard. I watched as guards descended on the cells. Most of the prisoners shrank away from where they had been holding onto the front of their cell.

I watched as one prisoner held their position at the bars, the guard trying to push them back with some sort of baton and when the prisoner didn't move, they were struck with the baton again. This time a blue light flashed from it and I watched as the prisoner, a young woman with the blackest hair I had ever seen, recoiled in pain. She leaned back against the wall in her cell, baring her teeth at the guard, looking as though she would pounce in his direction, but instead, she turned her gaze back to me.

I continued my descent and the prisoners' song slowly faded away. I could see Moses up ahead and below him, the faint glow of a red light. I pushed myself harder and faster, swimming further and further down into the cavern until I had all but caught up with him. I followed his feet as we neared the bottom of the cavern and under the glow of the red light, I could see a gap in the wall. Moses stopped in front of it and waited until I did the same. He pointed at me and then into the gap, then pointed upward, indicating for me to go first. I looked back up the way we had just come down. The cells loomed so high above me, I could no longer make out where the surface of the water was.

I peered into the gap in the wall. It was almost completely dark, with only the glow of the red light above it illuminating enough for me to see where I had to go. With my hands either side of the gap, I pulled myself into it. As I stepped inside, I felt out in front of me with my hands and came to a wall. I turned my head upward and could see a faint light high above me. I felt around above me and could make out the circular opening of the tunnel. I bent my legs and pushed away from the floor, kicking my feet. I kept my arms above my head at first, but on each kick my feet or knees hit the sides of the tunnel surrounding me. I eventually gave up kicking and used my arms to pull myself up bit by bit.

Looking down, I could see nothing below me. Was Moses there? Had he followed me or not? Looking back up, the light above me seemed to be getting no closer. My arms soon began to ache with the constant pulling and not being able to stretch out to the sides, just up and down, up and down. I looked down again, still no sign of Moses below me. Where was he? What had happened to him? I slowed down, trying to kick with my legs again, but the tunnel was just too narrow. I either hit one side with my knees or the other with my feet. I stopped where I was, bracing myself between the sides of the tunnel. I looked up again, the light seemed as though it was fading.

Had I gotten any closer to it at all? Where was Moses? I felt panic rising in me, my stomach clenched hard and I felt as though I might vomit. Then, I heard a faint ringing in my ears. Was it ringing? Or was it that singing again? The sadness of those voices was just so… But it was louder now, it was definitely inside my head, wasn't it? The urge to vomit pushed my chest forward and my head suddenly felt very light, like it wasn't attached to me anymore.

What was I doing here? Why was I in a tunnel? Why was I stuck here? I could feel hands on my legs and then my shoulders. Moses was here. I could feel his body against mine, his hands were on my face and he was looking at me, shaking me. Where was Morgan? Moses was looking at me, singing to me. But I just wanted to go to sleep. Why was Moses here? He had such beautiful eyes. But why was he here? I was just trying to go to sleep.

28.

Una

Sereia was really, really rubbish at building
sandcastles. We had gotten to The Cove early today and
had already swam for an hour. When we had got back to
shore it was nearly nine in the morning and we were out
of the water and building castles in the sand just in time
to see small groups of people hauling their beach stuff
down the path from the top of the cliff.

'It will be busy today Una' Sereia said. 'The
weather forecast said it would be hot all day, so no doubt
this beach will be packed by half ten.'

'So we can't go out swimming again?'

'Not the way we would want to. We would just
have to play in the waves like everyone else does.'

Sereia smiled at the sulky face I pulled.

'What would you like to do instead? We can do
anything you like.'

My face changed into a big cheesy grin.

'Let's go to The Colony!'

Sereia laughed out loud.

'Well that's impossible I'm afraid. I don't know how to get there.'

'Your Keeper that went there, didn't she tell you how to find it?'

Sereia shook her head as I used my finger to write my name in the wet sand.

'Keepers aren't allowed to tell anyone about how to get to The Colony. They can only show the children of The Colony how to return.'

Sereia stared out toward the water and the wind blew her bright red hair across her eyes for a moment before she tucked it away behind her ear. Turning back toward me, she smiled and her eyes narrowed in the way that they did when she was about to let me do something I shouldn't, like staying up late to watch movies with her.

'But she did say one thing about it to me. I was very young, so I reckon she didn't think I would remember, it was such a long time ago.'

I sat up excitedly.

'What did she say?'

'Well,' Sereia looked around dramatically, as if checking that no one else could hear her, even though we were still all alone on the beach. 'She said I had to look for it where I would find myself.' She sat back with a confused look on her face. 'What do you think that could mean?'

I turned her words around in my head for a while.

'I don't really know' I said, 'like a mirror or something?'

Sereia shrugged.

'You know that's not a bad guess, but how would a mirror tell us how to get there?'

I looked up toward the cliff path as the first of the beach goers got to the sand.

'Maybe she wrote it on the back of one?'

'Maybe she did' said Sereia.

I suddenly remembered Kendra talking about a map in a mirror.

'It's got to be a mirror!' I couldn't quite contain my excitement as I said it. 'Kendra said a Keeper told her dad how to get to The Colony. They showed him a map in a mirror.'

'Well now I know that that isn't true, because a Keeper can't just tell anyone how to get there. Was Kendra's dad from The Colony?'

I shook my head.

'I don't think so.'

She nudged me with her arm.

'Well there you go then. Now come on, lets get home and get dressed.'

She pushed herself off the sand and grabbed my hands, pulling me up to my feet.

'We're going to the next best thing.'

'What's that?' I said as I followed her across the sand.

She looked down at me and smiled.

'The aquarium of course.'

The aquarium was really busy. Sereia had thought it would be relatively quiet because the weather was so nice, but she was wrong. We had gone in the back staff entrance the way I always did with Vivienne and Morgan and the staff members had barely noticed us come in. Everyone seemed so busy today. Someone I recognised, Megan, eventually noticed us.

'Ah Sereia, Una' she said. 'So nice to see you both. I hope Viv and Morgan are having a nice time away.'

She crouched down in front of me.

'Una, you're just in time for the morning turtle feeding, would you like to do it today?'

'Oh yes, I really would. Sereia, can I please go up and do the feeding?'

'Of course you can Una. I'll sit as close to the front as possible and watch with everyone else.'

I followed Megan to the end of the corridor and through a door marked staff only. I had done this before with Morgan, but I was still so excited. We went up the metal stairs that took us to the top level above the turtle tanks. Leaning over the top of the railing, I could see the turtles already swimming around below, they knew what was coming. I followed Megan to the roped entry way and she held a bucket out in front of me. It was filled with large, leafy vegetables. I reached in and pulled out a handful.

'Are you ready?' She said. 'Do you want the prongs?'

I shook my head.

'No it's okay, I can reach.'

I laid myself down so I could reach under the ropes and watched as the turtles came toward me, snapping their small beaks. One at a time I made sure they all got pieces of food.

'Careful' Megan said. 'Your mum and dad would never forgive me if I let you fall in.'

I looked up at her. Had she meant Vivienne and Morgan? She realised what she had said.

'Oh I'm sorry, I meant Viv and Morgan of course.' She looked embarrassed all of a sudden. 'I didn't mean to upset…'

'No that's okay Megan, I…'

How did I feel about that? It definitely didn't upset me, it just felt kind of normal. That's how I thought of them in my head after all. I smiled at her.

'You can call them that if you want to.'

She smiled too then, in fact she almost beamed.

She knelt down next to me and held out the bucket for me to grab more food. I took another handful, smiling to myself. I was so happy here, with Vivienne and Morgan. Being part of the life they had, the life they had now given me. I never thought that I would feel happiness like this again, not after everything that had happened since we were taken, since I had lost my mother and my brother. I'm so glad that I was wrong about that.

After feeding time was over, I followed Megan back downstairs to find Sereia. She was still sat in the turtle viewing area, with lots of families milling around her. She opened her arms wide when she saw me and I ran into them, squeezing her tightly.

'How was that? Did you have lots of fun up there?'

'I really did' I said. 'I think the turtles like it when I'm feeding them the best you know.'

'They do seem to get a lot more food when you are around' Megan said with a smile on her face. 'Sereia, do you want a coffee?'

'Oh that sounds great. Lets go to the cafe shall we? We don't want any of that rubbish from the staff room today.'

We all walked together in the direction of the cafe. Sereia and Megan walked ahead of me chatting quietly, while I looked at every display. I must have seen each tank at least a hundred times before, but I always found something new to notice. People walked around me and I stared into tanks along with other children and the people they were with.

'Ew what's that thing?'

I turned to look at the little boy who had said it, whilst pointing into one of the tanks.

'That's a Blobfish' I said. 'They're an endangered species. I think he's really cute.'

'He looks funny to me' the little boy replied, before moving along to the next tank.

'You really know what you're talking about don't you Una.'

I recognised the voice and a feeling of utter dread pulled on my stomach from the inside. I felt a cold hand slide into my own and squeeze tightly.

'Come on darling, it's time to go.'

I looked up into Dr Ayer's eyes. She had a wide smile across her face, but her eyes had an almost evil glare in them. I opened my mouth, ready to scream the place down for Sereia's attention.

'I wouldn't if I were you' she interrupted. 'If you make even the tiniest of sounds, that man over there will cut her throat before you can take another breath.'

I looked up to where I had last seen Sereia and Megan. They were still walking slowly, deep in conversation and just behind them a few paces back, a large figure followed, keeping pace with them. He turned around for a moment and when he noticed us looking at him, he gave a little wave.

Dr Ayers crouched down next to me, taking both my hands in hers, pulling me down in front of her until our faces were level.

'So, Una, my little darling.' She smiled again, almost sweetly this time. 'We are going to walk out of here quickly and quietly, do you understand? And if that happens, no one will get hurt. Not you, not Sereia, not anyone, okay?'

I clenched my jaw shut and nodded. She quickly stood up and pulled me along behind her by one hand. We moved fast through the crowded room. I turned and looked behind me, but I could no longer see Sereia, Megan or the man that had waved. What could I do? There was no way I could get out of this without attracting attention, without getting Sereia or someone else hurt. Brooke squeezed my hand tighter as we followed the signs to the exit.

She continued to smile sweetly, even nodding to people around her and thanking them as they made way for us to pass. I had no way to signal anyone. To them, I must just have looked like a grumpy little girl who had just had a tantrum. All I could do was hope that one of the staff members who knew me, would notice me and realise that I was with someone that they didn't know, but there was no one close by. Every time I did see someone, there were too many people around me for them to notice me and Dr Ayers knew it.

Her pace quickened the closer we got to the door. I looked around desperately, there really was no way out. I was pulled through the exit doors and the brilliant sunlight hurt my eyes in the few moments it took for them to adjust to the light. We walked past the car park, out to the main road. A small black van with blacked out windows was parked up on the curb. I heard footsteps running behind us and the man who had waved caught us up. He grabbed me as I turned to look at him and he lifted me easily, pulling open the sliding door of the van and throwing me inside it. Dr Ayers followed closely behind and was around the other side of the van and in the drivers seat as the man reached for the door.

'STOP THEM, STOP THOSE PEOPLE.'

I heard the words as a desperate scream in the distance. I looked up and saw Sereia running from the front door of the aquarium. Megan was behind her. Their faces were twisted in absolute terror. Sereia had tears streaming down her face. Megan shouted now too, pointing toward me.

'HELP, THEY'VE TAKEN HER, THEY'VE TAKEN THAT LITTLE GIRL!'

People turned and looked as they ran across the car park toward the van. I watched as a man dropped the bags he was holding and started to run toward the van too. More people realised what was happening and joined him, running toward us.

'Shut the fucking door and get in!'

Dr Ayers screamed the words from the front seat. The man pulled the door across and it shut with a loud bang before he opened the passenger side door at the front. The van was moving away before he had even got fully in.

'UNA!' I could hear Sereia shouting as we pulled away. 'UNA NO!'

But it was too late. The last door slammed shut as the van sped away.

29.

Vivienne

'Vivienne? Vivienne can you hear me?'

I could feel a hand on my shoulder and someone gently shaking me. I could feel that I was laid on my side on a hard, uneven surface.

'Vivienne? We're out of the tunnel now, are you okay?'

Out of what tunnel? Where was I? I recognised the voice, it was Moses Cain, but what was I doing with him. I opened my eyes slowly and his face came into focus in front of me.

'You passed out in the tunnel Vivienne, but you're out now. There's nothing to be scared of.'

Why would I have been scared of a tunnel? What was he talking about? Where on earth was I? I pushed myself up into a more upright seated position, leaning on one hand. Moses was kneeling in front of me wearing some kind of wetsuit. I looked down at myself and I was dressed the same way. Slowly I began to remember, we were in Hadian, the Asrai prison. I was here to see someone. There had been a tunnel, it was dark and small and I had panicked.

'How… how did you get me out of the tunnel?'

Moses smiled.

'I had to pull you up myself. You gave me a bit of a fright there Vivienne. You had some sort of anxiety attack and forgot to keep breathing, I think. I did warn you that the enclosed space of the tunnel wasn't for everyone.'

'I don't know why I did that. I don't normally get claustrophobic. I'm sorry Moses.'

'It's okay, we're on the other side now. We'll just give you a few minutes to compose yourself and then we will go and talk to Kelvin.'

I nodded, looking around. We were sitting inside a small cave. I could see what must have been the tunnel hole to one side of me and on the other, another submarine type door.

'I'm okay, I'm ready' I said.

'Okay.'

Moses stood up and reached his hands out toward me. I let him pull me up from the floor. My head swam for a second and it must have shown. He grabbed my arms, steadying me.

'Are you sure you're alright? I think your brain must have been starved of oxygen for a moment there.'

I nodded again.

'Honestly I'm fine. I'm ready to do this, really I am.'

He raised an eyebrow, but accepted my answer. He crossed the cave to the door and banged on it loudly with the side of his fist. The wheeled handle in the middle began to turn slowly at first, before spinning around faster and faster, until the door eventually popped open. I followed Moses through and we were greeted by a guard and a short corridor. This guard was dressed in the same wetsuit looking attire as the ones under the water at the wet cells. There were doors on either side of the corridor, each with a small light glowing above them. The door closest to us had another guard stood in front, holding his baton like weapon across his chest.

'Mr Cain.'

The guard who had opened the door nodded as we stepped fully into the corridor. Moses returned the nod.

'How has the inmate been since being removed from his cell?'

'He still hasn't spoken, but he seemed oddly calm when we arrived for him. Almost like he was expecting us.'

'Have you told him who is coming to see him.'

'No, we've told him nothing.'

Moses nodded. The guard continued.

'Follow me Sir.'

He walked us toward the guarded door and pulling down on the handle, pushed the door inwards. I followed Moses into a well lit room, with only a table in the middle. On one side of the table sat a small figure. His elbows were resting on the table, his hands laid out in front, bound together with plastic handcuffs. On the opposite side of the table were two chairs. Moses motioned me ahead of him toward the table, whilst the guard entered the room last and closed the door behind him.   He stood off to one side of the door, his hands behind his back, his weapon slung around his waist.

Moses and I both took a seat at the table across from Kelvin Hudson, who now looked up and met our eyes.   Other than being on the thin side, you would not have immediately been able to tell that he had spent more than twenty years behind bars.   He was pale, having not seen any sunlight for all that time, but his skin had the same healthy glow that all Asrai seem to have and his light, shoulder length hair that had all but dried, shone brilliantly under the florescent lighting.   His eyes were the lightest green I had ever seen and they had a glassy sheen to them, as if he were on the verge of crying.   The skin around his eyes creased slightly and his chin wobbled as he pulled his lips into a short smile.

'Hello Kelvin' Moses said.

Kelvin nodded, but quickly averted his gaze to his hands.

'Can we have the handcuffs removed please.'

Moses indicated to the guard, who approached the table, quickly unlocked and removed the handcuffs, before returning to his position at the door.

'Kelvin, I trust you remember me?' Moses said.

Kelvin looked up again and nodded, but then his eyes dropped back to the table just as quick as before.

'Kelvin, do you know who this is with me?'

Kelvin nodded again, this time not lifting his head.

'We have come to talk to you about what happened, about why you are in here.' Kelvin continued to nod his head ever so slightly. 'I know you've been in here a very long time, but we need to know some information and I think you can help us. We think you know more about what Vivienne is, about where she came from?'

'I knew…' his voice croaked.

He stopped and cleared his throat, raising his head to look at me properly for the first time.

'I knew you would come. I've waited all these years, but they were right, they said you would come one day. I just had to wait, just wait here and not tell anyone anything and you would come to me.' A tear fell from his eye and he wiped it away quickly. 'I've waited all this time to see you again Vivienne. You are exactly as I imagined you would grow up to be. Just like your mother.'

'Did you know my biological father Kelvin?' I tilted my head to the side, keeping eye contact with him. 'You've told people in the past that I'm different to Asrai, that I'm something else. I know that I'm not half human. Do you know what I am?'

Kelvin looked down at his hands before he nodded slowly.

'I know what you are.'

'Tell me what you know, tell me from the beginning, tell me everything. Please.'

He cleared his throat again.

'The people that watch over us, the people that know what we are and what will happen, they're not supposed to fall in love. But David was different. I didn't know him, but I was told. He went against the people that know, he loved your mother. He loved you. He sacrificed his life for your mother and for you.'

Moses interrupted him.

'How do you know this Kelvin? Who are the people that watch over us?'

Kelvin's face creased slightly as he winced away from Moses' voice. His gaze returning to his hands.

'Jeremiah told me. He wanted to help you. He wanted to make sure that someone knew you were important and you had to be kept safe. He told me everything. But I had to be careful, he knew people would think I was crazy if I told them about him.'

'Is that who they say you killed, Kelvin?' I said. 'Is Jeremiah the one that was found at your home?'

Kelvin nodded.

'I don't know why he was there. He must have known they would come, he would have known what would happen.'

'Why Kelvin?' I said. 'Why would he have known what was going to happen?'

'Jeremiah and David. They were the same. People who watch over us, people who know. They know what will happen before it does. Jeremiah told me you were special. I had to protect you. You would save us all one day.'

'So why did you try to take her Kelvin?' said Moses. 'Surely the safest place was with her parents? With Marianne and Adrian.'

'I told someone, someone I thought that should know, someone important who could help me protect her.' His eyes moved to me. 'He told me I had to take you, I had to take you to him so that he could keep you safe. He was so worried about you, he thought something bad might happen to you if you stayed there. We had to make sure you stayed safe at all costs. Your mother and Adrian, they had no idea how important you were. No idea at all.'

'Who was worried about me Kelvin, who did you tell about me?'

'I told Lyle, Lyle Calder. He's a very important person, he could help you, he has resources. He could keep you safe.'

Moses and I looked at each other. If Lyle Calder was involved, it was looking more and more likely that he was responsible for the murder of Jeremiah.

'But I'm not important Kelvin, I haven't cured anything. Infertility in Asrai isn't cured.'

Kelvins brow furrowed in confusion.

'That's not why you're important.   You're not going to cure us, you're going to save us.'

Moses and I exchanged glances again.

'What do you mean Kelvin?' Moses said.

'We will need to be saved.   When the day comes that humans mean us harm, when we are on the verge of being wiped out, Vivienne will be the one to stop them.'

'But humans don't know about us Kelvin.' Moses continued in a gentle voice.   'Certainly not in enough numbers for it to be a threat to our existence.'

'How long will that last?   Jeremiah was certain, out of all the possibilities he was the most certain about this one thing. You will have to save us all Vivienne.'

'Did Lyle Calder know that part? Did you tell him that's why she was important?'

Kelvin shook his head.

'No I didn't.   I just told him that she would save us.   I didn't want to tell him too much, I couldn't risk him asking too many questions about Jeremiah.   But it was all for nothing, Jeremiah died anyway.'

He bowed his head again then screwed his eyes together tightly, as if trying not to let tears fall.

'Did you kill him Kelvin?'

His head shot upright. I looked him right in the eye, his face was creased in pain.

'I would never have hurt him. He was all I had, he was my only friend on this earth.'

'Why weren't you surprised to see us Kelvin?' Moses asked.

'He said this would happen. He warned me about the dangers of trying to protect Vivienne. He said that if this was the outcome, if I ended up here, that you would come to see me. He said that you would save me from this place.'

'What are they, Kelvin?' I asked. 'What are the people that know, how do they know?'

He shook his head.

'I don't know. They just seem to know what will happen, they are always watching us, always knowing what is coming next.'

'Where do they come from?'

'They don't come from anywhere, they just are.'

'And how do you know for certain that David was one of them?'

'Jeremiah would never have lied to me. He may not have been able to tell me everything all the time, but he would never tell me anything that wasn't true. You are one of them and Jeremiah said you had to be protected at all costs.'

'David and Jeremiah are dead, how do I find the rest of them? Where are they?'

'They aren't found Vivienne. They just watch, they just know.'

'How do they watch? How do they know what will happen?'

Kelvin shook his head.

'I don't know. I wish I could tell you more, I really do.'

I looked at Moses and gave the smallest shake of my head. I had nothing else to ask him. Moses acknowledged me with a curt nod of his head.

'Vivienne, would you mind excusing us just for a moment?'

Moses motioned toward the door as the guard pulled it open. I pushed my chair away from the table and stood up.

'Yes of course. Thank you for talking to me Kelvin.'

Kelvin smiled faintly.

'It was so nice to see you again Vivienne. I hope we will see each other again one day, under better circumstances.'

'Me too Kelvin' I said, before walking out of the door and having it closed firmly behind me.

I smiled awkwardly at the guard standing sentry on the other side, before pacing slowly up the corridor. So what did this all mean? That my biological father was some sort of psychic that was part of a group of mystics who could tell the future? This all sounded too crazy, even in a world where people could breathe underwater. But I honestly didn't think Kelvin was crazy, he just seemed so sincere.

I truly believed that he did not kill anyone. Something about him was just so gentle, so kind. I couldn't imagine that he would ever hurt anyone, even with knowing that he tried to take me as a baby. I just knew that he had never meant me any harm, being in the same room as him, I could somehow sense it, he was telling the truth about everything.

I heard the door open again and I turned around in time to see Moses step out. I followed him toward the huge metal door that led the way back to the tunnel. He pulled the heavy door open and I climbed through before him. Once on the other side, he pulled the door closed behind us.

'Everything okay?' I asked him.

'Do you think he is a killer, Vivienne?'

I shook my head.

'No I don't, Moses. I can't explain it, but I really do believe he's telling the truth.'

'Me too' said Moses. 'I'm going to have him relocated.'

'I think that's the right thing to do, Moses. But why did you sentence him all those years ago if you think he's innocent?'

'It was different at the time, Vivienne. He was so frantic, almost incoherent when we questioned him. He was caught in the act of trying to kidnap you, a harmless baby. Add that to the body found at his home, everything pointed to him being guilty and it was ultimately down to a vote. That's how our system works. Even if I had thought him innocent back then, the vote still wouldn't have gone in his favour.'

'How will the other members of The Council feel about you taking him out of here? Won't they have an issue with this?'

'I'll cross that bridge when I come to it. As it stands, in order to convince them of his innocence, I would need to explain everything to them. Tell them about David and Jeremiah being something other than human or Asrai, tell them about you being different. I don't think we should do that just yet. The less anyone else knows, the better.'

'Why not?' I said.

'I need to be sure of everything first, plus I'm worried what it would mean for you if others know about you and what you are. I don't want to give anyone else a reason to want to kidnap you, even if it is just because they think they have to keep you safe.' Moses looked down at the entrance to the tunnel. 'How do you think you're going to be going back down?'

'I'm okay now honestly. I think I was just so anxious about speaking to Kelvin, I let it all get to me. I really do feel like some sort of weight has been lifted off my shoulders, I feel like that's it now you know? I know that I'm different, my biological father wasn't human or Asrai, but it doesn't make a difference. It's not going to change my life. I have my family, we're happy and that's all that matters.'

Moses placed his hand on my shoulder and smiled softy.

'I'm glad you have that Vivienne.'

Shit. Here I was gushing about how none of this actually mattered because of how happy I was with my family, when he was all alone. Widowed decades ago and his daughter had been missing and presumed dead for the last fifteen years.

'Moses I'm sorry.'

He shook his head as if to stop me.

'No I mean I'm sorry for wasting your time. I really thought that this was so important, finding out why I was different, why my DNA wasn't the same as other Asrai and why I got pregnant once. But it's not important really is it? What's important is Morgan and Una. Like, what am I really doing here honestly? I feel like I've just wasted everyones time.'

Moses shook his head harder and his smile widened.

'You think this was all a waste of time? Vivienne no, it was quite the opposite. If it wasn't for you coming here, that man would likely have never spoken again. He would have stayed here for the rest of his life and that would have been an awfully long time. Kelvin will be freed because of you. A man innocent of murder will no longer be imprisoned and that's down to you.'

I smiled too then. It was good to know that I had actually helped someone. He patted me on the shoulder a couple of times.

'Now come on, lets get you back to your family.'

'They've taken Una.'

Morgan had been waiting right outside the door to the entrance to the prison.

'They've taken her from the aquarium, a woman and a man. It had to be Brooke.'

A hot wave of fear crashed over me, consuming my entire body.

'Morgan slow down' Moses said.

'We have to go, we have to get back to England right now.'

Morgan was almost shouting, his voice panicked. Moses put his hands on Morgans shoulders, forcing him to stand still.

'Morgan how do you know this, what's happening?'

Morgan took a deep breath, he looked to the ceiling, his face scrunched up in pain almost.

'Sereia called me, Una was taken by someone. It happened in broad daylight at our aquarium. The local police are involved, there were so many people there who saw. She was put in a van and they drove off with her.'

Moses nodded.

'If the local police are on this then that's a good thing. My people can use their systems, we can find out what they already know. The van could have been spotted on CCTV, on traffic cameras, we can use this. It's okay, she'll be okay. I just need to get my people on it right away.'

Moses let go of Morgan and strode off toward the room where he had changed earlier. I stayed where I was, the heat that had washed over me had subsided and I now felt cold to my bones. The sounds of the room around me became muffled. This was my fault. This wouldn't have happened if we had been with her. Why had I left her just to come here? Morgan looked at me, his mouth was moving but I couldn't hear what he was saying. The more his mouth moved, the angrier he began to look. He stepped toward me, bending down slightly to look into my eyes, his mouth still moving. What was he saying? I felt his hands take hold of my shoulders and he shook me. Not hard, but not gently either. My eyes met his and all of a sudden, the muffled sound of his voice disappeared and I could hear him clearly.

'Vivienne... Vivienne I said get dressed. We have to go, we have to leave right away.'

I swallowed hard, I felt like I couldn't breathe, like I wasn't feeling any air in my lungs whatsoever. I felt my chest rising and falling, faster and faster. The look on Morgans face changed from anger to confusion. His hands moved to my face, his eyes were inches away from mine.

'Vivienne, please…'

He pressed his forehead to mine, then squeezed his eyes shut.

'Vivienne, I need you to be *you* right now. Una needs us, she needs you.'

My breathing began to slow. Morgan pulled me into his chest, wrapping his arms around me. I could feel his heart thudding through his chest, I could hear him sniff as he held back tears. I heard a door open and close from across the room and Moses' voice. Morgan let me go and we both turned to see Moses striding back across the room, fully dressed with his mobile phone pressed against his ear.

'Come on Vivienne.'

Morgan took hold of my hand and pulled me across the room to where I had changed earlier. I walked slowly behind him for a few steps before I practically pushed him out of the way and ran toward the changing room.

30.

Una

We had been on the road for a long time. A really, really long time. It had got dark hours ago and I could see through the front window that we were no longer on a busy road. I could see stars twinkling in the night sky and there were no longer any street lights or lights from any other cars that I could see. Dr Ayres had driven the whole time and the man had passed me food to eat every now again. When I had complained about needing the toilet, they had pulled over away from busy roads and other cars and held me tightly by my arms whilst I crouched in a bush to pee. I had slept for at least a few hours, but I had no idea what time it was now.

I felt the van slow down and heard gravel under the tyres, before it came to a complete stop. The man got out of the front passenger side and slid the door to the side of the van open, pulling me out. He pulled me around to the front of the van while Dr Ayres got out from the drivers side. I looked around. Behind us were three small houses and in front of us was nothing. It was very dark, with no street lights, but the moon was bright enough for me to see that we were on some sort of moors or countryside. There were no trees at all and I could see the sparkle of water in the distance and there were low mountains beyond that.

It reminded me of my home before the laboratory, my home with my brother and my mother. There was a strong wind and it blew my hair all around me and across my eyes. I didn't see as Dr Ayres came around the front of the van and grabbed me by the arm. She steered me in the direction of the end house, pushing open the outside gate and walking me down a short path toward the front door. She let me go whilst she pulled keys from her pocket and fumbled with the door. I turned around, looking behind me only to find the man few feet away.

'Don't even think about it' he said.

Dr Ayres got the door open and stepped inside. I felt the man's hand on my back and stepped through behind her as she turned the lights on. We were in a small living room area with a sofa and arm chair surrounding a little fire place and a television.

'Dr Ayres, I need the toilet' I said.

'You can call me Brooke if you want to' she replied, almost with a smile. 'And it's this way.'

I followed her down a dark hallway and watched as she switched lights on along the way. She had been here before. Was this where she lived? She pushed open a door and pulled on a cord that lit up the room. It was a tiny bathroom with a toilet, sink and shower. There was also a small window.

'There you go' she said.

I walked through the door and tried to push it closed behind me. She stopped it with her hand.

'It stays open, Una.'

She turned her back toward me and leaned against the door frame. I huffed to myself before admitting defeat and going to the toilet. After I had finished and washed my hands, she escorted me back to the living room, where the man was sitting on the sofa with a mug in his hands.

'Are you hungry, Una?' Brooke said.

I shook my head.

'I imagine you're quite tired. We will go to bed in a bit. I just need to eat something.'

She turned around and went through another door where the light had already been turned on. I followed her through to the kitchen and watched as she took bread from a cupboard and made herself a sandwich with chocolate spread and drank wine from a glass. She drank the wine fast, refilling the glass after every few bites of her sandwich.

'Are you sure you don't want anything?'

I shook my head again. Brooke lifted her glass again, swallowing nearly all of it on one go.

'What are you going to do with me Brooke? Are you taking me back to that place?'

She seemed to laugh to herself.

'The lab? The lab is long gone Una. Your new mummy saw to that. All that research...' she shook her head. 'Just stopped... finished just like that. We were making such progress.'

She continued to shake her head as she chewed on her sandwich.

'I was there, I was right there on the edge of a cure and now… now I can't do anything.' She gulped at her wine again. 'I've got no lab, no subjects. I'm just running around on bloody fools errands for Lyle.'

She gulped at her drink again before refilling the glass from the bottle on the counter.

'What's a fools errand?' I asked her.

Brooke put down her glass and took another bite of her sandwich. After a few chews she answered with her mouth half full.

'It's a pointless task Una.' She was shaking her head as she said it. 'Lyle thinks Vivienne is still the answer to our problems. She's the missing piece to this puzzle and she could be for all I know, but you all had to go and escape before we could test for pregnancy. Years of money and research just wasted.'

'Is that what you were doing to Vivienne? Making her pregnant?'

'Lyle is confident that the last round would have worked. But instead, you lot disappeared. I've tried to tell him that she would have gotten rid of it at the first opportunity, so now we'll never know.'

'She wasn't pregnant when we left' I said.

Brooke scowled.

'Well she wouldn't tell you if she was would she, you're just a child.'

'I saw her bleeding. On a boat after we got away. I saw her washing herself and there was lots of blood. My mama told me about that before, it means you're not pregnant doesn't it?'

She gulped at her drink again before putting the glass down hard on the work top. She put both hands on the counter in front of her and looked down at me.

'That doesn't matter right now Una. You're here and Lyle knows she'll come after you.'

I knew that Brooke was right. We were a family now. Vivienne and Morgan would find me, they would do anything to try to save me, even if it meant they got hurt, or worse, in the process.

'So lets just make this easier for all of us shall we Una? Don't try anything funny. Don't try to escape. All the windows and doors are locked, there is no way to get out of this house unless I'm with you. We are miles away from any other people so even if by some miracle you do manage to get out, you've got absolutely nowhere to go, there is no one around to help you okay? Just do as you are told and this will all be over soon.'

31.

Vivienne

It was still light when we left Hadian, but the sun was getting low. It would take us six hours just to get back to Mauritius, where Moses' private plane was waiting for us. It would be late at night by the time we got there. We were literally half a world away from home and there was nothing we could do to get home any faster.

We couldn't do anything at all from here. Moses had arranged for all our belongings to be taken from the villa and put on the plane. He had also instructed his people to begin their investigation and they were going to be searching for Una and her abductors, but I still felt so absolutely helpless here, not being able to do anything to save her. My Una, she was all alone, she must be so scared.

'What if they've already hurt her?'

I didn't mean to say it out loud. Morgan and I were standing on the top deck of the boat, looking back the way we had come, watching Hadian Island slowly shrink into the distance behind us.

'They won't hurt her.'

Morgan's words jogged me out of the daze I was in.

'You don't think they will hurt her? You haven't seen what they're capable of, Morgan, what they've already done to hundreds of other children. Children who are all now dead.'

The volume in my voice had began to rise as I said it and he winced away from the words as they left my mouth. I watched as his hands gripped tightly on the railing at his hips.

'Well what am I supposed to say, Vivienne? Do you want me to tell you that I think they've probably already hurt her? That Brooke would probably treat Una even worse to get back at us? Is that what you want to hear?'

His knuckles turned white as he gripped the railing even harder. I shook my head and wiped a tear from my eye. I sniffed before replying.

'No of course not I... I just feel really helpless right now. We can't do anything to help until we get back to England and how long is that going to take us? Six hours on this boat, twelve on the plane, then however long to get from London back to Zennor. I just feel like we should be doing something, something that can help our little girl.'

I turned around and pulled myself up onto the corner of the railing, my feet on ledge underneath it. Morgan moved to stand in front of me and took my face in his hands.

'We have to stay positive Vivienne. We will get her back. She's going to be okay... We're all going to be okay, do you understand me?'

I nodded gently as I stared into his eyes. There was a fierceness to them as they glassed over. I sniffed again and wiped more tears from my own eyes. Out of nowhere, a deep rolling boom echoed around us. Over

Morgan's shoulder there was an explosion of sea water in the distance. Morgan turned around too.

'What was that?' I asked.

'One of the mines just went off I think' Morgan said.

'What could have set it …'

Before I could get the words out, another boom rang out, this time much closer, shuddering the boat from side to side. I tried desperately to grab for Morgan as I fell backwards. He turned back to me quickly, realising what had happened, but he was too late to get a good enough grip on me. I hit the water back first with a hard slap. As the sea closed around me, I could hear Morgan's muffled shouts. Before I had a chance to right myself, something hard hit me in the ribs and I was pushed away from the boat. I turned my head just in time to see a huge shark speeding toward me. I let out a silent scream in panic, before forcing myself downward and out of the path of the incoming shark. I watched its silhouette as it kept going in the other direction, before slowly turning around.

I had to get out of it's line of sight. I couldn't go upward, I would have to go down. I dived downward as quickly as I could, kicking my legs harder than I had ever done in my life. We were a mile out from the island, the water was already deep. I turned my head to look in the direction of the shark, it was still up above me. How would I get back to the boat? I continued downward, below me I could see something, some sort of structure. It was the wreckage of a boat. I willed myself to swim faster and faster until I felt my hands grab onto the rusted metal of the sunken vessel. I pulled myself into it through a square opening on the deck.

It was almost pitch black inside, I couldn't see anything further than my hand in front of my face. I felt my way forwards with my hands, pulling myself downward until I could go no further. I leaned back against a wall and pulled my knees in toward me, willing my heartbeat to slow down. What was I going to do, how do I get out of here? I had to get back to the boat. That's if it had even stopped. I had no idea if it still above me or not. Could I just wait here until the shark went away? I didn't know if the boat would wait for me.

I know Morgan wouldn't let them leave without me, but it's not like they could come down here looking for me, there could be more sharks. I felt my heartbeat begin to slow slightly. Think Vivienne, there had to be a way to get back to the boat.

I felt around the floor beside me with my hands, I could feel the rope of a fishing net of some kind. It was weighted down by something heavy, a large metal ball. I tried pulling it away from the net, but it wouldn't budge. I kept feeling around until my hand found something long and cylinder like. It was some sort of metal pole, light enough for me to pick up. The rusted ends felt sharp. I had no idea if it would help me against a shark, but right now it was all I had.

I felt my way back to the opening. I hovered where I was below the deck, trying to see if the shark was close by. I couldn't see the boat anywhere. I edged my head slightly out of the opening. I found the silhouette of the shark, at least ten meters above me. It swam in a wide circle, one, two, three times until at last, it swam away.

I waited for a little while longer before pulling myself through the opening completely. My eyes searched the surface of the water, off in the distance, at least a hundred meters away, I could see a large dark shadow. That had to be the boat, that's how far I had to get. I focused on the shadow. It wasn't a long distance, I could reach it in minutes, but I had to go now in case the shark returned. I pushed myself away from the ship wreck, metal pole still in my hand. Five meters, ten meters, I was crossing the gap quickly. To my right in the distance I suddenly saw it, the shark was coming back. I kept swimming, pushing myself forward as fast as I could. The shark seemed to be moving slowly, I don't think it had noticed me yet.

Something sharp suddenly grabbed the back of my lower leg, pain seared through me as I was yanked downward. I twisted my head around to look behind me, it was another shark. The hot pain in my calf felt like my leg had been set on fire. I was yanked from one side to another. I tried desperately to kick downward with my other leg, but I couldn't connect to the shark that had hold of me. The water around my legs began to turn red, making it harder and harder to see. I pulled myself into a ball and with both hands, brought the metal pole down as hard as possible. It connected with the shark square on the side of its face and it let go.

The pain in my leg was unwavering, but I pushed myself out of the cloud of blood as quickly as I could and I was soon closing the gap between myself and the boat again. I squeezed my eyes shut, willing myself to push harder, to swim faster in spite of the pain. When I opened my eyes again there were more of them, there were at least two sharks circling above me. I looked to my left, just in time to see a smaller shark swimming toward me. I held the pole up and outward in front of me just in time. The shark swam right into it, almost spearing itself. It shook itself off and seemed to float away in a daze. The circling sharks above me looked like they were getting nearer.

I continued toward the boat, still trying my best to go as fast as I could, but I was slowing down. I was losing blood quickly. I needed to get to the surface, try to signal to the boat. They would be looking for me up top, waiting for me to resurface. But the sharks above me, I had to get around them first. I pushed onwards, my whole leg numb with pain, I was willing it to move, but couldn't feel if it was or not. I dropped the metal pole so I could better use my hands and arms to move faster. I swam at an angle, heading toward where I thought the boat was and toward the surface at the same time. I must have been less than fifty meters away by now.

Then I saw it, coming at me fast. It was so big, there was no doubt in my mind it was a Great White. I froze where I was, not knowing which way to move. I looked up toward the surface, the circling sharks were gone, had the Great White scared the rest of them off? I felt paralysed as it came toward me head on. I could see its tail going from one side to the other either side of its head. I could move at the last minute, duck beneath it like I had with the first one, but then what? It was a Great White Shark for fucks sake, I couldn't out swim this thing. It was within feet of me now and then it was on me, I put my hands out in front of me and feeling its razor sharp rows of teeth on my fingers, I ducked down out of the way of its jaws. At the same time, something came at the Great White from the side, barrelling it into a roll.

I looked up to see a dolphin, then another and another. They were everywhere, surrounding me, surrounding the shark. More of them began to go after the shark, one at a time they accelerated toward it. I didn't wait around to see what would happen next. Swimming as fast as my injured hands and leg could take me, I once again headed for the boat, a cloud of blood following me. I was closer now and it was definitely a boat, I could see the clean, white underside and the motionless propellors. They were waiting for me, they had stopped the boat, they must be looking for me.

I was meters away when a body crashed through the surface into the water. When the bubbles cleared I could see it was Morgan. His hair swam around his face as he looked around, locking his eyes onto mine. It seemed as if everything was in slow motion as he swam toward me, before taking hold of me around the waist and pulling me back toward the boat. We were soon being pulled back onto the boat by Moses and his security guard.

'Watch her' Morgan shouted at them.   'She's bleeding. Get something, we need something to stop the bleeding. I need bandages, a towel, anything. Just get something now.'

Moses knelt down beside me, unzipping a large green bag and started pulling out bandages.

'She needs stitches' he said.

'Stitches?' Morgan said. 'Her fingers are hanging off Moses.'

I raised my hand up in front of me, blood was running down my palm. All four of my fingers were hanging awkwardly, the skin gaping at the knuckles, the tendons and bones visible.

'I can help her, but it's not going to be pretty.' Moses said.

'Just do it' Morgan replied.

Morgan was passed a towel from somewhere and wrapped it around my hand, soaking up the blood. Morgan pulled my body in toward his own.

'Are you okay Vivienne? I'm sorry. I'm so sorry that I let you go.'

He rocked me gently back and forth as Moses held another towel tightly around my calf.

'I'll need her to turn over. Let's get her below deck where I can do this properly.'

Morgan picked me up and carried me down stairs below deck. Moses laid more towels across one of the cushioned benches and Morgan gently lowered me onto it, stomach first. I winced as the wound on my leg was rinsed with alcohol and I felt every sting of the needle as Moses began to put stitches in my leg.

'What happened down there Vivienne?' Moses said.

'Fucking sharks, that's what happened Moses' I replied. 'Underwater mines and fucking sharks.'

32.

Una

I had woken at the sound of a door closing gently. I had fallen asleep quickly the night before, it must have been very late when we had arrived here. I had fallen asleep in a sleeping bag on top of Brooke's double bed whilst she had tapped away on a laptop next to me. She wasn't in bed now and her laptop was nowhere to be seen either. I unzipped myself from the sleeping bag and climbed off the bed, before stepping quietly across the room to the window. I pulled one of the curtains aside. It was a brilliantly clear day, the sky was so blue. It reminded me of the sky from home.

The sun was shining brightly and the water in the distance sparkled. It looked like some sort of lake and it was beautiful. I pushed the curtains open wider and pushed myself up onto the window sill. I could see figures on the other side of the water, there were people there.   Brooke was wrong, there were other people around.

I pushed myself onto my knees and tried the window's handle. I pressed the button in as hard as I could and pulled harder at the handle but it wouldn't budge. So she hadn't been lying about all the windows being locked then. I slid off the window sill and made my way toward the door. I listened by it for a moment, hearing a muffled voice from somewhere else in the house. The door was closed and I pulled gently on the door handle, unlatching the door silently and pulling it open.

With no window, the hallway was quite dark, the only light coming from the door to the living and kitchen areas, which was half closed. I moved as slowly as possible, using the tips of my fingers to stop the door closing behind me with any sound. I took a few steps toward the kitchen door, keeping my feet as soft as possible on the thick carpet.

'Lyle, why can't we just start fresh, we don't need Vivienne.   We got so many samples from her, I can continue from where I left off without her. Just get me a new lab, some test subjects, we can be back up and running in no time at all.'

She was quiet for a while, she must be on the phone, listening to someone.

'I just don't think it's worth all of this Lyle. You had us take her in broad daylight. The police could turn up here at any minute. This house is in my name, if they tell the police my name...'

She went quiet again for a moment.

'And what if they bring help? It's just the two of us here with the girl, you think we can go up against Moses and his resources? Look what happened to Abraham at site A. Moses has capabilities that we cannot match... yes but... yeah I get that but...'

She went quiet for much longer. I stepped even closer to the door, peering through the gap. She was standing over the worktop in the kitchen with her back to me, a mobile phone pressed to her ear.

'Understood.'

That was the last word she said before placing the phone down on the counter in front of her. She took a deep breath and sighed heavily.

'For fucks sake' she said.

'What did he say?'

It was the man who spoke now, from somewhere else in the room that I couldn't quite see. Brooke walked away from where she had been standing at the kitchen counter.

'He wants to go ahead with the original plan. Call Vivienne tomorrow, tell her to meet us alone at the airfield in a few days time, Lyle will be waiting there for us. We let Una go if Vivienne agrees to go with Lyle. We all fly off into the sunset, the end.'

'You don't think it's going to go down like that?'

'Of course it's fucking not. Lyle is deluded if he thinks he can engineer something like this. Honestly he's getting more and more unpredictable. She's never going to come alone, she won't trust that we will let Una go, she will have someone there with her to take Una at the very least. This is never going to work. He's adamant that the local police won't be involved, Moses will have seen to that he says, but I don't trust that one bit. We're in over our heads here. Whatever happens, whoever comes with her, if it looks like things aren't going our way, if it looks like Vivienne is going to get away… I need you to kill her.'

33.

Vivienne

In comparison to being thrown from a boat by an underwater mine explosion and being attacked by sharks, the rest of our journey home had been quiet. Moses spent almost the whole time on the telephone, telling us very little about his conversations and what information he had found out. Morgan and I sat in a stunned silence for the entirety of the plane ride back to the UK. Moses insisted on driving us straight home. We could arrange for someone to go get our car from the train station once we got back. We had arrived at Gatwick by midday and were met on the tarmac by another of Moses' security team in a large, black Range Rover. As soon as our luggage was loaded into the boot, we set off. I managed to doze off for a while in the car, but I was soon awoken as we neared home. As we pulled into our driveway, Morgan sat up straight.

'The police are here.'

I looked through the front seats and out of the windscreen ahead of me, where I could see a police car parked on the driveway in front of us. As we climbed out of the car, the front door opened and Sereia stepped out of the house. She had her arms clamped tightly around herself as if she was feeling the cold and her eyes were sunken and red. Fresh tears were running down her face and she used her sleeved hand to quickly wipe them away.

'Vivienne…' she sniffed as I walked toward her. 'I'm sorry.' She started shaking her head. 'I'm sorry, this is all my fault. She was behind me, I wasn't watching her.'

She dropped her head and used one hand to cover her eyes as her shoulders shuddered with her sobs. Morgan and Moses were now stood either side of me as a uniformed police officer stepped from the house, followed by a woman in ordinary clothes. She stepped forward.

'Mr and Mrs Whiddon? I'm Detective Inspector Kerensa Snell. I'm in charge of the investigation into the abduction of your daughter. Please, shall we go inside?'

I nodded and followed her back through the front door and into the house. I was surprised to find Megan from the aquarium sat in the kitchen.

'Megan,' I said. 'What are you doing here?'

'I… I was there when it happened. I've been here with Sereia since… since it happened.' She watched as everyone else entered the house behind me. 'I'll put the kettle on.'

She got up from her seat at the kitchen table and reached for the kettle.

'Please, Mrs Whidden' Detective Snell said. 'Please come and have seat.'

She motioned to the living room. I walked in and took a seat on the sofa. Morgan took a seat next to me, taking my bandaged hands in his. Detective Snell sat in the arm chair next to the fireplace, underneath the mirror.

'What happened to your hands Mrs Whidden?'

I looked down at my hands, straitening my fingers out, looking at the bandages. It was Moses who answered, from where he leaned in the doorway.

'Fire Coral. They were snorkelling. It gives a nasty burn if you touch it. She didn't realise what it was.'

'And who are you exactly?'

Detective Snell eyed Moses suspiciously.

'I'm a close family friend. I arranged their late honeymoon, travelling with them for parts of it. We all travelled back together as soon as we were informed about what happened.'

'And your name?'

Moses looked down at his arms folded across his chest.

'My name is Moses Cain.'

'And do you reside here in Zennor also?'

'No' said Moses. 'I work in London. I just wanted to make sure they got back as soon as possible.'

The detective nodded to herself, before turning back to Morgan and I.

'We've got a few leads, we're currently tracing the route of the van once it left the area of the aquarium. It was picked up by traffic cameras on the M6 outside of Birmingham, so we know for a fact that they're heading North.'

I watched Moses as he pulled his mobile phone from his pocket and looked intently at the screen as he scrolled through it. The detective seemed not to notice.

'We've got intelligence working on finding out exactly where it went next and I assure you, we'll do everything we can to get Una back. To help in our investigation, I do need to ask you both some questions if that's okay?'

Morgan and I both nodded and the detective continued.

'We understand that the person who took Una is known to you, Sereia thinks she recognised her?'

'I didn't really recognise her' Sereia interrupted from the doorway. 'I never met Brooke, but from how you described her, I think she was there, she drove the van away.'

Sereia gave me the briefest look of widened eyes. Sereia had no idea what Brooke looked like, she had never met her or seen her picture, but we all knew it was Brooke that had done this. Morgan swallowed hard. We needed to be very careful with what we told the police, we couldn't tell them anything about the lab, the experiments, my kidnapping, we couldn't have them looking too deeply into what really happened.

'Is this her?'

The detective held a photograph out toward Morgan and I. We both leaned forward and looked at the CCTV still of Brooke and Una walking toward the exit of the aquarium. Morgan nodded and cleared his throat.

'Yes, that is my ex-partner Brooke Ayres. I was with her before Vivienne and I were married. There is a lot of animosity between us, owing to the fact that I broke off our relationship shortly after Vivienne came to live here in Zennor. She thinks that Vivienne stole me from her I guess. Although that really isn't the case, as our relationship had been over for a long time as far as I was concerned.'

'So Brooke's surname is Ayres? Is that spelt A. Y. R. E. S?' The detective had a pen poised over a small notepad on her lap.

'Ayers yes, her name is Brooke Ayers. Dr Ayers technically.'

'When did you break up exactly?'

'Just over two years ago, in the July.'

The detectives brow furrowed and her pen stopped writing as she looked up.

'But Una is what seven? Eight years old?'
Morgan and I looked at each other. The more we had to explain, the more questions would be asked.

'Yes, Una is eight. We adopted her' I said. 'She is a distant relation of my parents, who are both now deceased. Una lived alone with her mother and when her mother died earlier this year, we decided to adopt her.'

The detective nodded to herself, accepting our answer.

'And do you think Brooke would take your daughter to get revenge against you?'

'It's possible' Morgan said. 'She took our breakup quite badly and she had always had quite a dramatic temper, so I just don't know.'

'Do you think she is capable of hurting a child Mr Whidden?'

Morgan and I looked at each other. We both knew the answer to that, we both knew about the hundreds of children she had inflicted horrendous pain on and ultimately killed, but we couldn't say that to this detective, to this human who had no idea what any of us really were. Morgan shook his head a little.

'I really don't know. I don't know if her mental health has deteriorated since our break up, I don't know what else she's been through. I really wish I knew what was going through her head right now but I don't. I just have to hope for Una's sake that Brooke is just trying to scare us, that she just wants to hurt us to get us back for the pain she has felt.'

'Do you know where she lives now?'

Morgan shook his head.

'She lived in St Ives when we were together. After we broke up, she moved away for her work. We haven't spoken since the night we broke up, so I don't know where she went.'

'Okay' the detective said as she stood up. 'I'll be able to look into Brooke back at the station. In the meantime, if you have any contact from her or anyone else at all, call me straight away. Lets find your daughter.'

She handed me a card with her details on. Morgan and I stood up and followed her from the living room. The uniformed police officer opened the front door before stepping out ahead of the detective, who stopped and turned back toward us.

'Moses Cain. I have seen your name before, in more than one investigation report, I'm sure of it. But you say you don't live here?'

Moses stepped forward.

'No, I don't live in this area. I have strong connections to the community here and I have provided additional resources to your Chief Constable on several occasions to assist with investigations.'

'So you have experience with criminal investigations?'

'I will always help where I can.'

The detective seemed to be considering his words, her suspicion on her face plainly obvious for anyone to see. Moses put his hand in his pocket and pulled out a small black card, then held it out to her.

'If there is ever any help that I could provide…'

His words hung in the air for a moment until eventually she nodded and took the card from his grasp. Then she turned her head toward us.

'Mr and Mrs Whidden, I'll be in touch soon.'

She took her final steps out of the door and closed it behind her. Megan emerged from the kitchen door behind us.

'I've made a pot of tea if anyone wants one?'

'Megan' Morgan said. 'Thank you for staying with Sereia until we got back. We'll get you home now.'

'My assistant will take you' Moses said. 'Sereia can go too and can pick up your car from the train station on their way back.'

We all nodded in agreement as Megan put her coat on and I rummaged in my bag for car keys to give to

Sereia. The two women followed the man out of the house.

'Thank you again Megan' I said, pushing the door softly closed behind them.

'So Brooke is taking Una back to Scotland' Morgan said it as soon as the door was closed.

'But the lab has been closed down' I replied. 'They wouldn't take her back there again surely?'

'No' Moses said. 'It will be somewhere else up there. Brooke will likely have a residence in Scotland if that's where she was working.'

I walked back into the living room and sat down again.

'How do we find out where?'

Moses and Morgan had followed me. Moses sat in the chair opposite, where the detective had just been sitting.

'I'll get my team on it straight away. We can leave for Scotland tonight.'

He pulled his phone back out of his pocket and began tapping away at the screen again.

'What if that detective comes back?' I said. 'Won't she think it's strange that we're not here when our daughter is missing?'

I looked at Morgan as he stood in the doorway. He knew what I would ask him and I could see the pain in his eyes as he spoke his next words.

'I'll stay.' He crossed his arms across his chest. 'I'll stay here with Sereia and deal with the police, you two go. Go and save our daughter.'

Moses nodded, before standing with his phone to his ear and disappearing to the kitchen. I didn't want to do this without Morgan, but I knew I had to. I had to be the one to save her, to face Brooke and whoever else stood in between me and my daughter. The fear of what could already have happened to her suddenly weighed down on me. I leaned back where I sat and covered my eyes with my hands, willing the tears to go away. Morgan was soon crouched in front of me, gently pulling my hands away from my face, pulling me down toward him.

'Vivienne, Viv it's okay. Una is going to be okay. We will find her.'

'What if she's already hurt her Morgan? What if this isn't about the lab and finding cures and using children as medication? What if this is just because she wants to hurt us and she knows that she can do that by hurting Una?'

He held my face in his hands, almost tightly.

'We can't think like that Vivienne. We have to believe that she will be okay. *I* have to believe it, okay?'

I felt the tension in his hands. He was scared, just as scared as I was. He stood up, leaving me where I was on the sofa. He paced the living room, one hand on his hip, the other on his head. I needed to get out of this room, it was killing me to see him like this. I knew we should be together, supporting each other, but I needed air. I felt nauseous over all of this, like I would actually throw up if I didn't get outside. I needed to not worry about him on top of everything else. Was that selfish of me?

'I need some air' I said as I stood up.

Morgan turned away from me, leaning over the fireplace, his hands either side of the mantle with his head lowered between his shoulders.

'Okay' was all he replied.

It was windy on top of the cliff overlooking the sea. I had walked toward the path that led down to The Cove, but I could see the beach full of families enjoying the sunshine and sand. I walked instead along the top of the cliff where I could be alone, just for a few minutes, just so I wouldn't feel like I was about to throw up. I walked slowly, feeling the cool wind across my skin as I looked out across the sparkling water. I stopped when I reached the place where I had last seen Emmy. This is where I had watched Abraham throw Emmy from the cliff, as if she was nothing. Despite that awful memory forcing its way into my head, the nausea eventually began to subside.

I longed for Emmy to be with me now. She would know exactly what to say to sooth this pain, this pain of having the child I loved taken from me. She would probably know how to deal with Morgan better than me right now, she would know what to say to him. I was just making him upset. I hadn't been able to stop Abraham before it was too late. Was I going to be too late to stop Brooke too? It felt like this was history repeating itself again. Tears stung at my eyes and I wiped them away. Crying wasn't going to help me, but I couldn't help it. I had lost Emmy, was I going to lose Una too? And what would this do to Morgan and I? I wasn't sure if I believed our marriage could survive this. Could we get through losing Una or would I lose Morgan too?

I wiped my face again and sniffed away the tears. I had to stop, I had to be stronger than this. I had to stop crying. I could see in my peripheral vision two people meandering along the path toward me. I wiped my eyes one more time, before turning back toward the cottage. I readied myself for a cheery smile and hello, so that they wouldn't see that I had been crying and try to ask me what was wrong. I knew for a fact that I would not be able to hold back the tears if kind strangers asked me if I was okay or not. I tucked my hair behind my ears as I walked toward them, waiting for the right moment to make eye contact. As I looked up to acknowledge them, the two women came to a stop in front of me.

'Hello Vivienne.'

I stopped where I was and looked between them. I didn't know either of these women. I couldn't recall seeing them in the village, could I have met them at the aquarium before? They were quite a bit older than me, in their late forties or early fifties. They were dressed in plain jeans and t-shirts and both had mousy brown hair. One woman wore hers loose, just above her shoulders, the other had her hair pinned in a soft bun on the back of her head. She had her hands clasped in front of her, as if she was welcoming me to some kind of church. In fact, they both looked like they could have been a vicars wife, with warm, friendly smiles.

'Hello.'

It was all I could say, whilst I racked my brains trying to figure out how they knew who I was.

'I'm Carol' the one with the hair down touched her hand to her chest. 'And this is Julie'. She motioned to the woman with the bun. 'Do you mind if we talk for a moment?'

I started to shake my head.

'Now's not really a good time.' I stepped out, ready to walk around them. 'I'm needed urgently at home.'

'We know' said Julie.

The words made me stop still again.

'That's why we're here' she continued. 'Please, come sit with us for a moment.'

She pointed to the bench a few feet away from us. I had no idea who these women were and how they knew what was going on with Una. Were these women part of Brooke and Lyle's operation? Were they part of Una's abduction? I could feel my heart rate speed up as I turned and walked toward the bench. I took a seat and the women sat themselves either side of me. Julie was the next one to speak.

'Jeremiah was not good at dealing with the things he knew.'

Jeremiah? Kelvin Hudson had spoken of Jeremiah only yesterday. What did this have to do with a man that died years ago?

'He could not separate the emotional weight of what he knew and he tried to intervene.' She spoke

slowly and concisely, every word soft, but clear. 'He
wanted to make sure that what was predicted, became a
certainty.'

I looked between the women, they wouldn't have
been noticed anywhere. Their quiet, yet assured
demeanour and completely ordinary appearance would
have kept them off anyone's radar. No one would think
to take any notice of them in the street. Were these
women part of the people that Kelvin Hudson had told
me about? Were these the watchers, the people that
know?

'Who are you?' I said.

Julie looked out toward the horizon.

'We don't have a name, yet we are referred to by
many different words.'

'Watchers? The People That Know? Guardian
Angels?' I said.

Carol nodded as the words left my mouth.

'Yes, those words have been used to describe us.
But they shouldn't. We shouldn't be talked about in
such a way, because we shouldn't tell anyone what we

know. Unfortunately, there are some of us, who find the weight of their knowledge too hard to bare alone.'

'Like Jeremiah?' I said.

Julie nodded.

'Yes, like Jeremiah and like your natural father, David.'

'Did… did you know him?' Both women nodded. 'Look' I continued. 'This is all so confusing, I don't know what to believe. Kelvin Hudson told me about you, but I really don't know what is real anymore. Can you please, just start from the beginning, tell me everything. If I really am half… half whatever it is you are, then you have to tell me everything. What are you? How do you know things?'

Carol looked around, her eyes pointing upward toward the bright blue sky.

'No one really knows how we came to be' she said in her soft voice. 'I'm sure that if we were more widely known about, many would like to believe we were sent from above to watch over you all. But all we know with certainty is that we are genetically very similar to humans, but like Asrai, have something extra in our genetic make up. As a child, we will be notably different. If we attend school, we will be assumed to have some sort of Savant Syndrome. Our ability to predict certain events hinge on our capability to assess the probability of every possible outcome. We know what is most likely to occur and we can manipulate this ability to help us look much further ahead in time. Although there is never complete certainty in what we predict, we are seldom wrong. In most cases, we can narrow it down to just two outcomes and one will be correct.'

Julie continued the train of thought.

'David met your mother and fell deeply in love with her. Love is not an emotion we would normally have to deal with, but it affects everyone differently I suppose. Women of our kind don't tend to suffer with the affliction. We choose another to procreate with for the sole purpose of continuing our lineage.'

She stopped and smiled to herself, then Carol continued.

'Some of the men however do have a much higher range of emotions and are much more susceptible to falling in love and suffering the consequences that that means for us.'

'What consequences are there for falling in love?' I asked.

'Well' Julie said. 'Can you imagine loving someone and knowing almost exactly when and how they would die? If you knew with almost certainty when your husband would die, would you not do anything in your power to stop it?'

'Of course I would' I nodded.

Carol nodded slowly.

'Exactly, but that's not why we know what we know. We are not supposed to change what is predicted. David knew the two most probable outcomes for when your mother visited Abraham Lean, to try to convince him to leave the side of the Promotors. It would either result in her death and therefore the death of his unborn child, or it would result in his death. He knew he couldn't convince her not to go, not without revealing how or why he was certain that they were in danger. So he went with her and he made sure that his death was the outcome. He made sure that you would be saved.'

'It was a sacrifice that would continue to cost us dearly' Julie said. 'It started a domino effect. Soon after you were born, Jeremiah decided he needed to intervene, he needed to make the same sacrifices as David in order to keep you safe. The burden of what he knew was simply too much for him.'

'But why?' I interrupted. 'Why do I need to be kept safe? I get why David would want to save my mother, because he loved her. But I hadn't even been born, what is so important about me? I know I'm not the magical cure to Asrai infertility that Abraham and Lyle Calder thought I was, so what is it?'

'We cannot tell you that at this time Vivienne' Julie said. 'For we do not fully understand it yet ourselves. Of all the probable outcomes for the future, we only know of one inevitability, which is that you play a pivotal role in preserving the survival of humanity.'

All the air in my body left me suddenly. I could barely take a breath.

'I what?'

'There will come a time when the decisions you make and the actions you take affect the survival of everyone on this earth' Carol said.

I took a moment to let her words sink in. This couldn't be reality. What they were saying was just... just completely implausible. But most of what had happened to me over the past few years had been that way, why should this moment be any different?

'You said you nearly always had two possible outcomes, what are they?'

I saw the women look at each other across me, Carol nodded slightly, as if instructing Julie on her next words. I looked at Julie, staring intently into her eyes.

'Either billions of people are saved' she said. 'Or they aren't.'

I shook my head. This was crazy. I stood up, putting my hands to my head, trying to get what they were saying out of my mind. I didn't have time for this, Una was more important than all of this right now.

'I can't... I can't deal with this right now. I have to go, I have to save my daughter.'

'We know. That is why we are here. Una is of great importance to you Vivienne. Although we do not like to intervene, we are here to help you save her. She has her own role to play in the survival of this world.'

Carol stood up in front to me, gently taking hold of my wrists and pulling my hands away from my face.

'She will be okay Vivienne' she said. 'Go to Loch Shin.'

I met Carol's eyes as tears began to fall from my own.

'That's where she is?' I sniffed. 'Loch Shin?'

Carol nodded.

'Moses and indeed the police would have found this out later today anyway. We are just giving you a head start. Accept help when it is offered Vivienne and you will both return home.'

I pulled my arms slowly from Carol's grasp.

'Thank you.'

I whispered the words before turning around and running faster than I had ever ran, back to the cottage.

34.

Una

I stared out of the window of the bedroom, sitting on the window sill with my legs pulled into my chest. Brooke had given me a t-shirt to wear to bed and I pulled it over my knees, stretching the material as far as it would go. I watched the surface of the water in the distance. The sky was clear again today and the early morning sun shone down on it, reflecting back brightly from the water. I wished I could be in the water, in any water in fact. I'd been allowed to have a shower yesterday, but I hadn't been swimming since I had last been at The Cove with Sereia.

I felt so bad for Sereia, she would blame herself for this. I know she already felt bad enough about her boyfriend Adam being the one who took me from my home, even though she didn't even know him back then. I knew she would be crying now, about this, thinking it was all her fault. But it wasn't, there are just so many bad people in the world. People who do these things because they are greedy, or because they hate one another. I would tell Sereia when I saw her again that this wasn't her fault, none of this was her fault. Yes, that's the first thing I'll say to her when I see her, because I will see her again. I just had to get out of this house first.

This window was no good, it was locked tight and I wouldn't be able to break it without making an awful lot of noise. I looked around the room, there was definitely nothing in here that I could use to break it quietly. I looked at the wardrobes and for the first time, noticed that in the ceiling above them, was a hatch. It was painted the same colour as the ceiling, so it wasn't noticeable straight away. I got down from where I had been sitting on the window sill and walked closer to the wardrobes. There was definitely a way into that ceiling, maybe it was a sort of loft. The latch wasn't small, it was big enough for a grown up to fit through it. I quickly looked away from it as Brooke pushed open the bedroom door, some clothes in her hands.

'Una, get dressed please' she said, as she placed the clothes on the bed. 'Then come and have some breakfast. We're going to call Vivienne today. She's going to want to speak to you.'

She left the room without saying another word. So they were putting their plan in action today. She was going to tell Vivienne to give herself up for me and I knew that Vivienne was going to do it, I knew she would do anything for me. I had to get out of here before it was too late. I dressed myself as quickly as I could, Brooke had washed everything I had arrived in and I hurriedly put it all back on.

I had left my trainers next to the bed the first night we had arrived and I laced them tightly before climbing up onto the chest of drawers next to the wardrobe. I got up into a crouch and my knee knocked into a tall perfume bottle in front of me, pushing it over. I flinched as the glass bottle made a noise as it hit the wooden surface of the chest of drawers. I sat still where I was, ready to jump off if Brooke or the man came in to investigate the sound. But there was nothing. After a few seconds, I slowly stood up straight, being careful not to knock anything else over.

I could now just about see onto the top of the wardrobe. It was thick with dust and there were a couple of small cardboard boxes in my way. I placed my hands on the edge of it at the top and pulled myself up. It would have been easier to jump up, but that would have knocked more things off the chest of drawers that I was standing on and would have made a lot of noise. I managed to get up high enough to get a knee over the top and slid my way further across the top until I was completely on.

I pushed the boxes out of my way. The lid came off one of them and I could see inside it. There were photos in there, lots of photos of Brooke and someone else. I pulled out a photo, Brooke was smiling. I'd never seen her look this happy. Next to her in the photo, his arm around her waist, was Morgan. He looked quite different, with no hair at all on his head, but it was definitely him. They had been together once.

I remembered Vivienne asking Brooke, when we were in the lab, if she had loved Morgan. I remember thinking how upset Brooke had seemed. I remember I had thought that surely, someone who could do all the things she has done, can't be capable of really loving someone. Someone who does the things she has done, had to be completely heartless. But in this picture, she looked so happy, so full of love. Maybe that's why she did it all, because she no longer had the love she had felt. She was so angry at Morgan now, so angry that she was going to kill Vivienne. I couldn't let Vivienne be taken by Brooke. I heard the sound of muffled conversation and dropped the photograph back in the box, putting the lid back on quickly.

I reached out to the hatch in the ceiling and pushed it gently with my hand. It lifted away from the framing and I was able to move it over to one side. Once I had made a gap big enough for me to fit through, I put my hands inside the frame of the hatch and pulled myself inwards. I got my body all the way in and pulled my legs in one by one, being careful to be as quiet as possible. I had done it, I was inside the loft. I looked around, it wasn't completely dark and I could see a few boxes in front of me. I pushed the hatch cover slowly back over the gap. I hoped they wouldn't immediately work out that this was the way I had gone once they noticed I was missing. That's if there was even a way out of here.

I turned myself around on the spot, looking all around the small space. There was light coming in from somewhere. I stood up on one of the beams and looked over the boxes in front of me. At the other end of the loft space was a small window. Definitely big enough for me to fit through. I walked across the beams, keeping my balance by holding onto the supporting beams as I stepped across the floor ones one by one, until I made it to the window. It was facing the other direction to the one in the bedroom, so I couldn't see the water. I was looking out of the other side of the house toward the road. The road was straight and flat and went all the way off into the distance. I stared at it for a while, almost not believing what I could see... because I could see a car coming toward the house.

35.

Vivienne

Moses and I had left Zennor with his security guard Dylan shortly before seven yesterday evening. We had shared the driving between us and had driven all night. We had stopped a couple of times for fuel and grabbed food and drink, the last time being an hour ago in Inverness. Another hour at most and we would be at Loch Shin, another hour until I would find Una. There weren't many residential buildings near Loch Shin. There was a hotel, some camping locations and fishing excursions, but other than that, it was very remote. Moses had found properties that were listed under Brooke's name. We knew exactly where to find them. But if Moses had been able to find out that information, the police would know soon too. We had to get Una and get out of here. But how easy would it be?

There hadn't been enough time for Moses to arrange for help to come with us, not like when he had rescued Morgan from Abraham. We had no idea what we would find there, whether Brooke would be armed with a gun or not. As far as we knew, it was just her and one other who took Una, but would there be more people here? It wasn't a stretch to worry that only three of us could possibly be outnumbered.

Dylan was driving, whilst Moses sat in the front seat, holding his phone in his lap, looking down at the screen.

'The team has finally been mobilised' he said, his face still looking at the screen. 'The closest team we could arrange was from Manchester. It will take them just over an hour to reach the location.'

My heart began to beat faster, not knowing whether the three of us would be enough, whether we would get there in time to save Una or not. Somehow Moses sensed my renewed anxiety. He turned in his seat to look at me.

'Vivienne we will get there. Please, don't worry. We will save her.'

An hour later, the minutes were passing slowly as I watched from the backseat, the map screen in the car moving onwards. We were getting closer and closer. I held my hands out in front of me and gently unwound the bandages from my palms and fingers. The cuts were all but gone, leaving only soft pink skin where the wounds had been. It almost looked like scars, but they would soon be gone too. My leg still hurt to stand on, but like my hands, the wounds would soon be completely gone. I sat up straighter, I could see the loch, I could see buildings in the distance. We were here. Moses leaned forwards and pointed.

'Those small buildings up there, up the hill a little bit, that's the location. How many vehicles can you see?'

I leaned forward through the gap between the seats, squinting to make it out.

'Looks like just the one to me?' Dylan said.

'Should we drive up close?' I said. 'Or should we hide the car further away, so they don't realise we're coming?'

'No' Dylan said. 'If we are spotted and they manage to get away in the car and we are on foot, we've got no chance of catching them up.'

'We'll drive all the way up' Moses said. 'Block in their vehicle. Hopefully just having the van that they took her in on the drive means it's still only the two of them with Una.'

Dylan slowed the car as we came closer to the building. We were less than a few hundred meters away.

'Who's that?' Dylan almost shouted the words, leaning forward over the steering wheel. 'Someone is outside the house.'

He was right, there was a small figure, running away from the house, hair blowing widely in the wind, small legs sprinting toward the road. It was Una.

'UNA!"

I cried out loudly, reaching for the door handle.

'There's someone else.'

Moses' words made me look back up. Running behind Una was a large figure. Una was nearly a hundred meters from the house and he was catching up with her fast. My hand was on the handle of the car door, Dylan had put his foot down again, but I jumped out as soon as the door opened, slamming it shut behind me.

'UNA' I screamed again, louder this time. 'UNA RUN!'

Her face was screwed up as she pushed her legs back and forth with everything she had, but it was't enough. He was on her in seconds, scooping her up into a bear hug from behind, lifting her feet clear off the ground. She screamed and kicked out as he stopped running and began taking steps backwards, away from us.

'Let her go.' I spat the words at him as I came to a stop in front of him. 'Get your hands off her.'

He lowered her down so that her feet touched the floor again and put one hand on her shoulder and the other around her neck.

'Don't come any closer' he said. 'Or I'll snap her neck.'

I heard the car come to a stop behind me, then the doors opening and closing. Moses and Dylan were soon standing either side of me.

'Come on' Moses said. 'Just let us take the girl home, there's three of us, we've got more people coming. There's no need to do this.'

'There may be three of you, but none of you have got her neck in your hands have you? Don't come any closer.'

I heard the door of a house close behind him, then the sound of footsteps on gravel. Brooke stepped out from behind the van that was concealing the front door. She walked up to where the man holding Una was standing and came to a stop next to him.

'Hello Vivienne. So lovely to see you again.' I ignored her pleasantries, so she quickly continued. 'You are rather early though. I honestly didn't think you'd make it up here so quickly, so we are ill prepared I'll admit. But you're here and that's the main thing.' She turned her attention to Una. 'And how on earth did you get out little Una? We had that house locked down.'

Brooke turned around and looked at the house. I followed her gaze and could see a small window in the roof, which looked like it was broken. Brooke turned back toward me and nodded.

'Ah the attic. Very clever.'

'Let Una go.' I said.

'Oh I have every intention of letting Una go. In fact I've been ordered to do so by the powers that be. But there's a catch. You see they still want you. They still believe that you are of the utmost importance in saving our species. So Una can by all means go, but only if you come with me.'

'She's not going anywhere with you.' Moses said.

'Oh I'm sorry' Brooke said, cocking her head to one side. 'I don't think we've met before. Get back in your car, you and your friend. Then reverse down the street, right to the end of it.'

Nobody moved.

'I mean it, you two back in the car or Una *will* get hurt.'

I looked at Moses from the corner of my eye and gave the tiniest of nods. He motioned to the car with his head, before both he and Dylan walked slowly backwards. I turned and watched as they both got in the front seats. The engine started up and the car began to reverse slowly away. It came to a stop about twenty meters away. I looked back at Brooke as she raised her hands and waved the back of her fingers toward the car. The car reversed slowly again, until it was another twenty meters away.

'That's better.' She said. 'No Morgan with you today Vivienne?'

'Is this why you've done this Brooke?' I said. 'Have you done this to cause him pain? To get back at him for hurting you?'

Brooke's eyes looked toward the sky, her lips pursed together.

'I'm reminded every day that I was never enough for him.' Her eyes returned to me, narrowed and angry. 'But you? You were special, you were enough. He married you in what? A year after you met? And now you're playing happy families with your little rescued orphan? You two honestly make me feel sick. I will happily get back at Morgan for what he did to me by keeping you locked in a tank for the rest of your life, orders or no orders. Now unless you get in the fucking van in the next thirty seconds, Una's neck is going to be snapped in half. It's your choice Vivienne. I really do not care either way.'

She knew I would have no choice. I would do anything to save Una again. I didn't come all this way just to watch her die, we didn't go through everything we did escaping the lab just for her to die now. I stepped forward, watching Una's eyes widen as I did so. I opened my mouth, ready to agree to Brooke's terms when Una's hands shot up, grabbing her captor's bare arm, her fingers digging in hard to his skin. She pulled his arm forward as his hand released her neck, then before he could react any further, she clamped her mouth down hard on his forearm. The man wailed in response, whether from pain or shock, but it was enough to make him let go of her completely.

'GO UNA!' I shouted. 'THE WATER, GO!'

She was away from the driveway before I even finished shouting at her, gone in the direction of the water. Brooke took off after her whilst the man stood clutching his bleeding arm.

'Do it' she shouted as she went. 'Do it now.'

It only took him two strides to reach me and his hands were around my neck, squeezing tightly. He lifted my feet from the floor and slammed me down on to the hard ground. He knelt beside me, both hands still around my neck. I clawed at his skin, trying to get a grip on his arms, trying to pull his hands away but he was too strong, I couldn't get his hands away from my neck. I couldn't breathe, no air was getting in. I felt my head start to swim and my vision blurred. The edges began to fade, I was going to pass out.

I heard a thud echo inside my head and suddenly there were no longer hands around my neck. I gulped in the air, coughing and spluttering as I did. Moses was stood above me, looking down. He crouched down beside me and pulled on my arms, sitting me up. I shook my head and scrunched my eyes open and closed, until my vision cleared. I looked around and saw Dylan grappling with the man on the ground.

'Go' Moses said. 'Go, get Una, now!'

I scrambled to my feet, pushing myself away from the dusty gravel with my hands. I managed to get upright and started to run in the direction of the loch. I could see Brooke ahead of me, she was halfway to the water. I ran faster and faster. I could see Una on the shoreline. She turned to look behind herself before running into the water and diving under once it got to her knees. Brooke kept running, but she was slower than me. I caught up quickly, tackling her from behind. She let out a scream as she hit the rocky ground beneath her.

She kept moving and made it to her feet again before I shoved her hard in the back. She was ready this time and didn't go down fully. Instead, she took a few steps forward and managed to right herself, before turning to face me. She opened her mouth as if to speak, but before she got the chance to get a word out, my fist hit her square on the nose. She stumbled backwards, her hands at her nose. When she regained her balance, she pulled her hands away, looking down at them, taking in the bright red blood. I hit her again, this time connecting with her eye socket. She teetered back once more, this time losing her balance and falling to the floor.

I left her where she was and ran toward the water. I had to find Una, I had to make sure she was safe. I was a few feet from the water when I felt hands wrap around my thighs from behind. I toppled forwards, putting my hands out to stop the impact, but my face still hit the ground with a thud. My ears rang loudly. I could hear a voice, someone shouting, but it sounded watery, like when someone talks to you when your head is under water. My face throbbed on one side and I could taste blood. The voice I could hear was becoming clearer, like it was closer than before. I felt hands on my shoulder, pulling me over. I was on my back now, looking at the clear blue sky. I couldn't move my arms, something was on them, someone was straddled across my chest.

Brooke's face came into view. She was leaning over me, reaching for something on the ground, past my head. She looked down at me, her long hair almost completely covering her face, but I could see her eyes, I could see the blood dripping from her nose. She pulled her arms back to her chest, her hands holding something between them. It was a rock, a rock the size of a bowling ball. She held it in the air above her, her chest rose up and down quickly as she breathed heavily in and out. I watched as her mouth turned into a grimace and she raised the rock even higher above her head. Her face twisted almost in pain and her lip curled at one side. I stared into her eyes, trying to remain defiant in accepting what was about to happen.

Her chest heaved as she took a huge breath and fully extended her arms above her head, but before she had the chance to bring the rock down on me, she was struck from the side suddenly by a long black baton. I watched as she toppled sideways and I felt the weight of her body leave my arms. I rolled in the opposite direction and found Detective Kerensa Snell doubled over, hands on her thighs, still holding the extendable baton in one hand. She was out of breath and raised her empty hand to her chest. I pushed myself backwards, away from where Brooke lay face down on the ground. She began to groan and feel around her with her hands.

'Your daughter' the detective said. 'She went into the water, you have to help her.'

The detective dropped the baton and knelt down beside Brooke, taking her arms and holding them behind her back, her chest still heaving, trying to regain her breath. She reached behind her back and pulled handcuffs from her belt.

'Quickly, you have to find her now. She's been under for too long. GO… NOW!'

I pushed myself up off the ground, now standing above the detective as she held Brooke down. How would I explain this? The detective must have seen Una dive in, as I had told her to. Had the detective heard me say that to her? I couldn't bring myself to move. I was trying, but my legs were not responding to my thoughts. I just stood where I was staring at the spot where the detective had Brooke pinned down on the floor.

She looked from me, to Brooke and then toward the water, before dropping the handcuffs and standing up. She ran toward the water, her breath having nearly returned to normal. At the waters edge she pulled her shoes and jacket off, discarding them behind her. She waded into the water, looking down in front of her. She kept going until the water was up to her chest.

'I can't see her!'

She shouted the words without looking up, her voice sounding panicked. Her head disappeared under the surface of the water, leaving only air bubbles in her place. I heard the sound of shoes on gravel behind me and turned in time to see Brooke up and running. I was still frozen in place and my legs had turned to jelly, my head felt light and airy. I had to sit down. As the detective resurfaced, my legs gave way beneath me and I hit the floor, rear end first. The detective took a deep breath and disappeared back underneath the water once more. Brooke was still running in the opposite direction of the house, getting further and further away from us. I heard the fast pace of a run behind me and turned to find Moses careering toward us. The detective came out of the water again, noticing Moses when she looked back at me.

'Mr Cain' the detective said. 'The girl, she's in the water. We have to do something. I think Vivienne is in shock.'

Moses stood still and looked between me and the detective. She submerged herself again. Moses and I both looked back in the direction that Brooke had ran as she disappeared over the top of a small hill. Moses looked at me, opening his mouth to speak but the detective resurfaced again.

'I can't find her, I can't see anything down there.' She said.

She began wading back toward the shore.

'Vivienne… I'm sorry Vivienne…' The detective reached the small pebbly beach. 'She's been under for such a long time…by the time we get search equipment here… I… I think we're too late…'

'Mum?' The tiny voice made everyone look. 'Is it safe to come out now?'

Away from where the detective still stood in the water, little fingers where visible on the side of a cluster of rocks. Slowly, a small blonde head peered out from behind them.

'Una!' I leaned forward on one hand, reaching my other hand out and motioned her toward me. 'Yes Una it's safe, you can come out.'

The detective had a look of utter relief on her face as Una came out from behind the rocks and made her way toward me on the shore. Once she was far enough out of the water, she broke into a run. I managed to sit up on my knees, my arms open wide. Una flung herself at me, her arms wrapping tightly around my neck.

'Mummy are you okay? You're bleeding.'

My breath caught in my chest, choking me up as I heard her say it again. She had called me mummy.

'I'm fine Una' I said, my face buried in her hair. 'We're all fine now, everything is okay.'

I continued to squeeze her as the detective climbed out of the water. She crouched down beside us, her hand on Una's shoulder.

'Una are you okay? Are you hurt anywhere?'

Una pulled away from me, shaking her head. She held out her hand.

'I thought I cut my hand when I broke the window, but it's okay.'

I looked at her hand, I could see a line across the back of it where it obviously had been cut, but had now healed. I took her hand in mine, shielding it from the detective's view.

'Did they hurt you? Did they do anything else to you?'

Una knew what I meant. Even though there was no longer a lab, that didn't mean they wouldn't try to take something from her, just like they had done hundreds of times at the lab. Una shook her head again.

'No mummy, I'm okay.' She said.

I was suddenly aware of Moses' soft voice talking quietly behind me. I turned to see him still stood behind me, but he now had a phone pressed to his ear.

'She's on foot... yes she's alone. We've apprehended the other one. She's heading south along the top of the loch.'

Una looked at my forehead, brushing the hair from my wound and pushing it behind my ear.

'Can we just go home? Please?' She said.

'Yes' I nodded. 'Yes we can go home right now.'

'Now wait just a moment' said Detective Snell. 'I need to ask you all some questions first. What were you all doing here? How did you find Una before me?'

Moses and I looked at each other again. I should leave this to him to answer.

'Let me take Una to the car at least, I need to get her into some dry clothes, she's freezing.'

I gave Una a soft nudge and she quickly pulled her arms around herself in the pretence of being cold.

'Yes, okay' the detective nodded. 'But you can't leave, not yet anyway.'

I got slowly to my feet, Una pulling me by the arm to help me. We left Moses where he was, on his phone and walked back to the house where Una had been held. As we got closer, we could see Dylan crouched down next to the man that had helped Brooke kidnap Una. The man was face down on the ground, his hands tied behind his back with a zip tie, Dylan kneeling on top of him. Dylan also had a phone pressed to his ear.

'How far out?' He said before pausing for a moment. 'Searching for what?'

I ushered Una past them as the man struggled on the ground, Dylan leaned forward, pushing more of his weight down onto him. We made it to the car and found another, smaller car parked behind it, which must have belonged to Detective Snell. I opened the boot of Moses' car before lifting Una and sitting her inside, her legs dangling over the edge. I had packed changes of clothes for us and I helped her change into some dry clothes and tried to wipe my own face clean of blood. Once Una was changed, I took her face in my hands.

'Are you sure they didn't hurt you? It's okay, you can tell me, I won't get upset, I promise.'

She smiled up at me.

'They didn't hurt me.' Her smile faded suddenly. 'But they said they were going to kill you. I shouldn't have run away like that, I knew they would try to hurt you. I'm sorry mummy.'

'No, no, no Una. You did the right thing. You had to get away, I wanted you to get away from them. What you did saved us both. You got away and they didn't take me away or kill me. You were very, very brave Una. Braver than I could ever be.'

I pushed her long hair out of her face.

'Who was that other lady?'

I turned around, sitting myself down next to Una in the boot of the car.

'That's a Police Detective, her name is Kerensa. She was in charge of investigating your abduction.'

'What are you going to tell her about everything that happened?'

'I think I'm going to leave that to Moses for now. The less you or I talk to her the better. Moses is used to this sort of human, Asrai relations type thing.'

Una looked up at me.

'Can we go home soon?'

I nodded and put my arm around her, pulling her in tight and giving her a squeeze.

'Yes we can. Are you hungry? We'll find somewhere nice to have breakfast on the way home shall we? You can have whatever you want.'

'Can I have pancakes?' She said.

I nodded.

'You can have as many as you like.'

'With ice-cream?'

'For breakfast?' I put on a mock shocked voice.

'Yep' she said. 'Ice-cream and syrup.'

I looked down at her, smiling.

'If that's what you want, then thats what you shall have.'

I heard footsteps on the gravel nearby and stood up from where I was sitting in the boot. I stepped around the car and watched as Moses and Detective Snell, carrying her coat and shoes, walked toward us. Moses crouched down next to the man that Dylan had restrained and then he and Dylan took the man by each arm and pulled him to his feet. I could hear a gentle thudding sound in the distance and then felt Una tug at my clothes.

'Mummy look, what's that?'

I turned to look up at the direction she was pointing. There was a helicopter, hovering about a mile away from us, near the edge of the loch.

'I take it that's my ride to Hadian' the man said, looking toward the sky.

The detective turned toward the sound too, a confused look on her face and then looked back at Moses.

'Ride to where?'

I don't know what Moses had already told her, but he certainly wouldn't have divulged the name or location of the Asrai prison. I changed the subject before he could answer.

'Detective Snell, you're soaking, would you like some dry clothes?'

She looked like she would fit in the change of clothes I had brought for myself. I signalled to the car and the bags I had open in the boot.

'Please Vivienne, call me Kerensa. But yes, that would be wonderful, thank you.'

Kerensa stood behind the car and changed quickly into the clothes I had given her. She was just pulling a t-shirt over her head as I watched the helicopter spin around in the sky and head off in another direction.

'Who is he exactly?'

Kerensa nodded in the direction of Moses, Dylan and the man they still held between them.

'Who? The man who took Una? I have no idea, I've never seen him before today.'

'No, I mean Moses' she said. 'When we spoke earlier, he told me he would take Brooke's accomplice into custody. I said he couldn't. He told me he had authorisation and I just had to check my phone. I looked at it and sure enough, there was a message from my boss telling me to do as Moses says.' She paused for a while, still watching the helicopter. 'He's also managed to get a helicopter here to search for Brooke. Yet other than his name cropping up in a few case notes, I've never really heard of or seen him before during my career in the force.' She looked at me expectantly. 'What kind of person can just tell the Chief Constable that he's going to take a criminal… a child abductor no less, into custody himself?'

I shrugged, avoiding her questioning glare.

'I don't know him that well to be honest. He's an old family friend of my grandmother. I only met him for the first time after my parents died a few years ago.' I swallowed hard. 'Since my grandmother is no longer with us either…' I folded my arms tightly around across my chest, still watching the helicopter. I cleared my throat, the lump in it getting heavier. 'Since she died, Moses has been in touch a bit more. He arranged our honeymoon for us as a wedding gift, but it was the first real time we'd spent with him.'

It wasn't all a complete lie, but I tried my best to keep my face completely neutral as she studied it, looking for a give away.

'And do you know what he does? Why he would have such influence?'

I turned to face her, keeping my expression as indifferent as I could.

'What do any London business men do? I haven't got a clue really. He doesn't talk to us about his work too much.'

Once again, this wasn't a complete lie. Kerensa nodded to herself chewing on her lip slightly. A wave of nausea passed over me. She was asking too many questions. I wasn't equipped to deal with this, I was terrible at being vague, even worse at lying. The helicopter seemed to move off in another direction as Moses turned and walked toward us. I felt Una's hand on my elbow and looking down at her, I took her hand in mine.

'Now can we go home?'

As I nodded, the nausea rolled up through my insides and I barely had time to turn around and face away from Una before the vomit left my mouth.

'Oh shit!' I heard Kerensa say. 'Una, stand back a second.'

I felt hands around my hair, pulling it away from my face as I wretched again. A hand then rubbed my back in small circles.

'We need to get you to a hospital as soon as we can. You've had a few knocks to the head, it could be a concussion.'

'I will take her.' Moses was with us now. 'I can take her to a doctor right away, I know where the closest one is.'

Kerensa continued to rub my back and I heaved again.

'She needs a hospital, I can radio for an ambulance.'

I spat out the last dribbles of vomit, trying to find my voice.

'It's okay, honestly I'm fine. It's not a concussion.'

I stood up straight and wiped my mouth with my sleeve.

'You need to see someone, you may even need stitches.'

She raised her hand to my forehead, where I still had blood from falling and hitting the ground face first. I knew I wouldn't need stitches. The wound would be barely there soon. I got my hand there first, covering the blood.

'It's okay, really. It's just a graze from the rocks and I felt sick before all this happened, probably just travel sickness from the drive up here. We drove all night, plus I haven't slept and we were on a plane yesterday. It's just travel sickness, I don't need a hospital. I'm okay, really I am.'

Kerensa seemed to finally accept my protests. She turned around and crouched in front of Una.

'And what about you? Are you hurt?'

Una shook her head. Kerensa looked at me as she stood up again.

'It's standard procedure in this type of situation for kids to be checked out by a doctor. Even if it's just to check for signs of shock. We should take her to be safe.'

'I don't want to go to hospital!'

The words came out of Una's mouth fast and loud, making   Kerensa almost jump in surprise.

'Please don't make me go. Please. I just want to go home.'

Kerensa pursed her lips, almost grimacing to herself as she considered Una's plea.

'Okay' she finally said. 'But I will have to come and see you in a few days, to make sure you really are okay and to take a full statement... from all of you.'

She looked at all three of us. Moses and I both nodded our agreement.

'Okay' she said again. 'I will see you all back in Zennor, soon.'

The sound of the helicopter grew louder and we all looked up in time to see it fly over our heads. It touched down on a patch of flat grass on the other side of the road. Dylan pushed the man forward and frog marched him to the helicopter. We all watched as the man was pulled onboard by someone sat inside and Dylan climbed on behind him. I squeezed Una's hand as the helicopter took off again and headed back in the direction of the loch, presumably continuing its search for Brooke. Our attention was turned back to the road as we all heard the faint wail of a police siren.

'My back up has finally arrived.' Kerensa said. 'We will have to secure the scene and collect evidence. You guys better get on the road.'

We all got in the car, Moses behind the wheel, myself and Una in the backseat. I watched Kerensa out of the window as Moses turned the car around and drove slowly past her. She lifted the phone to her ear, but her eyes followed the car.

'Is she going to cause problems for us Moses? She seems very suspicious of you and the fact that her boss told her to let you take people into custody.'

'I know. But it's alright. The Chief Constable and I go way back. He'll smooth it over with her. Probably tell her I'm MI5 or something and it was all part of a bigger undercover case.'

He looked in the rearview mirror and smiled. I couldn't help smiling back at him.

'Is that really how you cover up our existence? With stories like that?'

He caught my eye in the rear view mirror again and raised an eyebrow.

'Sometimes.'

36.

Everyone had stayed asleep for a long time today.
It had been the early hours of the morning when we had
gotten home, but I couldn't stay asleep for long, not after
everything that had happened. I stood in the doorway of
Una's room, watching the shape of her shoulders lift
slowly up and down as she breathed deeply. She slept so
soundly.   After everything she had been through, she
seemed so at peace. A wave of dread pulled through my
stomach as I thought about what could be next for her.
The Watchers, The People That Know had said it
themselves.   She was important, she had a purpose.
What role was she going to play in saving the world?

I couldn't even fathom what those words had
meant for me, let alone her. She was just a child. Yes,
she's been through more hurt and pain than most adults
experience in their lives, but still, she is only a child. I
had to try not to think about that part of her future right
now. Whatever role she is to play in saving the world,

we would think about that when the time came. If there is nothing we can do to change it, then we have to just not think about it... *I* have to not think about it. Una will enjoy the rest of her childhood. It won't be long until she is grown and together we will face our inevitabilities.

I felt a light hand on my shoulder. I put my own on top of it, before turning to face Morgan. We stood for a moment, just smiling at each other, before he leant down and gently kissed my lips. I had missed him. I had missed loving him without the threat of our family being torn apart.

'Come on' he said. 'I'll make you a tea.'

Una had not stayed asleep for much longer. By late morning the house was full of people again. Moses had stayed the night in the guest bedroom and Sereia had come by with croissants and jam. We had all piled our plates high and eaten in silence, a strange quiet that was neither awkward or uncomfortable. Everyone seemed subdued, but content to be so. I began to clear the table, the tiredness I suddenly felt making me move slowly. Morgan watched as I rubbed my eyes at the sink.

'Vivienne, you should go back to bed, you've had next to no sleep since we left Hadian.'

I put the dishes down and stifled a yawn.

'I'm fine honestly. I think I just want to chill out on the sofa today and not have to do or think about anything.'

Una stood up and took my hand.

'If we're not going swimming today, can we watch films? All day long?' She said.

'Of course we can' I smiled. 'I'll even let you choose which ones.'

She pulled me into the living room and I plonked myself down on the sofa. Una sat on the floor in the middle of the room and busied herself switching on the television, then scrolling through the menus, looking for a film. Morgan, Sereia and Moses soon joined us.

'So what are the next steps Moses?' Morgan said. 'Brooke wasn't found yesterday, will you keep searching for her?'

'Yes of course. We believe she will likely lay low in that area and await for help from Lyle Calder. There's been no activity on her mobile phone since yesterday morning, but that doesn't mean she hasn't been able to contact him some other way. My team are working on it and we will do everything we can to apprehend her.'

'I don't want to be rude Moses,' I said. 'But you said that when Una and I escaped the laboratory, yet Brooke was able to come here and kidnap Una with the help of just one other person. What makes you think you can get her this time?'

'I'll be honest with you Vivienne, I don't know if we can. Lyle likely has access to resources much similar to mine. We've just got to hope that we can, because what is the alternative for you? Living the rest of your lives here under twenty four hour surveillance in case Brooke, or Lyle or whoever else comes for you again?'

I pulled my knees up into my chest on the sofa.

'I don't know' I said. 'I'm sorry, I didn't mean it like that I just... we've been through a lot these past few days... months even. I know you're doing everything you can.'

'Vivienne, it's okay.' He leaned forward, his elbows on his knees. 'You have every right to be worried about the future, to be mad at me about everything that happened. I'm the one who let this all happen. I had no idea about what they were doing up there. You told me what you had seen at the other laboratory, the video images of the children and I did nothing. I let all those children down. I should have done something, needle in a haystack or not.'

He looked down at his hands, clasped together.

'It's not your fault Moses. None of this is. I'm just worrying. Knowing that this isn't really over yet. It's never really over, is it?'

Morgan took one of my hands in his and squeezed it gently.

'Just like humans' Moses said, 'our race is at odds with itself at times. I just wish there was more I could do to keep the peace, to make sure we were all protected.'

Sereia sighed loudly from her chair.

'It makes you just want to go and hide somewhere doesn't it.' She said.

I smiled at her.

'Wouldn't it be amazing if we could all just disappear together? Get away from all this? Enjoy a nice quiet life?'

I watched as everyone in the room nodded to themselves.

Una turned around to face us suddenly.

'We could all go to The Colony.'

She said it so hopefully.

'If only we knew the way' said Sereia, almost wistfully.

'We can' Una said. 'We just need to find a map.'

I loved her eternal optimism despite everything she had been through. She must get that from spending so much time with Sereia. Moses was smiling now too. Una seemed to have that effect on everyone.

'Do you know where a map is Una?' He said.

Una nodded and everyones smiles grew wider, enjoying the innocence of an optimistic child.

'Oh really? Where will we find it?'

'In a mirror' she said. 'Sereia told me her Keeper said she had to look for it where she would find herself and Kendra said her dad had told her how to get there, because he had seen a map in the mirror.' A shadow of sadness passed across her face. 'She didn't get to tell us anything else before...'

She looked downward, averting her gaze from me. I tried to lighten the mood.

'Una, I bet you're right, it is a mirror and one day, we will find it.'

I held my arms out and she came crossed the room quickly. I pulled her in to my arms on the sofa, stroking her hair gently.

'Olivia had a mirror just like that.' Sereia pointed at the mirror above our fireplace. 'Almost exactly the same. The hands, the hair, all the same characteristics, but not identical.'

'Your Keeper had one too?' Moses said, sounding shocked. 'I thought that that one was unique.'

'It is' I said. 'Or at least that's what Emmy told me. She said it had been hand made and passed down through the family.'

'Check the back' Una said. 'See if theres's a map on it.'

Sereia stood up and walked over to the fire place.

'I'm sure Emmy would have noticed a long time ago if there was anything on the back of it' she said.

She pulled at the mirror from the bottom and peered behind it before shaking her head.

'Nope. Nothing. Good idea though Una.'

Morgan stood and quickly left the room. He returned quickly, holding a cleaning spray bottle.

'What's that for?' Sereia asked.

'Vivienne, remember what happened when you sprayed it with this? Show them.'

He walked over to me and held the cleaning spray out in front of me. I left Una on the sofa and stood up slowly, before taking the bottle from Morgan's hand. Everyone watched me as I crossed the room and stood in front of the mirror.'

'What is it Vivienne?' Sereia said. 'What's going to happen?'

'Just watch' I said, as I began to spray the cleaner all across the mirror.

Just like before, as soon as the liquid hit the mirrored glass, it bang to sparkle as if I was spraying glitter directly onto it. Moses and Sereia both stood up and came closer to the mirror.

'How is it doing that?' Moses said.

'We've got no idea. There's no glitter in the cleaner. It's just a normal glass cleaner. It only does this when we spray it on the mirror, it doesn't do the same thing on the windows or other mirrors in the house.'

Moses got closer, inspecting the mirror. He lifted his hand and touched it gently, before rubbing his fingers and thumb together.

'Vivienne, can we have a large glass of water please?'

'To drink?' I said.

Moses smiled widely and shook his head.

'I'll get it!'

Una was up and out of the room before I had a chance to ask anything further.

'Morgan, help me get the mirror down' Moses said.

Morgan stepped forward and he and Moses took a corner of the mirror each and gently lifted it from where it hung on the wall. They crouched down and laid it face up on the soft rug in the middle of the room. Una returned quickly and handed a large glass of water to Moses. We all gathered low on the floor around the mirror and watched as Moses slowly poured the water onto the mirror. We watched as the water spread across the mirror exposing a golden sheen of glitter as it did so. More colours were soon visible, green and then blue. The further the water went, the clearer the image beneath it became. It was a map.

A map of the world.

37.

Una

I wasn't scared, not anymore. I knew I would always be safe here, with Vivienne and Morgan. My mum and dad. I liked calling them that and I could tell they liked it too. Dad's face had been so happy when we had got back. He had opened the door and ran out to us. He picked me up so fast and had squeezed me so tightly when I had called him daddy, telling him that I had missed him.

They had all stayed up late last night, talking about the map, working out what it meant. Now we knew how to get to The Last Colony. Sereia was so excited, she almost cried. I really hoped we would get to go soon, but it was a long, long way away daddy had said. He said we would have to talk about it, a lot. Mummy had looked worried, she said it would be dangerous, but I was excited to go, just like Sereia.

No one else was awake yet today. I had had a long, cold bath when I had first woken up and now I was hungry. I stepped quietly through the house to the kitchen. I didn't want to wake anyone up, I wanted to let them sleep as long as possible. So I had made myself cereal and tidied away after myself, then got dressed and put my shoes on.

I wanted to swim, but I knew I wouldn't be able to go by myself. It was seven in the morning, mummy would normally be up by now. She must be so tired after all that driving. I would go and see if anyone was on the beach and then as soon as someone else woke up, we could go swimming. I wrote a note to say where I was, just in case anyone woke up before I got back. I didn't want anyone to worry.

Opening the door, I was met with a cloudy sky. It was dark and moody and it looked like it could even rain. That was good, because it meant there would be fewer people at The Cove. I skipped down the drive way and onto the path toward The Cove. The wind was strong on the top of the cliff, it almost felt cold against my skin. Hopefully no one would be down on the sand today. I stopped at the top of the path, looking at the sand below. No one was there, only seagulls flying above the waves, screeching in the wind. I looked up and down the cliff top. There were two people walking toward the bench seat further along the cliff edge.

One by one, they both stopped, turned and looked right at me. It was two older women, they were looking at me and smiling. Something told me that these women were kind, I didn't need to be afraid of them. They both wore coats and at the same time, they lifted their hoods and pulled them tight around their faces. We stared at each other for a moment, their kind faces, still smiling right at me. I looked up at the sky and saw the clouds had grown darker and then I felt the first drops of rain that fell from the sky and hit my skin. How did they know it would…

'UNA!'

Daddy's voice rang out from behind me. I turned around and ran back toward the house, watching as he waved to me from the end of the driveway.

Back at home, everyone was now awake and in the kitchen, drinking their teas and coffees.

'Can we go swimming? There's no one on the beach. It's raining, no one will be on the beach today. Can we go? Please?'

'Yes, we can go' daddy said. 'But let's let everyone have something to eat first. Viv, do you want some toast?'

I watched as mummy shook her head.

'I'm not really hungry' she said.

'Are you still feeling a bit sick? You seem to be suffering with the travel sickness a bit don't you?'

'I'll be fine once I've had a swim and stayed away from long car journeys for a few days.'

'Moses, will you come and swim with us?'

I was excited to swim with someone new again.

'Oh I don't know' he said. 'I don't really swim with anyone anymore. Not since... well I just... haven't had anyone to swim with for a long time.'

'You have us today though don't you?'

I smiled at him and as he smiled back, I saw his eyes flick to Sereia and then quickly back to me.

'Yes, I do have all of you today don't I.' He nodded to himself. 'I will come swimming with you all too. But I will need that toast first.'

'I'll make it!'

I jumped across the kitchen and got to work making lots of toast for everyone to share. I put the butter and spreads on the table along with plates and knives and piled the toast high in the middle. Everyone except mum was eating when there was a knock on the door.

'I'll get it!'

I jumped up and ran to the door before anyone had a chance to stop me. I pulled the front door open before anyone else had even gotten out of their seat. It was Detective Snell.

'Hi Una' she said softly. 'Can I come in?'

I stood back, pulling the door with me.

'We're having breakfast. Do you want some toast?'

She stepped past me and gently patted my head.

'No I'm fine, but thank you for the offer.'

I closed the door and followed her into the kitchen.

'Hello everyone, good morning. Sorry to come by so early.'

She stood still as everyone looked at her.

'Please' Sereia said. 'Take a seat. Can I get you a drink?'

'Oh no thank you' she said. 'This won't take long. I just wanted to check that everyone was okay. Vivienne, how's your…'

She was looking at mummy, her eyes squinting as if she was trying to get a better look. Mummy put her hand to her head, where the blood had been the last time the detective had seen her.

'Your wound it's… it's gone.'

Mummy unhooked her curly hair from behind her ear, letting it fall across the side of her face.

'Um… Like I said, it was just a graze. Nothing a bit of make up couldn't cover up.'

Detective Snell nodded.

'I see. Well I'm glad you're not too hurt. How are you feeling other than that?'

'Not great actually' mummy said, standing up from the table. 'In fact I think I need to go and…' she pointed toward the door and shuffled around the detective to reach the door. 'Kerensa, thank you so much for everything you did for us.'

Mummy moved quickly toward the door, covering her mouth with her hand as she urged. Sereia dropped the piece of toast she had been about to bite into and followed her out. Detective Snell looked at Daddy once they had disappeared from the room. She took a deep breath and sighed a little.

'So I've been given orders to close down your case from my office. It's being dealt with by another department apparently.' She looked at Moses and then back to daddy. 'I've been told not to take your statements today, so I just wanted to come and check you were all okay, but it seems like you're all doing fine. Well, as fine as can be I suppose. So I... I guess this is goodbye really.'

She held out her hand to Moses and he stood up from his chair. He held out his hand too and they shook for a moment. Their hands stopped shaking but they didn't let go straight away. They just looked at each other until daddy made a coughing sound and held out his hand.

'Thank you detective' he said.

She let go of Moses' hand suddenly then grabbed hold of daddy's hand, shaking it quickly.

'Oh um.. no thank you, no um… I mean, you're welcome. It was my pleasure.'

Her cheeks suddenly looked a little pinker then before. Daddy looked at me and smiled, raising his eyebrows.

'I'll see you out' Moses said.

She nodded and stepped back as he walked past her. She held out her hand for me to shake.

'Goodbye Una. Well done for being so brave.'

I shook her hand, squeezing it tightly.

'Thank you.'

She let go of my hand and used her hands to straighten out her hair as she left the room. I peered around the kitchen door and watched as she walked through the front door that Moses held open for her. She stopped on the front step and turned back to face him.

'Thank you again Moses.'

'Thank you detective' he nodded in return.

He closed the door behind her and walked back into the kitchen, taking his seat at the table again.

'I'm going to get my swimming stuff ready' I said.

I walked along the hallway and could hear mummy and Sereia's voices from the bathroom. I stopped a few steps away from the door, which had been left slightly open.

'Look it's not that, it's just travel sickness. There's no point doing this, this is silly Sereia.'

It was mummy's voice that I heard first.

'Look it's just for my own piece of mind. Lets just rule it out okay?' Sereia was talking softly.

'Why do you even have this?'

'I went and got it yesterday. You told Morgan you had been sick when you called him on your way back. I went right out and got it, you know, just in case.'

'How long has it been?'

'Only sixty seconds.'

'How long do we have to wait?'

'We have to wait for ninety seconds.'

They both went quiet. What were they doing?

'Right, that's got to have been ninety seconds. Can you look now?'

Mummy was talking to Sereia again.

'I'm looking, I'm looking. Pass me the box, I just need to check something.' Sereia was quiet again for a while.

'Vivienne… Vivienne look. You're pregnant.'

Pregnant? Mummy was going to have a baby? I stepped slowly away from the door, not wanting to get caught listening. I put my hands over my mouth, trying to not squeal. This was… this was perfect. I would have a little brother or sister. I walked into the living room and watched the detective's car through the window as it pulled away from the driveway in the rain.

Mummy would be so happy, daddy would be so happy too. There would be a little baby here and we would all be happy, everything would be perfect. I smiled to myself. Suddenly I thought about my brother Jordan and how much I missed him. Jordan would have loved this place and the life we have here. I hoped the baby would be a boy.

'Una? Una are you getting ready?'

It was daddy's voice coming from the hallway.

'Not yet' I replied.

I ran back through the house towards my bedroom and grabbed my bag and towel. I already had my swim suit on underneath my clothes. Mummy and Sereia were no longer in the bathroom and I could hear the sound of drawers opening and closing coming from mummy and daddy's room. Daddy walked out and held one of his swim suits in his hand. He opened the door to the guest room.

'Here you go Moses, these should fit you.' He turned and looked down at me. 'Are you ready Una?'

I nodded.

'Yes, I'm ready.'

'Why are you smiling so much?' He said.

'I'm just really happy to be home' I said.

'Good' he said, before ruffling my hair.

Mummy and Sereia came out of mummy and daddy's room. I ran to the front door, opening it quickly and running outside onto the drive way. I was so happy as the rain hit my face and I laughed out loud.

'UNA No! Stop.'

Mummy's voice stopped me in my tracks, she sounded so scared and then I realised why. The doctor was here. Brooke stood at the end of the drive way. Her wet hair stuck to her face, her clothes were soaked through and clung to her body. Her chest heaved as if she was out of breath and in one hand she held a long, silver knife.

'Una get back here!'

I began to walk backwards slowly, one step at a time. Brooke stepped forward. I heard footsteps on the gravel behind me as more people came out of the house. Brooke opened her mouth and began to speak.

'I should have killed you a long time ago Vivienne.' She lifted her arm up and pointed the knife toward mummy. 'You ruined EVERYTHING.'

I was next to mummy now and we both stepped back, slowly. Mummy put her hand on my shoulder and I felt her push me slightly, until she was in front of me, shielding me. I looked around her and watched as Brooke stepped closer, the knife still pointing toward mummy. She drew her arm back behind her head.

'NO!' I screamed.

I heard more footsteps behind me, but it was too late. Brooke swung her arm forward, releasing the knife. Everything slowed down as it spun in circles in the air towards us. I heard mummy scream and Sereia was shouting something. Mummy was trying to push me back, but I pushed my arms forwards and around her, pulling her in at the middle. I didn't want to hurt the baby, but I had to protect them. I pulled mummy down over my leg, knocking her feet out from underneath her. As she fell back I spun around. I could see Sereia, her hands over her mouth. Then daddy was running out of the front door. He looked like he was shouting, but I couldn't hear what he was saying either. Moses was with him, his phone lit up in his hand.

My neck felt wet. Wet and warm. It was still raining, but this felt different. This was something else. I lifted my hand to the back of my neck and touched my fingers to it, I could feel something there, something that shouldn't have been. I pulled my hand away and held it in front of my face, my fingers were red with blood and then I couldn't move my fingers anymore, even though I was really trying to. I think I had been hurt. Mummy's arms were now around me, we were on the floor. I don't know how I got here.

I looked at her face, she was shouting, crying. One of her hands was touching my face as she looked down at me, her face was smeared with blood. Was she hurt too? I let my head turn the other way. I could see where Brooke had been standing, but now she was on the floor too. Someone was on top of her, holding her down. It was the detective, Kerensa. I thought she had already left. Mummy turned my face back toward her, she was talking. Her voice was getting louder, I could hear her again.

'Una, Una stay here, stay with me.'

'We need to get her in the water, now.' Moses was crouched down next to us now. 'We don't have time to wait for help.'

Then I could hear daddy's voice.

'Get them up, get them up now' he said. 'Quickly.'

I felt more hands on me as mummy stood up.

'What are you doing? Where are you taking her?' The detective was shouting now. 'We need to call an ambulance right now.'

But mummy didn't stop. She held me in her arms tightly and we were moving, she was running fast. I just wanted to close my eyes, I just needed to rest for a moment.

'Una no, stay awake. Don't do this.'

She was running faster now, holding me tightly in her arms. Then I felt like I was falling. I opened my eyes and I could see the grey sky above me and the grey rock of the cliff. We weren't falling, we were on the cliff path. She was taking me to The Cove. I could hear mummy breathing heavily. She was crying still. Her blood stained face was streaked with tears. I could smell the sea now, the salt in the air.

Mummy was running again, running really fast, not loosening her grip on me for a moment. I could hear the water, the waves and the gulls up above us. Then I could feel the water around us. We were in the sea. Mummy waded out and then plunged us under. The water around me was cloudy red. I closed my eyes again. The water was cold, the way it always was, but I felt so much colder, cold on the inside, cold in my bones. I'd never felt cold like this before. I had never felt anything like this.

Printed in Great Britain
by Amazon